W9-AZX-802

Journey to the Centre of the Earth

JULES VERNE

Journey to the Centre of the Earth

JULES VERNE

ARCTURUS

This edition published in 2015 by Arcturus Publishing Limited
26/27 Bickels Yard, 151–153 Bermondsey Street,
London SE1 3HA

Introduction by Brian Busby
Typesetting by Palimpsest Book Production Limited
Cover image: *Well of the Steps, Jerusalem*, 1871 (w/c & pencil on paper),
Simpson, William 'Crimea' (1823-99)/Palestine Exploration Fund, London,
UK/The Bridgeman Art Library

ISBN: 978-1-84837-610-6

AD001541EN

Printed in Germany

Introduction

The great early pioneer of science fiction, Jules Verne was celebrated for his *Voyages Extraordinaires*. His heroes travelled around the world, to the moon and, in this volume, to the centre of the earth. It is therefore fitting that the author began life – on 8 February 1828 – in the busy, bustling French harbour city of Nantes.

Drawn to a life of adventure, at twelve Verne was beaten by his father when found hiding on a ship bound for India. After this bitter experience, the future writer famously resolved to travel only in his imagination.

The troubled relationship with his father marked much of Verne's early literary career. Upon learning that his son was writing, rather than studying law, the elder Verne withdrew all support. For over a decade, the author worked as a stockbroker, while attempting to interest publishers in his work. Verne's fortunes changed when he met Pierre-Jules Hetzel. An editor and publisher, in 1863 he published Verne's first novel, *Five Weeks in a Balloon* (*Cinq Semaines en Ballon*). *Journey to the Centre of the Earth* (*Voyage au centre de la Terre*), published the following year, proved to be one of the author's most enduring works. Verne came to be celebrated the world over for such classic novels as *Twenty Thousand Leagues Under the Sea* (1870) and *Around the World in Eighty Days* (1873). He died on 24 March 1905.

Editor's Note

The text published here is a modernization of the Rev F A
Malleson's 1876 translation of Verne's *Voyage au centre de la
Terre*, the main purpose of this reworking of Malleson being
to update it in terms of style and vocabulary. While Verne's
Voyage has been constantly at the editor's elbow to allow him
where necessary to check the original French before settling on
a rewording of Malleson's text, this book is by no means a new
translation but simply an updating of an out-of-date English
version which no longer did justice to Verne. However, since
Verne's book itself was published in the mid-1860s, it would
have been inappropriate to have fully altered the language
of the 19th-century English translation to the idiom of the
21st century. The editor hopes he has struck the right balance
between the modern and the slightly old-fashioned.

From a scientific point of view, there are some errors of fact
in Verne's book, and Malleson helpfully provided a number
of footnotes correcting these mistakes. However, since they
have no relevance to the story, and in some cases have been
overtaken by advances in scientific knowledge, these notes
have for the most part been dropped from the present book.
What Verne wrote was a novel, not a textbook, and nothing
stands or falls on the accuracy of his science. The same is
true for his historical accuracy: for example, it may be rather
implausible that the British scientist Sir Humphry Davy would
have visited Otto Lidenbrock in 1825 (see page 33) when
Lidenbrock would only have been 12 years old (he is stated
to be 50 in 1863) in order to discuss matters of science with
him, but the implausibility in no way affects the story. Verne's
purpose is simply to establish Lidenbrock as a respected
authority in his field.

The reader will find a great deal of geological and
mineralogical terminology in this book. This is hardly
surprising, as it is supposedly written about the underground
explorations of an eminent geologist and mineralogist by
a nephew who is himself competent in these sciences. In
order to enjoy the story, however, one does not need to know
more about feldspar, syenite, porphyry, trachite or tufa than
is explained in the story itself, and the present editor felt it

unnecessary to add notes on these or other minerals mentioned. Similarly, no attempt has been made to check whether what Verne wrote about geological periods such as the Tertiary and the Quaternary conforms to modern scientific knowledge or usage.

On the other hand, the editor, aware that a 21st-century reader is likely to be less well versed in Latin and Greek literature and mythology than the readership Verne and Malleson had in mind, has added a number of notes where, for example, quotations in Latin or allusions to Greek myths might not be understood, to the detriment of the story.

The chapter headings are Malleson's, not Verne's (hence, for example, the quotation from Shakespeare used as the heading for Chapter 24). Similarly, as will be seen from the notes, Malleson included in his translation other quotations from English literature that have no basis in the French text. Most of those have been left as Malleson wrote them, since there seemed to be no good reason to remove or replace them.

GEORGE DAVIDSON

CHAPTER 1

THE PROFESSOR AND HIS FAMILY

On the 24th of May, 1863, a Sunday, my uncle, Professor Lidenbrock, came rushing back to his little house, No. 19 in the Königstrasse, one of the oldest streets in the oldest part of the city of Hamburg.

Martha, our maid, must have thought that she was running well behind time, as the dinner was only just beginning to bubble on the kitchen stove.

'Well, now,' I said to myself, 'if my uncle, that most impatient of men, is hungry, what a fuss he'll make!'

'Professor Lidenbrock back so soon!' cried poor Martha in great alarm, half opening the dining-room door.

'Yes, Martha, but it's quite all right for the dinner not to be ready, because it's not two o'clock yet. Saint Michael's clock has only just struck half past one.'

'Then why has the master come home so soon?'

'He'll probably tell us that himself.'

'Here he is, Mr Axel. I'm going to hide while you try to reason with him.'

And Martha retreated to the safety of her culinary laboratory.

I was left alone. But how could a man of my wavering character reason successfully with so irascible a person as the Professor? With this in mind, I was preparing to retreat to my own little room upstairs when the front door creaked on its hinges; heavy feet made the whole flight of stairs shake, and the master of the house, passing rapidly through the dining-room, dashed into his study.

However, during his rapid passage through the house, he had flung his stick into a corner, his broad-brimmed hat on to the table and these commanding words at his nephew:

'Axel, follow me!'

I had scarcely had time to move when the Professor was again shouting impatiently to me:

'What? Not here yet?'

And I rushed into my formidable master's study.

Otto Lidenbrock was not a bad man, I freely admit that, but unless he changes as he grows older, which is not likely, he'll have a reputation as a fearful eccentric by the time he dies.

He was a professor at the Johannaeum, and delivered a course of lectures on mineralogy, during which lectures he regularly got into a terrible temper at least once or twice. Not that he was at all concerned about his students' attendance, or about the degree of attention with which they listened to him, or about any success of theirs which might eventually crown his labours. Such little matters of detail never troubled him much. His teaching was, as German philosophy calls it, 'subjective'; it was to benefit himself, not others. He was a learned egotist. He was a well of scientific knowledge, but the pulley rather creaked when you wanted to draw anything out. In a word, he was a learned miser.

Germany has not a few professors of this sort.

It was my uncle's misfortune that he was not gifted with a smooth, flowing articulation – not an affliction when he was talking at home, of course, but certainly when speaking in public. And it is a lack much to be deplored in a public speaker. The fact is, that during the course of his lectures at the Johannaeum, the Professor often came to a complete stop. He would struggle with some wilful word that would not pass his struggling lips, a word that refused to be uttered, swelled up in his mouth, and then at last broke out in the unasked-for form of a most unscientific oath: hence his fury.

Now in mineralogy there are many half-Greek, half-Latin terms which are very hard to articulate and which would be very trying even to a poet. I don't wish to say a word against so respectable a science; far be it from me. But in the august presence of rhombohedral crystals, retinasphaltic resins, gehlenites, Fassaites, molybdenites of lead, tungstates of manganese and titanite of zirconium, why, even the most fluent of tongues may be allowed a slip now and then.

It therefore happened that this minor fault of my uncle's came to be pretty well known around the town, and people took an unfair advantage of it. The students waited for him to arrive at difficult passages, and when he began to stumble, loud was their laughter – which is not in good taste, not even in Germans. And if there was always a full audience for the Lidenbrock lectures, who knows how many came only to have a laugh at my uncle's expense?

Nevertheless, my uncle was a man of deep learning – a fact I am most anxious to assert and reassert. Sometimes he might irretrievably damage a specimen by his excessive ardour in handling it, but nevertheless in him were united the genius of a true geologist with the keen eye of the mineralogist. Armed with his hammer, his steel chisel, his magnetic needles, his blowpipe and his bottle of nitric acid, he was a powerful man of science. He would refer any mineral to its proper place among the six hundred elementary substances now known, according to the way it fractured, its appearance, its hardness, its fusibility, its sound, its smell and its taste.

The name of Lidenbrock was therefore spoken of with honour in colleges and learned societies. Humphry Davy, Humboldt, Captain Sir John Franklin and General Sabine never failed to call upon him on their way through Hamburg. Becquerel, Ebelman, Brewster, Dumas, Milne-Edwards and Saint-Claire-Deville frequently consulted him on the most difficult problems in chemistry, a science which was indebted to him for many discoveries, as in 1853 there had been published in Leipzig an imposing folio by Otto Lidenbrock, entitled 'A Treatise on Transcendental Crystallography', with plates (a work which, however, failed to cover its costs).

In addition, let me add that my uncle was the curator of the museum of mineralogy created by Mr Struve, the Russian ambassador, a most valuable collection, famous across the whole of Europe.

Such was the gentleman who addressed me in that impatient manner. Imagine a tall, spare man, with an iron constitution and a fair complexion which took a good ten years off the fifty he had to admit to. His restless eyes were constantly moving behind his full-sized spectacles. His long, thin nose was like a knife blade. Some people were heard to remark that that organ of his was magnetized and could attract iron filings. But this was merely a mischievous story; the only thing it attracted was snuff, which it seemed to draw to itself in great quantities.

When I have added, to complete my portrait, that my uncle walked in mathematically exact strides of one yard, and that while walking he kept his fists firmly closed, a sure sign of an irritable temperament, I think I'll have said enough to disenchant anyone who might by mistake have desired much of his company.

He lived in his own little house in Königstrasse, a structure half brick and half wood, with a gable cut into steps. It looked out on to one of those winding canals which intersect each other in the middle of the ancient quarter of Hamburg which the great fire of 1842 had fortunately spared.

It's true that the old house stood slightly off the perpendicular, and bulged out a little towards the street. Its roof sloped slightly to one side, just like a student in the 'League of Virtue'[1] wore his cap down over one ear, and its lines lacked balance, but nonetheless it stood firm, thanks to an old elm which buttressed it at the front and which often in spring pushed its fresh blossoms through the windows.

My uncle was tolerably well off for a German professor. The house was his own, and everything in it. The living contents were his goddaughter Gräuben (a young girl of seventeen who came from Virland[2]), Martha and myself. As his nephew and an orphan, I had become his laboratory assistant.

I freely admit that I was extremely fond of geology and all its kindred sciences. The blood of a mineralogist was in my veins, and I was always happy among my specimens.

In a word, a man could live happily enough in the little old house in the

Königstrasse, in spite of the restless impatience of its master, for although he was a little too excitable, he was very fond of me.

But the man had no idea of patience. Nature herself was too slow for him. In April, after he had planted the terracotta pots in his sitting-room with mignonette and convolvulus seedlings, he would go and give them a little pull by their leaves to make them grow faster.

In dealing with such an odd individual, there was nothing for it but prompt obedience. I therefore rushed after him to his study.

CHAPTER 2

A MYSTERY TO BE SOLVED
AT ANY PRICE

That study of his was a veritable museum. Specimens of every substance known to mineralogy lay there, placed in perfect order and correctly named in accordance with the three great divisions of inflammable, metallic and lithoid minerals.

How well I knew all these bits of science! Many a time, instead of enjoying the company of boys my own age, I had preferred dusting these graphites, anthracites, coals, lignites and peats! There were bitumens, resins and organic salts to be protected from the slightest speck of dust; there were metals from iron to gold, metals whose market value meant nothing in their absolute equality as scientific specimens; and there were stones too, enough to completely rebuild the house in Königstrasse, even with an extra room, which would have suited me admirably.

But on entering this study now, I was thinking of none of these wonders. My uncle alone filled my thoughts. He had flung himself into a velvet easy-chair, and was holding a book which he was studying with intense wonder.

'What a book! What a book!' he kept repeating.

These exclamations brought to my mind the fact that my uncle was liable to occasional fits of bibliomania, but no old book had any value in his eyes unless it had the virtue of being unfindable or, at the very least, unreadable.

'Well? Well? Can't you see? I discovered this priceless treasure this morning while I was rummaging about in old Hevelius the Jew's shop.'

'Oh, that's wonderful!' I replied, with forced enthusiasm.

What was the point of all this fuss about an old quarto bound in rough calfskin, a yellowish tome with a faded bookmark hanging from it?

But there was no end yet to the Professor's exclamations of admiration.

'Look,' he went on, both asking the questions and supplying the answers. 'Isn't it a beauty? Yes, it's absolutely splendid! Did you ever see such a binding? Doesn't the book open easily? Yes, it lies flat open at any page. But does it shut equally well? Yes, because the binding and the leaves are flush, all in a straight line, with no gaps or openings anywhere. And look at its spine, not a single crack in it after seven hundred years! Why, Bozerian, Closs or Purgold[3] would have been proud of such a binding!'

While making these comments, my uncle kept opening and shutting the old tome. I just had to ask about its contents, although I really hadn't the slightest interest in what it was about.

'And what's the title of this marvellous work?' I asked with an affected eagerness which he must have been absolutely blind not to see through.

'This work,' replied my uncle, with renewed enthusiasm, 'this work is the *Heims-Kringla* of Snorre Turleson, the famous twelfth-century Icelandic writer! It's the chronicle of the Norwegian princes who ruled in Iceland.'

'Indeed?' I cried, keeping up the pretence of enthusiasm. 'And of course, it's a German translation?'

'What?' replied the Professor sharply. 'A translation? What would I be doing with a translation? Who cares about a translation? This is the Icelandic original, in the magnificent idiomatic vernacular, which is both rich and simple and admits of an infinite variety of grammatical combinations and verbal modifications.'

'Like German,' I ventured.

'Yes,' replied my uncle, shrugging his shoulders, 'but, in addition to all that, Icelandic has three genders like Greek and declensions of proper nouns like Latin.'

'Ah!' I said, shaken a little out of my indifference, 'and is the type good?'

'Type! What do you mean by talking about type, you clown? Type? Do you imagine it's a printed book, you ignorant fool? It's a manuscript, a runic manuscript.'

'Runic?'

'Yes. Do you want me to explain what that is?'

'Of course not,' I replied in a tone of wounded pride. But my uncle continued nevertheless, and told me, whether I liked it or not, many things I had no interest in knowing.

'Runic characters were in use in Iceland in times past. They were invented, it is said, by Odin himself. Just look at them, you impious young man. Admire these letters, the creation of the mind of a god!'

Well, not knowing what to say, I was going to prostrate myself before this wonderful book, a way of answering equally pleasing to gods and kings and which has the advantage of never causing them any embarrassment, when a little incident happened which diverted our conversation down a different path.

This was the appearance of a dirty piece of parchment, which slipped out of the book and fell on the floor.

My uncle pounced on this scrap with understandable eagerness. An old document, enclosed from time immemorial within the folds of this old book, had for him immeasurable value.

'What can this be?' he exclaimed.

And he carefully spread out on the table a piece of parchment, about five inches by three, on which were some lines of mysterious characters.

Here is the exact facsimile. I think it is important for these strange signs to be publicly known, for they were to lead Professor Lidenbrock and his nephew to undertake the strangest expedition of the nineteenth century.

The Professor studied this series of characters for a few moments; then, raising his spectacles, he stated:

'These are runic letters, they're exactly like those of Snorre Turleson's manuscript. But what on earth does it mean?'

Since runic letters seemed to my mind to be an invention of the learned to mystify the rest of us poor souls, I was not sorry to see that my uncle was himself utterly mystified. At least, so it seemed to me, judging from his fingers, which were beginning to work uncontrollably.

'But it's definitely Old Icelandic,' he muttered between clenched teeth.

And Professor Lidenbrock must have known that, for he was acknowledged to be quite a polyglot. Not that he was fluent in the two thousand languages and four thousand dialects which are spoken across the world, but he did nevertheless know his fair share of them.

Faced with this difficulty, I could see he was going to give way to all the impetuosity of his character, and I was expecting a violent outburst, when the little clock over the fireplace struck two o'clock.

At that moment Martha opened the study door, saying:

'The soup is ready!'

'The Devil take your soup,' shouted my uncle, 'and the person who made it, and those who will eat it!' Martha fled. I followed close behind, and, hardly knowing how I got there, I found myself seated in my usual place.

I waited for a few moments. No Professor came. Never within my memory had he missed the important ceremony of dinner. And what a good dinner it was, too! There was parsley soup, a ham omelette garnished with sorrel and nutmeg, and a fillet of veal with compote of prunes; for dessert, sugared fruit; and the whole thing washed down with a good Moselle.

All this my uncle was going to sacrifice for a bit of old parchment. As an affectionate nephew, I considered it my duty to eat for him as well as for myself, which I did most conscientiously.

'I've never known such a thing,' said Martha. 'Professor Lidenbrock not eating!'

'Who'd have believed it?' I said.

'It means something serious is going to happen,' said the old servant, shaking her head.

In my opinion, it meant nothing more serious than the awful scene that would arise when my uncle discovered that his dinner had been eaten. I had just got to the last of the fruit when a loud voice tore me away from the pleasures of my dessert. I bounded out of the dining-room into the study.

CHAPTER 3

THE RUNIC WRITING EXERCISES THE PROFESSOR'S MIND

'It's undoubtedly runic,' said the Professor, frowning, 'but there's a secret in it, and I mean to discover what it is. Otherwise . . .'

A violent gesture completed his sentence.

'Sit there,' he added, gesturing towards the table with his fist. 'Sit down there, and write.'

I was seated and ready in an instant.

'Now I'll dictate to you every letter of our alphabet which corresponds to each of these Icelandic characters. We'll see what that will give us. But, by St Michael, don't you dare make a mistake!'

The dictation began. I concentrated hard on my task. Every letter was called out to me one after the other, with the following incomprehensible result:

mm.rnlls	esreuel	seecJde
sgtssmf	unteief	niedrke
kt,samn	atrateS	Saodrrn
emtnaeI	nuaect	rrilSa
Atvaar	.nscrc	ieaabs
ccdrmi	eeutul	frantu
dt,iac	oseibo	KediiY

When this work was completed, my uncle snatched the paper from me and examined it attentively for a long time.

'What does it all mean?' he kept repeating.

I swear to you I couldn't have enlightened him. But he didn't ask me anyway, and went on talking to himself.

'This is what is called a cryptogram,' he said, 'in which the letters have been deliberately mixed up to hide the meaning, and which if properly arranged would form an intelligible sentence. Just think, there may lie concealed here the clue to some great discovery!'

As for myself, I was of the opinion that it meant nothing at all, though, of course, I was careful not to say so.

Then the Professor took the book and the parchment, and compared the one with the other.

'These two writings are not by the same hand,' he said. 'The cryptogram is of a later date than the book, an undoubted proof of which I can see immediately. The first letter is a double m,[4] a letter which is not to be found in Turleson's book, and which was only added to the alphabet in the fourteenth century. Therefore there are at least two hundred years between the manuscript and the document.'

I won't deny that this seemed a perfectly logical conclusion to me.

'I am therefore led to think,' continued my uncle, 'that someone who possessed this book wrote these mysterious letters. But who was that possessor? Is his name nowhere to be found in the manuscript?'

My uncle raised his spectacles, picked up a strong magnifying glass and carefully examined the blank pages of the book. On the back of the second page, the half-title page, he noticed a sort of stain which looked like an ink blot. But examining it very closely, he thought he could make out some half-effaced letters. My uncle at once latched on to this as the main area of interest, and he worked on that blot until, with the help of his magnifying glass, he managed in the end to make out the following runic characters, which he read out to me with no hesitation:

ᚦᛐᛉᚠ ᚼᛆᚠᛚᚦᚤᚤᛐᚼ

'Arne Saknussemm!' he cried in triumph. 'Why, that's the name of another Icelander, a sixteenth-century scholar and celebrated alchemist!'

I looked at my uncle admiringly.

'Those alchemists,' he went on, 'Avicenna, Bacon, Llull, Paracelsus, were the real, indeed the only, scientists of their time. They made discoveries which still rightly astonish us. Is it not possible that this Saknussemm has concealed in his cryptogram some surprising invention? It must be so. It is so!'

The Professor's imagination caught fire at this hypothesis.

'No doubt,' I ventured to reply, 'but why would he have hidden so marvellous a discovery in this way?'

'Why? Why? How should I know? Didn't Galileo do the same with regard to Saturn? We shall see. I'll get to the secret of this document, and I'll neither sleep nor eat until I have.'

My comment on this was a half-suppressed 'Oh dear!'

'Nor will you, Axel,' he added.

'Oh, good Lord!' I said to myself. 'It's a good thing I ate enough for two today!'

'First of all we must find out what language this cipher is written in. That can't be difficult.'

At these words I looked up quickly. My uncle went on with his soliloquy.

'There's nothing easier. In this document there are a hundred and thirty-two letters, seventy-nine consonants and fifty-three vowels. This is the proportion found in southern languages, whilst northern tongues are much richer in consonants; therefore this is in a southern language.'

These were sensible conclusions, I thought.

'But what language is it?'

Here I expected a display of learning, but what I got instead was profound analysis.

'This Saknussemm,' he went on, 'was a well-educated man. Now, since he was not writing in his own mother tongue, he would naturally select the one which was currently adopted by the leading spirits of the sixteenth century. I mean Latin. If I'm mistaken, I can try Spanish, French, Italian, Greek or Hebrew. But the scholars of the sixteenth century generally wrote in Latin. I therefore have the right to say, *a priori*, that this will be Latin.'

I almost jumped up from my chair. My memories as a Latin scholar revolted against the notion that these barbarous words could belong to the sweet language of Virgil.

'Yes, it is Latin,' my uncle went on. 'But it's a confused and mixed-up Latin.'

'Fine, then,' I thought. 'If you can bring order out of that confusion, my dear Uncle, you're a clever man indeed.'

'Let's examine this carefully,' he said again, picking up the sheet I had been writing on. 'Here is a series of one hundred and thirty-two letters in apparent disorder. There are words consisting of consonants alone, such as 'mm.rrlls'; others, on the other hand, in which vowels predominate, as for instance the fifth, 'unteief', or the last but one, 'oseibo'. Now this arrangement has evidently not been planned; it has arisen *mathematically* in obedience to some unknown rule which has governed the ordering of these letters. It seems certain to me that the original sentence was written properly, and then scrambled according to a rule which we have yet to discover. Whoever possesses the key to this cipher will read it fluently. But what is that key? Axel, have you got it?'

I said not a word, and for a very good reason. My eyes were fixed on a charming picture hanging on the wall, the portrait of Gräuben. My uncle's ward was at that time at Altona, staying with a relative, and in her absence I was very sad, for I may confess to you now, the pretty Virland girl and the professor's nephew loved each other with a patience and a calmness that were so very German. We had become engaged without my uncle's knowledge; he was too much taken up with geology to be able to understand feelings like ours. Gräuben was a lovely blue-eyed blonde, a rather serious girl but that did not stop her from loving me deeply. As for me, I adored her, if there is such a word in the German language. So it was that the picture of my pretty Virland girl instantly carried me away from the real world to a world of daydreams and memories.

Once again I could see the faithful companion of my labours and my leisure. Every day she helped me arrange my uncle's precious specimens; she and I labelled them together. Miss Gräuben was an accomplished mineralogist; she could have taught scientists a few things. She was fond of investigating abstruse scientific questions. What pleasant hours we'd spent in study together, and how often had I envied the very stones which she handled with her delightful fingers.

Then, during our leisure hours, we would go out together and walk along the shady paths beside the Alster, and wander happily side by side up to the old windmill which looked so splendid at the head of the lake. On the way we would chat hand in hand; I would tell her amusing tales which would make her laugh heartily. Then we would reach the banks of the Elbe, and after having said good-bye to the swans swimming gracefully among the white water-lilies, we would come back to the quay on the steamer.

That is just where I was in my daydreaming when my uncle thumped the table with his fist, dragging me violently back to the realities of life.

'Right,' he said, 'the very first thought that would come into anyone's head if they wanted to scramble the letters of a sentence would be to write the words vertically instead of horizontally.'

'That's an idea,' I said to myself.

'Now we must see what the effect of that would be, Axel. Write down any sentence you like on this piece of paper, only instead of arranging the letters in the usual way, one after the other, place them in succession in vertical columns, so as to group them together in five or six vertical lines.'

I understood what I was to do, and immediately produced the following literary masterpiece:

```
I y y l u
l o l e b
o u i G e
v , t r n
e m t ä !
```

'Good,' said the professor, without reading what I had written, 'now write those words in a horizontal line.'

I did as I was told, with the following result:

Iyylu loleb ouiGe v,trn emtä!

'Excellent!' said my uncle, grabbing the paper out of my hands. 'This is beginning to look just like an ancient document: the vowels and the consonants are grouped together in equal confusion, and there are even capitals in the middle of words, and commas too, just like in Saknussemm's parchment.'

I considered my uncle's remarks highly ingenious.

'Now,' said my uncle, looking straight at me, 'to read the sentence which you've just written, and with which I am wholly unacquainted, all I have to do is take the first letter of each word, then the second, then the third, and so on.'

And my uncle, to his great astonishment, and even more to mine, read out:

'I love you, my little Gräuben!'

'What's this?' exclaimed the Professor.

Yes, indeed, without realizing what I was doing, like an awkward and unlucky lover I had compromised myself by writing this unfortunate sentence.

'Ah! You're in love with Gräuben, are you?' he said, sounding just like a guardian should.

'Er, yes! Er, no!' I stammered.

'You love Gräuben,' he went on once or twice, as if in a dream. 'Well, let's apply the procedure I've suggested to the document in question.'

My uncle, becoming absorbed once again in his contemplations, had already forgotten my imprudent words. I say 'imprudent', because the great mind of so learned a man had of course no room for love affairs. Fortunately the important business of the document was more pressing.

As the very moment for the crucial experiment arrived, the Professor's eyes flashed through his spectacles. There was a quivering in his fingers as he grasped the old parchment. He was deeply moved. At last, he gave a preliminary cough, and with profound gravity, calling out in succession the first letter, then the second letter of each word, and so on, he dictated the following series of letters to me:

       mmessunkaSenrA.icefdoK.segnittamurtnecertser
       rette,rotaivsadua,ednecsedsadnelacartniiiluJsira
       tracSarbmutabiledmekmeretarcsilucoYsleffenSnI

I must confess I felt extremely excited when we reached the end. These letters that my uncle had called out, one at a time, conveyed no meaning to my mind, so I was waiting for the Professor to pompously unfold the magnificent but hidden Latin of this mysterious sentence.

But who could have foreseen what was going to happen? A violent thump made the furniture rattle and spilt some ink, and my pen dropped from between my fingers.

'That's not it,' shouted my uncle. 'It doesn't make any sense at all.'

Then shooting across the study like a cannonball and going down the stairs like an avalanche, he rushed out into the Königstrasse and ran off.

CHAPTER 4

THE ENEMY TO BE STARVED INTO SUBMISSION

'Has he gone?' called Martha, running out of her kitchen at the noise of the violent slamming of doors that had shaken the whole house.

'Oh, yes,' I replied, 'completely gone.'

'But what about his dinner?' said the old servant.

'He's not having any.'

'And his supper?'

'He's not having any.'

'What?' cried Martha, clasping her hands.

'No, my dear Martha, he will eat nothing more. No one in the house is to eat anything at all. Uncle Lidenbrock has put us all on a strict diet until he has succeeded in deciphering an undecipherable scrawl.'

'Oh, Heavens! Are we all to die of hunger, then?'

I couldn't bring myself to admit that, with so absolute a ruler as my uncle, such a fate was inevitable.

The old servant, visibly disturbed, returned to her kitchen, moaning pitifully.

Alone once more, I thought of going and telling Gräuben all about it. But how could I leave the house? The Professor might return at any moment. And supposing he called for me? Supposing he wanted to start work on this word-puzzle again, a puzzle which would have taxed even old Oedipus[5]. And if I wasn't there to answer his call, who knows what might happen?

The wisest course was to remain where I was. A mineralogist in Besançon had just sent us a collection of siliceous geodes, which I had to classify. So I set to work, sorting and labelling all these hollow specimens and arranging them in a glass case. Inside each hollow geode was a nest of little crystals.

But this work didn't occupy my whole attention. The business with that old document kept going round and round in my brain. My head was throbbing with excitement and I felt vaguely uneasy. I was gripped by a feeling of impending disaster.

An hour later, my geodes were all arranged on the shelves. Then I flopped into the old velvet armchair, with my head back and my arms hanging over the sides. I lit my long curved pipe, the bowl of which was carved in the likeness of a reclining water-nymph; then I amused myself watching the tobacco turn into carbon, a process which was also slowly turning my nymph into a negress. Now and then I listened for those well-known footsteps on the stairs. But there wasn't a sound. Where could my uncle be? I imagined him running along under the magnificent trees which line the road to Altona, gesticulating wildly, shooting at the walls with his cane, thrashing the long grass, cutting the heads off the thistles and disturbing the peace of the solitary storks.

Would he return in triumph or discouragement? Which of the two would get the upper hand, him or the secret? Sitting pondering such questions, without thinking I picked up the sheet of paper on which I had written the incomprehensible succession of letters, and I repeated to myself 'What does it all mean?'

I tried to group the letters so as to form words. Quite impossible! Whether I put them together in twos, threes, fives or sixes, I got nothing but nonsense. Certainly, the fourteenth, fifteenth and sixteenth letters made the English word 'ice'; the eighty-fourth letter and the next two made 'sir'; and in the middle of the document, in the second and third lines, I noticed the Latin words 'rota', 'mutabile', 'ira', 'nec' and 'atra'.

'Right,' I thought, 'these words seem to justify my uncle's idea about the language of the document. In the last line I could see the word 'luco', which means a sacred wood. In the same line there was the word 'tabiled', which looked like Hebrew, and also the French words 'mer', 'arc' and 'mere'.

It was enough to drive a poor fellow crazy. Four different languages in this ridiculous sentence! What connection could there possibly be between such words as 'ice', 'sir', 'anger', 'cruel', 'sacred wood', 'changeable', 'mother', 'bow' and 'sea'? The first and the last might have something to do with each other; it was not at all surprising that in a document written in Iceland there should be a mention of a sea of ice. But it was quite another thing to get to the meaning of this cryptogram from so small a clue.

So I was struggling with an insurmountable difficulty. My brain was overheating, my eyes were blinking over that sheet of paper; its hundred and thirty-two letters seemed to flutter and fly round me like those silvery drops which float in the air around your head when there's a sudden violent rush of blood to the brain. I was prey to some kind of hallucination; I was suffocating; I needed air. Absent-mindedly I fanned myself with the bit of paper, the back and front of which alternately passed before my eyes. Imagine my surprise when, in one of those rapid movements, just as the back of the paper was turned towards me, I thought I could make out perfectly readable words such as the Latin words 'craterem' and 'terrestre'.

Suddenly, the penny dropped! These mere hints gave me the first glimpse of the truth – I had discovered the key to the cipher! To read the document, it would not even be necessary to read it through the paper. It could be spelt out with ease just as it was, just as it had been dictated to me. All those ingenious professorial combinations were coming to fruition. He was right about the arrangement of the letters. He was right about the language. He had been within a hair's-breadth of reading this Latin sentence from beginning to end; but the crossing of that hair's-breadth, chance had given to me!

Was I excited? I certainly was. My eyes were blurring so much, I could hardly see. I had spread out the paper on the table. I would only have to glance over it to know the whole secret.

At last I became calmer. I made myself walk twice round the room quietly to settle my nerves, and then I sat down again in the huge, deep armchair.

I took a deep breath, and then said to myself 'Now, let's read it.'

I leaned over the table, placed my finger on every letter in turn, and without a pause, without a moment's hesitation, I read out the whole sentence.

What amazement, and what terror, overwhelmed me! It was as if I had received a sudden mortal blow. What? Had what I had read really, actually been done? A mortal man had had the audacity to penetrate . . .

'Oh, no!' I cried, jumping up. 'No! No! No! My uncle must never know about such an incredible journey. He'd insist on doing it too. He's such a determined geologist, ropes couldn't hold him back! He'd start out in spite of everything and everybody, and he'd take me with him, and we'd never get back again. No, never! Never!'

My agitation was beyond all description.

'No! No! I won't let it happen,' I declared emphatically. 'And since it's in my power to prevent knowledge of it reaching the mind of my tyrant, I'll do it. By dint of turning this document round and round, he too might discover the key. I'll destroy it.'

There was a little fire left in the hearth. I picked up not only the piece of paper but Saknussemm's parchment as well. Feverishly, I was just about to fling it all on to the coals and utterly destroy this dangerous secret when the study door opened and in walked my uncle.

CHAPTER 5

FAMINE, THEN VICTORY, FOLLOWED BY DISMAY

I only just had time to put the wretched document back on the table.

Professor Lidenbrock seemed to be completely preoccupied. His obsession was giving him no rest. Evidently he had gone deeply into the matter, with careful thought and analysis. He had brought all the resources of his mind to bear upon it during his walk, and he had come back to apply some new combination to the cypher.

He sat in his armchair, and pen in hand he began to write what looked very much like algebraic formulae. My eyes followed his trembling hands, I noted every movement. Might not some unexpected result come of this? I too trembled, but quite unnecessarily since the true key was in my hands and no other key would unlock the secret.

For three long hours my uncle worked on without a word, without even looking up, rubbing out what he had written, beginning again, then rubbing it all out again, and so on a hundred times.

I knew very well that if he succeeded in writing down these letters in every possible relative position, he would eventually create the correct sentence. But I also knew that twenty letters alone could form two quintillion, four hundred and thirty-two quadrillion, nine hundred and two trillion, eight billion, a hundred and seventy-six million, six hundred and forty thousand combinations. Now, there were a hundred and thirty-two letters in this sentence, and these hundred and thirty-two letters would give a number of different sentences, each made up of at least a hundred and thirty-three letters, a number almost larger than one could imagine.

So I felt reassured as far as this heroic method of solving the problem was concerned.

Time passed. Night came; the noises in the street ceased. My uncle, bent over his task, didn't notice a thing, not even Martha half-opening the door; and he didn't hear a sound, not even the voice of that worthy woman saying:

'Will Sir not have any supper tonight?'

And poor Martha had to go away unanswered. As for me, after a long struggle against it, I was overcome by sleep and dropped off at the end of the sofa, while Uncle Lidenbrock went on calculating and then rubbing out his calculations.

When I awoke the next morning, that indefatigable worker was still at his post. His red eyes, his pale complexion, his hair tangled between his feverish fingers, the red spots on his cheeks, all revealed his desperate struggle with this impossible task and the weariness of spirit and mental exertions he must have undergone all through that unhappy night.

To be honest, I pitied him. In spite of reproaching him, which I considered I had every right to do, I was beginning to feel sorry for him to some extent. The poor man was so entirely taken up with this one idea that he had even forgotten how to get angry. The full strength of his feelings was concentrated on one thing alone, and as the usual vent for his feelings was closed, I was afraid that the extreme tension might lead to an explosion sooner or later.

With one action, with just one word, I might have loosened the vice of steel that was crushing his brain, but that word I would not speak.

Yet I wasn't a hard-hearted person. Why did I stay silent at such a time of crisis? Why was I so insensible to my uncle's interests?

'No, no,' I repeated to myself. 'I'll say nothing. He would insist on going; nothing on earth could stop him. His imagination is a volcano, and he would risk his life to do something that other geologists have never done. I'll say nothing. I'll keep the secret which mere chance has revealed to me. To reveal it would be to kill Professor Lidenbrock! Let him discover it by himself if he can. I will never have it laid at my door that I led him to his destruction.'

So resolved, I folded my arms and waited. But I hadn't reckoned on one little incident which transpired a few hours later.

When Martha wanted to go to the market, she found the door locked. The big key was gone. Who could have taken it out? Undoubtedly, it was my uncle, when he had returned the night before from his hasty walk.

Had he done it on purpose? Or was it a mistake? Did he want us to suffer starvation? That would be going too far! What? Were Martha and I to be the victims of a state of affairs in which we had not the slightest interest? It was true that, a few years before this, while my uncle was working at his great classification of minerals, he went forty-eight hours without eating, and the whole household was obliged to share in this scientific fast. I remember that, for my part, I got severe stomach cramps, which hardly suited the constitution of a hungry, growing boy.

Now it seemed that there was going to be no breakfast, just as there had been no supper the night before. But I made up my mind to be a hero, and not to give in to the pangs of hunger. Martha took it very seriously, and, poor woman, was very upset. As for me, being unable to leave the house distressed me much more, and for a reason you may well understand. A caged lover's feelings may easily be imagined.

My uncle went on working, his imagination rambling through the ideal world of combinations. He was far away from the real world, and far away from worldly needs.

About noon, I began to feel real pangs of hunger. Martha had, without thinking anything about it, used up all the food in the larder the night before, so now there was nothing left in the house. Still I held out; I made it a point of honour.

The clock struck two. This was getting ridiculous; no, worse than that – unbearable. I began to tell myself that I was exaggerating the importance of the document; that my uncle would surely not believe what it said; that he would take it as mere nonsense; that if it came to the worst, we would restrain him and keep him at home if he thought of setting out on the expedition; that, after all, he might himself discover the key to the cipher, and that there would then have been no point to my involuntary abstinence.

These seemed excellent reasons to me, though I would have rejected them indignantly the previous night. I even went as far as to condemn myself for my stupidity in having waited so long, and I finally resolved to let my uncle in on the secret.

I was wondering how to approach the subject, not wanting to do so too suddenly, when the Professor jumped up, put his hat on and was about to go out.

Surely he was not leaving the house and shutting us in again? Oh, no! I wasn't having that.

'Uncle!' I cried.

He seemed not to hear me.

'Uncle Lidenbrock!' I cried, raising my voice.

'Eh?' he answered, like a man suddenly waking up.

'Uncle, the key!'

'What key? The door key?'

'No, no!' I cried. 'The key to the document.'

The Professor stared at me over his spectacles. No doubt he saw something unusual in my expression, because he took hold of my arm and wordlessly questioned me with his eyes. Never was a question more forcefully put.

I nodded my head.

He shook his pityingly, as if he was dealing with a lunatic. I made a more affirmative gesture.

His eyes flashed, his hand became threatening.

This silent conversation in such circumstances would have held the attention of the most indifferent spectator. And the fact really was that I dared not speak now, for fear that my uncle might smother me in his first joyful embraces. But he became so insistent that I was at last obliged to answer.

'Yes, that key. Chance . . .'

'What are you saying?' he shouted with an intensity of emotion that is hard to describe.

'There, read that!' I said, handing him the sheet of paper I had written on.

'But there's nothing there,' he answered, crumpling up the paper.

'No, nothing – until you read it backwards.'

I hadn't finished my sentence when the Professor gave a cry, or rather a roar. He had seen the light! He was transformed!

'Ah, you clever man, Saknussemm!' he cried. 'First you wrote your sentence backwards.'

And snatching up the paper, with vision blurred with tears and a voice choked with emotion, he read the whole document from the last letter to the first.

This is how it went:

In Sneffels Yoculis craterem kem delibat
umbra Scartaris Julii intra calendas descende,
audas viator, et terrestre centrum attinges.
Kod feci. Arne Saknussemm.

Which rather bad Latin may be translated as follows:

Descend into the crater of the jokul of Sneffels,
which the shadow of Scartaris touches before the calends[6] of July,
and you, bold traveller, will reach the centre of the Earth;
which I, Arne Saknussemm, have done.

On reading this, my uncle jumped as if he had touched a Leyden jar[7]. His courage, his joy and his certainty were magnificent to behold. He walked up and down, he held his head in his hands, he pushed the chairs around, he piled up his books; incredible as it may seem, he even juggled with his precious flint geodes; he punched this and he thumped that. Finally, he calmed down and sank back exhausted into his armchair.

'What time is it?' he asked after a few moments of silence.

'Three o'clock,' I replied.

'Is it really? Dinner-time went by quickly, and I didn't notice. I'm dying of hunger. Come on, and after dinner . . .'

'Well?'

'After dinner, pack my trunk.'

'What?' I cried.

'And yours!' replied the merciless Professor, going into the dining-room.

CHAPTER 6

EXCITING DISCUSSIONS ABOUT A UNIQUE UNDERTAKING

At these words, a shiver ran through me. But I controlled myself. I even resolved to put a good face on it. Only scientific arguments could stop Professor Lidenbrock. And there were good arguments against the practicability of such a journey. To penetrate as far as the centre of the Earth? What nonsense! But I kept my battery of arguments in reserve for a suitable opportunity, and gave my whole attention to the meal.

There would be no point in telling you here of my uncle's anger and oaths when he found himself faced with an empty table. Explanations were given, and Martha was set free again. She ran to the market, and managed so well that an hour later my hunger was assuaged, and I was able to go back to contemplating the gravity of the situation.

Throughout dinner my uncle was almost merry. He indulged in some of those learned jokes which never do anybody any harm. But when dessert was over, he beckoned me into his study.

I obeyed. He sat down at one end of his desk, and I sat down at the other.

'Axel,' he said in a kindly voice, 'you're a very clever young man. You've done me a great service, just when, weary of the struggle, I was about to give up. Who knows where I would have ended up. I'll never forget this. And you shall have your share in the glory to which your discovery will lead.'

'Right!' I thought. 'He's in a good mood. Now's the time to discuss that very glory.'

'Most of all,' my uncle went on, 'I must insist on absolute secrecy, you understand? There are not a few people in the world of science who envy me my success, and many of them would be ready to undertake this journey. Our return must be the first news they have of it.'

'Do you really think there are many people bold enough?' I said.

'Certainly. Who would hesitate to gain such fame? If that document became public knowledge, a whole army of geologists would be ready to hasten in the footsteps of Arne Saknussemm.'

'I'm not so sure of that, Uncle,' I replied, 'because we've no proof of the authenticity of this document.'

'What! Given the book we found it in?'

'All right. I'll admit that Saknussemm may have written these lines. But does it follow that he really accomplished such a journey? May it not be that this old parchment is simply intended as a joke?'

I almost regretted having uttered this last word. I said it in an unguarded moment. The Professor's shaggy brows formed into a frown, and for a moment I feared for my safety. Luckily no harm came of it. A vague smile formed on the lips of my stern companion, and he replied:

'That is what we shall see.'

'Oh!' I said, rather put out. 'But do let me go through all the possible objections against this document.'

'Speak, my boy, don't be afraid. You are quite at liberty to express your opinions. You're no longer only my nephew, but my colleague. Please go on.'

'Well, in the first place, I'd like to know what Jokul, Sneffels and Scartaris are. I've never heard these names before.'

'Nothing easier. Not long ago I received a map from my friend, Augustus Petermann, in Leipzig. It couldn't have come at a better time. Take down the third atlas in the second shelf in the large bookcase, series Z, shelf 4.'

I got up, and with the help of such precise instructions couldn't fail to find the required atlas. My uncle opened it, and said:

'Here is one of the best maps of Iceland, Handersen's, and I think this will provide the answer to all your questions.'

I bent over the map.

'Look at this volcanic island,' said the Professor. 'Notice that all the volcanoes are called 'jokuls', a word which means glacier in Icelandic, and that given the northerly latitude of Iceland nearly all the active volcanoes discharge through beds of ice. Hence this term 'jokul' is applied to all the volcanic mountains in Iceland.'

'Fine,' I said, 'but what about Sneffels?'

I was hoping that this question would be unanswerable, but I was mistaken. My uncle replied:

'Follow my finger along the west coast of Iceland. Do you see Reykjavik, the capital? You do? Well, move up past the innumerable fjords that indent those sea-beaten shores, and stop at the sixty-fifth degree of latitude. What do you see there?'

'I can see a peninsula that looks like a thigh bone with the knee bone at the end of it.'

'A very reasonable description, my boy. Now, do you see anything on that knee bone?'

'Yes, a mountain rising out of the sea.'

'Right. That's Snæfell.'

'That's Snæfell?'

'Yes. It's a mountain five thousand feet high, and one of the most remarkable in the world if its crater does lead down to the centre of the Earth.'

'But that's impossible,' I said, shrugging my shoulders, furious at such a ridiculous supposition.

'Impossible?' said the Professor severely. 'Why, may I ask?'

'Because the crater would obviously be filled with lava and burning rocks, and therefore . . .'

'But suppose it's an extinct volcano?'

'Extinct?'

'Yes. The number of active volcanoes on the surface of the globe is at the present time only about three hundred. But there's a very much larger number of extinct ones. Snæfell is one of them. In the historic period, there has only been one eruption of this volcano, in 1219. From then on, it has quietened down more and more, and now it is no longer counted among active volcanoes.'

To such definite statements, I could make no reply. I therefore took refuge in other mysterious passages in the document.

'What's the meaning of this word 'Scartaris', and what have the calends of July got to do with it?'

My uncle took a few minutes to consider. For one brief moment I felt a ray of hope, but it was quickly extinguished, as in a minute he replied with these words:

'What is darkness to you is daylight to me. This shows the care and ingenuity with which Saknussemm has indicated his discovery. Sneffels, or Snæfell, has several craters. It was therefore necessary to point out which of these leads to the centre of the world. What did the Icelandic sage do? He observed that at the approach of the calends of July, that is to say in the last days of June, one of the peaks, called Scartaris, threw its shadow down the mouth of that particular crater, and he committed that fact to his document. Could there possibly have been a more exact guide? As soon as we have arrived at the summit of Snæfell, we need have no hesitation over the proper path to take.'

There was no doubt about it, my uncle had answered every one of my objections. I saw that his position with regard to the old parchment was impregnable. I therefore stopped pressing him on that part of the subject, and since the most important thing was to convince him, I moved on to scientific objections, which in my opinion were far more serious.

'All right, then,' I said. 'I'm forced to admit that Saknussemm's sentence is clear and leaves no room for doubt. I will even allow that the document bears every mark and evidence of authenticity. That learned philosopher did get to the bottom of Sneffels, he has seen the shadow of Scartaris touch the edge of the crater before the calends of July, he may even have heard legends told in his day about that crater reaching to the centre of the world; but as for reaching it himself, as for making the journey, and returning, if he ever went, I say no – he never, ever did that.'

'And what reason do you have for saying that?' said my uncle in a mocking tone.

'All the theories of science declare such a feat to be impracticable.'

'The theories say that, do they?' replied the Professor in an affable tone. 'Oh, those nasty theories! Those theories will really hold us back, won't they?'

I could see that he was just laughing at me, but I continued all the same.

'Yes. It's perfectly well known that the internal temperature of the Earth rises by one degree for every 70 feet you go down from the surface. Now, admitting this proportion to be constant, and the radius of the Earth being fifteen hundred leagues[8], there must be a temperature of more than 200,000 degrees at the centre of the Earth. Therefore, all the substances that compose the body of this Earth must exist there in a state of incandescent gas, for the metals that most resist the action of heat, gold and platinum, and the hardest of rocks could never be solid or even liquid at such a temperature. I have therefore a perfectly good reason for asking if it is possible to penetrate through such a medium.'

'So, Axel, it's the heat that's bothering you?'

'Of course it is. Were we to reach a depth of even 25 miles, we would have arrived at the limit of the terrestrial crust, because there the temperature would be more than 1,300 degrees.'

'And you're afraid of being melted?'

'I'll leave it to you to answer that question,' I replied, rather sullenly.

'This is my answer,' replied Professor Lidenbrock, putting on one of his grandest airs. 'Neither you nor anybody else knows with any certainty what is going on in the interior of the Earth, since not a twelve-thousandth part of its radius is known. Science is always improvable, and every new theory is soon driven out by a yet newer one. Was it not always believed until Fourier that the temperature of interplanetary space decreased indefinitely? And is it not now known that the greatest cold of the ethereal regions is never lower than 40 or 50 degrees below zero? Why should it not be the same with the internal heat? Why should it not be the case that, at a certain depth, it reaches an impassable limit instead of rising to such a point as to melt the most solid metals?'

Since my uncle was now talking hypotheses, there was of course nothing to be said.

'Well, I will tell you that true men of science, amongst them Poisson, have demonstrated that if a heat of 200,000 degrees existed in the interior of the globe, the fiery gases arising from the fused matter would acquire a force that the crust of the Earth would be unable to resist, and that it would explode like the plates of a bursting boiler.'

'That's Poisson's opinion, Uncle, nothing more.'

'Granted. But it is likewise the opinion of other distinguished geologists that the interior of the globe is neither gas nor water, nor any of the heaviest minerals known, for in none of these cases would the Earth weigh what it does.'

'Oh, you can prove anything with figures!'

'But it's the same with facts! Is it not known that the number of volcanoes has decreased since the first days of creation? And if there is central heat, may we not therefore conclude that it too is decreasing?'

'My dear Uncle, if you're entering the realms of speculation, there's nothing more to be said.'

'But I have to tell you that the greatest names have come round to supporting my views. Do you remember a visit paid to me by the celebrated chemist, Humphry Davy, in 1825?'

'Not at all, since I wasn't born until nineteen years after that.'

'Well, Humphry Davy did call on me on his way through Hamburg. We spent a long time discussing, amongst other problems, the hypothesis of the liquid structure of the nucleus of the Earth. We agreed that it couldn't be in a liquid state for a reason which science has never been able to confute.'

'What is that reason?' I said, rather astonished.

'Because this liquid mass would be subject, like the ocean, to lunar attraction, and therefore twice every day there would be internal tides which, by pushing up the terrestrial crust, would cause regular earthquakes!'

'Yet it's evident that the surface of the globe has been subject to the action of fire,' I replied, 'and it is quite reasonable to suppose that the external crust cooled down first, whilst the heat took refuge down at the centre.'

'You would be wrong in that assumption,' replied my uncle. 'The Earth has been heated by combustion on its surface, and that's all. Its surface was composed of a great many metals, such as potassium and sodium, which have the peculiar property of igniting when they come into contact with air and water. These metals ignited when the atmospheric vapour fell on the ground as rain, and by and by, when the water penetrated into the fissures of the crust of the Earth, it caused fresh combustion with explosions and eruptions. This was what caused the numerous volcanoes when the Earth was formed.'

'That's a very clever hypothesis!' I exclaimed, somewhat in spite of myself.

'And one which Humphry Davy demonstrated to me by a simple experiment. He formed a small ball of the metals I have mentioned, making a very fair representation of our globe. Whenever he caused a fine spray of rain to fall on its surface, it swelled up, oxidized and formed tiny mountains. A crater broke open at one of its summits, an eruption took place, and transmitted such heat to the whole of the ball that it could not be held in one's hand.'

In truth, I was beginning to be swayed by the Professor's arguments, to which he was giving additional weight by his usual ardour and fervent enthusiasm.

'You see, Axel,' he added, 'the state of the nucleus of the Earth has given rise to various hypotheses among geologists. There is no proof at all of this internal heat, and my opinion is that there is no such thing, that there cannot *be* such a thing. In any case, we shall see for ourselves, and, like Arne Saknussemm, we'll know exactly what the truth is concerning this important question.'

'Very well, we shall see,' I replied, carried away by his contagious enthusiasm. 'Yes, we shall see. That is, if it's possible to see anything there.'

'And why not? May we not depend on electrical phenomena to give us light? May we not even expect light from the atmosphere, the pressure of which may cause it to be luminous as we near the centre?'

'Well, yes,' I said. 'That too is possible.'

'It is certain,' exclaimed my uncle in a tone of triumph. 'But not a word, do you hear? Not a word about this whole subject. We don't want anyone to get the idea of discovering the centre of the Earth before we do.'

CHAPTER 7

A WOMAN'S COURAGE

So ended this memorable session. That conversation threw me into a fever. I came out of my uncle's study quite stunned, so much so that it was as if there was not enough air in all the streets of Hamburg to put me right again. I therefore made for the banks of the Elbe, close to the quay for the steamer that plies between the town and the Harburg railway line.

Was I convinced of the truth of what I had heard? Had I not simply given way under the pressure of Professor Lidenbrock's forceful personality? Was I to believe that he was really in earnest in his intention to penetrate to the centre of this massive globe? Had I been listening to the mad speculations of a lunatic or to the scientific conclusions of a lofty genius? Where did truth end? Where did error begin?

I was all adrift amongst a thousand contradictory hypotheses, and I couldn't grasp any one of them firmly.

But I remembered that I had been convinced, although my enthusiasm now was beginning to cool. I felt a desire to make a start at once, and not to lose time and courage by calm reflection. I had at that moment quite enough courage to simply pack my case and set off.

But I have to confess that in another hour this unnatural excitement abated, my nervous tension lessened, and from the depths of the Earth I climbed back to the surface again.

'It's absolutely crazy!' I shouted out. 'There's no sense in it. No sensible young man should consider such a proposal for a moment. Nothing of that is real. I've had a bad night, it's all a bad dream.'

By this time, I had walked along the banks of the Elbe and crossed the town. After passing the port as well, I reached the Altona road. Something led me there, some intuition that was soon to be justified, for I shortly caught sight of my little Gräuben returning with her light step to Hamburg.

'Gräuben!' I shouted while still some way away.

The young girl stopped, rather frightened perhaps to hear someone call her name on the public highway. In ten strides, I was beside her.

'Axel!' she exclaimed in surprise. 'What, then? Have you come to meet me? Is that why you're here?'

But when she looked at me, Gräuben couldn't fail to see my uneasiness and distress.

'What's the matter with you?' she said, holding out her hand.

'What's the matter with me, Gräuben? You have no idea!' I said.

In two seconds and three sentences my pretty Virland girl was fully informed of what was going on. For a time she was silent. Was her heart beating like mine? I don't know, but I do know that her hand wasn't trembling in mine. We walked on a hundred yards without speaking.

At last she said, 'Axel.'

'My darling Gräuben.'

'That will be a wonderful journey!'

These words made me jump.

'Yes, Axel, it's a journey worthy of the nephew of a scientist. It's a good thing for a man to gain fame by some great undertaking.'

'What, Gräuben, aren't you going to try to dissuade me from setting out on such an expedition?'

'No, my dear Axel, and I would willingly go with you, except that a poor girl would only be in your way.'

'Are you serious?'

'Quite serious.'

Oh, women, girls, the female mind, how hard it is to understand you! When you're not the most timid of creatures, you're the bravest. Reason has no influence over you. What was she saying? Was this child encouraging me to undertake such an expedition? Would she really not be afraid to take part in it herself? And she was urging *me* to do it, me, the one she loved!

I was disconcerted and, to tell you the truth, I was ashamed.

'We'll see whether you'll say the same thing tomorrow, Gräuben.'

'Tomorrow, dear Axel, I will say exactly what I have said today.'

Gräuben and I continued on our way, hand in hand but in silence. The emotional turmoil of the day had exhausted me.

After all, I thought, the calends of July are a long way off, and between now and then many things could happen that would cure my uncle of his desire to travel underground.

It was night when we arrived at the house in Königstrasse. I expected to find the house quiet, my uncle in bed as usual, and Martha giving the dining-room a last touch with the feather duster.

But I hadn't taken into account the Professor's impatience. I found him shouting and getting himself all worked up amidst a crowd of porters who were all depositing various loads in the hallway. Our old servant was at her wits' end.

'Come on, Axel, you miserable wretch!' shouted my uncle as soon as he saw me. 'Your cases aren't packed, and my papers aren't in order. I can't find the key of my carpet bag. And I haven't got my gaiters.'

I stood thunderstruck. My voice failed. My lips could scarcely utter the words:

'Are we really going?'

'Of course we are! I never dreamed that you would go out for a walk instead of getting a move on with your preparations.'

'So we're really going?' I asked again, my hopes fading.

'Yes, the day after tomorrow, early.'

I couldn't listen to any more. I fled to my little room for refuge.

All hope was now gone. My uncle had spent the whole afternoon buying some of the tools and apparatus required for this desperate undertaking. The hallway was packed with rope ladders, knotted cords, torches, flasks, grappling irons, alpenstocks, pickaxes, iron-tipped sticks, enough for ten men to carry.

I spent a terrible night. Next morning I was called early. I had quite decided not to open the door, but how could I resist the sweet voice which was always music to my ears, saying, 'Axel dear'?

I came out of my room. I thought my pale countenance and my red and sleepless eyes would have some effect on Gräuben's sympathies and change her mind.

'Oh, Axel, my dear,' she said, 'I see you're better. A night's rest has done you good.'

'Done me good?' I exclaimed.

I rushed to the mirror. Well, in fact I did look better than I'd expected. I could hardly believe my own eyes.

'Axel,' she said, 'I've had a long talk with my guardian. He's a dedicated scientist and a man of immense courage, and you must remember that his blood flows in your veins. He has told me of his plans and his hopes, and why and how he hopes to attain his objective. I have no doubt he will succeed. My dear Axel, it's a wonderful thing to devote yourself to science! What honours await Professor Lidenbrock, and they will reflect on his companion too. When you return, Axel, you will be a man, his equal, free to speak and to act independently, and free to . . .'

The dear girl could only finish this sentence with a blush. Her words revived me. But I refused to believe we would be starting so soon. I dragged Gräuben into the Professor's study.

'Uncle, is it true we're going?'

'Why do you doubt it?'

'Well, I'm not doubting it,' I said, not wanting to annoy him, 'but what need is there for all this hurry?'

'Time! Time that's flying by with a speed that nothing can change.'

'But it's only the 16th of May, and the end of June is . . .'

'You ignoramus! Do you think you can get to Iceland in a couple of days? If you hadn't gone off and left me, like a fool, I would have taken you to the office of Liffender & Co. of Copenhagen and then you would have learned that there's only one sailing every month from Copenhagen to Reykjavik, on the 22nd.'

'Well?'

'Well, if we waited for the 22nd of June, we would be too late to see the shadow of Scartaris touch the crater of Snæfell. So we must get to Copenhagen as fast as we can in order to secure our passage. Go and pack!'

There was nothing I could say to this. I went up to my room. Gräuben followed me. She set to to pack everything I would need on my trip. She was no more affected than if I had been starting out on a little trip to Lübeck or Heligoland. Her little hands moved without haste. She talked quietly. She kept giving me sensible reasons for our expedition. She charmed me, and yet I was angry with her. Now and then I felt like exploding into a temper, but she took no notice and went on as methodically as ever.

Finally the last strap was buckled. I went downstairs again. All that day the suppliers of scientific instruments, guns and electrical equipment kept coming and going. Martha was being driven distracted.

'Is the Professor mad?' she asked.

I nodded my head.

'And is he going to take you with him?'

I nodded again.

'Where to?'

I pointed down towards the floor.

'Down into the cellar?' exclaimed the old servant.

'No,' I said. 'Lower than that.'

Night came. But I didn't notice time passing.

'Tomorrow morning, at six o'clock sharp,' said my uncle. 'That's when we're setting off.'

At ten o'clock I fell on my bed, a mere lump of inert matter. All through the night terror gripped me. I dreamed of abysses. I was a prey to delirium. I felt myself held by the Professor's sinewy hand, dragged along, hurled down, shattered into little bits. I dropped down unfathomable precipices with the accelerating velocity of bodies falling through space. My life became one unending fall. I awoke at five, trembling and weary, with my nerves shattered. I went downstairs. My uncle was already at the table, gobbling down his breakfast. I stared at him with horror and disgust. But my dear Gräuben was there, so I said nothing. But I couldn't eat a thing.

At half-past five there was a rattle of wheels outside. A large carriage had arrived to take us to the Altona railway station. It was soon piled up with my uncle's trunks and cases.

'Where's your case?' he cried.

'It's ready,' I replied in a faltering voice.

'Then hurry up and bring it down, or we'll miss the train.'

It was now clearly impossible to continue to struggle against fate. I went up to my room again and let my case slide down the stairs, following quickly after it.

At that moment, my uncle was solemnly handing over control of the household to Gräuben. My pretty Virland girl was as calm and collected as ever. She kissed her guardian, but couldn't hold back a tear as she touched my cheek with her gentle lips.

'Gräuben!' I murmured.

'Go, my dear Axel, go! I'm your fiancée now, and when you come back I will be your wife.'

I hugged her in my arms and took my seat in the carriage. Martha and the young girl, standing at the door, waved their last farewell. Then the horses, urged on by the driver's whistling, swept off at a gallop on the road to Altona.

CHAPTER 8

SERIOUS PREPARATIONS FOR A VERTICAL DESCENT

Altona, which is just a suburb of Hamburg, is the terminus of the Kiel railway, which was to take us to the coast at the Belts[9]. In twenty minutes we were in Holstein.

At half-past six the carriage stopped outside the station. My uncle's numerous voluminous trunks were unloaded, moved, labelled, weighed and put into the luggage vans, and at seven we were seated face to face in our compartment. The whistle blew and the engine pulled away. We were off.

Was I resigned to my fate? No, not yet. Nevertheless the cool morning air and the rapidly changing scenes along the way to some extent drew me out of my sad thoughts.

As for the Professor's thoughts, they were running far ahead of the express train. We were alone in the carriage, but we sat in silence. My uncle checked all his pockets and his travelling bag with the minutest care. I could see that he hadn't overlooked the slightest detail.

Amongst other documents, there was a carefully folded sheet of paper bearing the heading of the Danish consulate and signed by Mr Christiensen, the Danish consul in Hamburg and a friend of the Professor's. This we would hoped would provide us with the means in Copenhagen of getting a recommendation to the Governor of Iceland[10].

I also caught sight of the famous document, carefully hidden in a secret pocket in my uncle's wallet. I cursed it, and then began to study the countryside. It was an interminable succession of uninteresting loamy and fertile flats, a very easy country to build railways on, and particularly suitable for the laying-down of these direct, level lines so dear to railway companies.

I had no time to get tired of the monotony, for in three hours we stopped at Kiel, close to the sea.

The luggage being labelled for Copenhagen, we had no need to concern ourselves with it, but nonetheless the Professor kept a careful eye on every item until all were safe on board. There they disappeared into the hold.

My uncle, in his haste, had so well calculated the connection times between the train and the steamer that we had a whole day to spare. The steamer *Ellenora* was not leaving until that night. This caused nine hours of feverish over-excitement in which the impatient irascible traveller (my uncle) consigned to hell the railway directors and the steamboat companies and the governments which allowed such intolerable delays. I was forced to back him up when he argued with the captain of the *Ellenora* on this very subject. He wanted to get him to stoke the boilers at once. The captain told him to clear off.

In Kiel, as elsewhere, a day passes eventually. What with walking along the verdant shores of the bay on which the little town stands, exploring the thick woods which make the town look like a nest hidden in a tangle of branches, admiring the villas, each with its own little bath-house, and by rushing about and grumbling, at last ten o'clock came.

The smoke from the *Ellenora*'s funnel rose up into the sky in thick curls and the bridge shook with the throbbing of the boiler. We were on board, and for a time possessors of two berths, one above the other, in the only saloon cabin on the ship.

At a quarter past ten, the ship cast off and started on its journey over the dark waters of the Great Belt.

The night was dark. There was a sharp breeze and a rough sea. Through the thick darkness, a few lights appeared on the shore. Later on, I don't know when, a dazzling light from some lighthouse threw a bright stream of fire across the waves. And this is all I can remember of this first crossing of ours.

At seven in the morning, we landed at Korsör, a small town on the west coast of Zealand. There we transferred from the boat to another railway line, which took us across a country every bit as flat as Holstein.

Three hours' travelling brought us to the capital of Denmark. My uncle hadn't shut his eyes all night. In his impatience, I do believe he had been trying to make the train go faster with his feet!

At last he caught a glimpse of the sea.

'The Sound[11]!' he shouted.

On our left was a huge building that looked like a hospital.

'That's a lunatic asylum,' said one of our travelling companions.

'Great!' I thought. 'Just the place to end our days in. But big as it is, that asylum isn't big enough to hold the complete madness of Professor Lidenbrock!'

At ten in the morning, we at last set foot in Copenhagen. The luggage was loaded on to a carriage and, with us too, taken to the Phoenix Hotel in Breda Street. This took half an hour, because the station is outside the town. Then my uncle, after a quick wash, dragged me after him. The porter at the hotel could speak German and English, but the Professor, as a polyglot, questioned him in good Danish, and it was in the same language that we were given directions to the Museum of Northern Antiquities.

The museum was a curious establishment, a collection of wonders – stone weapons, metal goblets and jewellery – by means of which one might reconstruct the ancient history of the country. Professor Thomsen, the curator, was a learned scholar and a friend of the Danish consul in Hamburg.

My uncle had a cordial letter of introduction to him. As a general rule, one scholar greets another with a certain coolness. But here it was different. Professor Thomsen greeted Professor Lidenbrock warmly like an old friend, and the Professor's nephew as well. I need hardly say that we kept our secret from the worthy curator: we were simply visiting Iceland out of harmless curiosity.

Professor Thomsen put himself entirely at our disposal, and with him we visited the harbour with the object of finding the vessel that was due to sail the soonest.

I was still hoping there would be no way of getting to Iceland, but no such luck. A small Danish schooner, the *Valkyrie*, was due to set sail for Reykjavik on the 2nd of June. The captain, a Mr Bjarne, was on board. His passenger-to-be was so overjoyed that he shook his hand so hard he almost broke it. The worthy fellow was rather surprised at this intensity. To him it seemed a very simple thing to go to Iceland, as that was his business, but to my uncle it was sublime. The worthy captain took advantage of this enthusiasm to charge us double for the trip, but we didn't bother ourselves over such trifles.

'You must be on board on Tuesday, at seven in the morning,' said Captain Bjarne, having pocketed the cash.

Then we thanked Professor Thomsen for his kindness and returned to the Phoenix Hotel.

'That's fine, that's fine,' my uncle kept saying. 'How lucky we are to have found this boat ready to sail. Now let's have some breakfast and wander round the town.'

First we went to Kongens-nye-Torw, an irregularly-shaped square in which there are two innocent-looking guns which wouldn't frighten anyone. Close by, at No. 5, there was a French restaurant owned by a chef by the name of Vincent, where we got an ample breakfast that cost us four marks each.

Then I took a childish pleasure in exploring the city. My uncle let me drag him around with me, but he took no notice of anything: not the insignificant king's palace; nor the pretty seventeenth-century bridge which spans the canal in front of the museum; nor that immense monument to Thorwaldsen, decorated with a horrible mural painting and containing within it a collection of the sculptor's works; nor, in a beautiful park, the chocolate-box Rosenberg Castle; nor the beautiful renaissance edifice of the Exchange, nor its spire composed of the twisted tails of four bronze dragons; nor the huge windmill on the ramparts, whose huge arms billowed in the sea breeze like the sails of a ship.

What delightful walks we would have had together, my pretty Virland girl and I, along the harbour where the double-decked ships and the frigates slept peacefully beside the red roofs of the warehouses, by the green banks along the strait, through the deep shades of the trees amongst which the fort is half concealed, where the guns are thrusting out their black throats between branches of alder and willow.

But, alas, Gräuben was far away, and I had no hope of ever seeing her again.

But if my uncle felt no attraction to these romantic scenes, he was very much struck by the sight of a certain church spire situated on the island of Amager, which forms the south-west[12] part of Copenhagen.

I was ordered to head in that direction. We embarked on a small steamer which plies the canals, and in a few minutes it pulled alongside the Dockyard quay.

After making our way through a few narrow streets where some convicts in yellow and grey trousers were at work under the supervision of warders, we arrived at the Vor Frelsers Kirk. There was nothing remarkable about the church, but there was a reason why its tall spire had attracted the Professor's attention. Starting from the top of the tower, an external staircase wound around the spire, circling upwards in spirals.

'Let's go right to the top,' said my uncle.

'I'll get dizzy,' I said.

'All the more reason why we should go up. We've got to get used to it.'

'But . . .'

'Come on, I tell you. Don't waste time.'

I had no option but to obey. A caretaker who lived at the other end of the street gave us the key, and our ascent began.

My uncle went ahead, treading carefully. I followed him rather anxiously, because I was very prone to dizziness. I had neither the sense of balance of an eagle nor the nerves of one.

As long as we were protected by being on the inside of the winding staircase up the tower, all went well enough; but after we had toiled up a hundred and fifty steps, fresh air hit me in the face, and we found ourselves on the platform at the top of the tower. There the outside staircase began its spirals, protected only by a thin iron rail, and the narrowing steps seemed to lead on up into infinite space!

'I'll never be able to do it,' I said.

'Come on, don't be a coward,' said my uncle, not showing a shred of pity.

I had no option but to follow him, clutching at every step. The cold air made me giddy; I felt the spire rocking with every gust of wind; my legs were turning to jelly. Soon I was crawling on my knees, then on my stomach. I closed my eyes; I seemed to be lost in space.

At last I reached the top, assisted by my uncle dragging me up by the collar.

'Look down!' he cried. 'Take a good look down! You must have a lesson in abysses.'

I opened my eyes. I saw houses squashed flat as if they had all fallen from the sky; they seemed to be drowning in a smoky fog. Above my head ragged clouds were drifting past, and by an optical illusion they seemed stationary, while the steeple, the ball and I were all scudding along at a fantastic speed. Far away to one side was green countryside, while on the other the sea sparkled, bathed in sunlight. The Sound stretched away to Elsinore, dotted with a few white sails like seagulls' wings; and in the misty east and away to the north-east lay outstretched the faintly-shadowed shores of Sweden. All this immensity of space whirled and swirled before my eyes.

But I was forced to get up, to stand up, to look. My first lesson in dizziness lasted an hour. When I got permission to come down and feel the solid street pavements beneath my feet I was aching all over.

'We'll do the same again tomorrow,' said the Professor.

And so it was. For five days in a row, I was made to undergo this anti-vertigo exercise. And whether I wanted to or not, I made definite progress in the art of 'looking down from high places'.

CHAPTER 9

ICELAND! BUT WHAT NEXT?

The day of our departure arrived. The day before that, our kind friend Professor Thomsen had brought us letters of introduction to Count Trampe, the Governor of Iceland, Mr Pictursson, the bishop's suffragan, and Mr Finsen, the mayor of Reykjavik. My uncle expressed his gratitude with the warmest of handshakes.

On the 2nd, at six o'clock in the morning, all our precious baggage having been safely stowed on board the *Valkyrie*, the captain led us to some very narrow cabins.

'Is the wind favourable?' asked my uncle.

'Excellent,' replied Captain Bjarne. 'A southeasterly. We'll sail down the Sound at full speed, with all sails set.'

In a few minutes the schooner, under her mizzen, brigantine, topsail and topgallant sail, cast off from her moorings and sailed at full speed through the straits. In an hour the capital of Denmark seemed to sink below the distant waves, and the *Valkyrie* was skirting the coast near Elsinore. In my nervous frame of mind, I half-expected to see the ghost of Hamlet wandering on the legendary castle terrace.

'You magnificent fool!' I said. 'No doubt *you* would approve of our expedition. Perhaps you would accompany us to the centre of the globe, to find the answer to your eternal doubts.'

But there was no ghostly shape on the ancient walls. In any case, the castle is much younger than the heroic prince of Denmark. It now serves as a sumptuous lodge for the guardian of the straits of the Sound, through which pass fifteen thousand ships of all nations, every year.

The castle of Kronborg soon disappeared in the mist, as well as the tower of Helsingborg on the Swedish coast, and the schooner passed lightly on her way, driven by the breezes of the Kattegat.

The *Valkyrie* was a splendid ship, but on a sailing vessel you can never be sure what to expect. She was carrying coal to Reykjavik, and household goods, earthenware, woollen clothing and a cargo of wheat. The crew consisted of five men, all Danes.

'How long will the passage take?' asked my uncle.

'Ten days,' the captain replied, 'if we don't encounter a northwesterly while we're passing the Faeroes.'

'But you aren't often delayed much, are you?'

'No, Mr Lidenbrock, don't you worry, we'll get there in good time.'

Towards evening the schooner rounded the Skaw at the northernmost point of Denmark, and then during the night crossed the Skagerrack, after which it skirted Norway with Cape Lindesnes to starboard and sailed into the North Sea.

Two days later we sighted the coast of Scotland near Peterhead, and the *Valkyrie* turned to head towards the Faeroe Islands, passing between Orkney and Shetland.

Soon the schooner encountered the great Atlantic swell. She had to tack against the north wind, and reached the Faeroes only with some difficulty. On the 8th, the captain made out Mykiness, the westernmost of the islands, and then set a straight course for Cape Portland, the most southerly point of Iceland.

Nothing unusual happened during the crossing. I wasn't troubled by seasickness; my uncle, on the other hand, to his great disgust and even greater shame, was ill for the whole voyage.

He was therefore unable to talk to the captain about Snæfell, how to get to it and what means of transport were available. He was obliged to put off these inquiries until our arrival, and spent the whole time stretched out in his cabin, the timbers of which creaked and shook with the pitching and tossing of the ship. I thought him not undeserving of this punishment.

On the 11th, we reached Cape Portland. The clear weather gave us a good view of Myrdalsjökull, which towers over it. The cape is merely a low hill with steep sides, standing alone by the beach.

The *Valkyrie* kept some distance from the coast, taking a westerly course amidst huge schools of whales and sharks. Soon we came in sight of an enormous rock with a hole in the middle of it through which the sea crashed furiously. The Westmann Islands seemed to rise out of the ocean like rocks sown in a field of liquid. From that point on, the schooner kept well out to sea and gave the land a wide berth as it rounded Cape Reykjanes, which forms the westernmost point of Iceland.

The rough sea prevented my uncle from coming up on deck to admire these battered and wind-beaten coastlands.

Forty-eight hours later, coming out of a storm which had forced the schooner to sail under bare masts, we caught sight to the east of us of the beacon on Skagen Point, where dangerous rocks stretch far out to sea. An Icelandic pilot came on board, and in three hours the *Valkyrie* dropped anchor close to Reykjavik, in Faxa Bay.

The Professor at last emerged from his cabin, rather pale and wretched-looking but still full of enthusiasm and with a look of satisfaction on his face.

The population of the town, thrilled by the arrival of a vessel from which everyone expected something, formed in groups on the quay.

My uncle hastened to leave his floating prison, or rather hospital. But before leaving the deck of the schooner he dragged me over, and pointing north of the bay to a distant mountain that formed a double peak, a pair of cones covered with perpetual snow, he shouted:

'Snæfell! That's Snæfell!'

Then motioning to me to say nothing about our secret, he got into the boat that was waiting for him. I followed, and soon we were standing on the very soil of Iceland.

The first man we saw was a decent-looking fellow in a general's uniform. But he wasn't a general, just a magistrate, the Governor of the island, Baron Trampe himself. The Professor realized at once who he was dealing with. He handed over his letters from Copenhagen, and there then followed a short conversation in Danish which, for a very good reason, I took no part in. But the result of this first conversation was that Baron Trampe placed himself entirely at the disposal of Professor Lidenbrock.

My uncle was just as courteously received by the mayor, Mr Finsen, whose appearance was just as military, and whose temperament and function just as peaceful, as the Governor's.

As for the bishop's suffragan, Mr Pictursson, he was at that moment engaged in an episcopal visit in the north, so we would just have to wait for the honour of being presented to him. But Mr Fridriksson, the science teacher at the Reykjavik school, was a delightful man, and his help became very important to us. This humble scholar spoke only Icelandic and Latin, and he came and offered us his assistance in the language of Horace. I felt we were well suited to understanding each other. In fact he was the only person in Iceland with whom I could converse at all.

This good-natured gentleman gave us the use of two of the three rooms in his house, and we were soon installed there with all our luggage, the quantity of which rather astonished the good people of Reykjavik.

'Well, Axel,' said my uncle, 'we're getting on, and now the worst is over.'

'The worst?' I said, astonished.

'To be sure, now we have nothing to do but go down.'

'Oh, if that's all, you're quite right. But nevertheless, when we've gone down, we'll have to climb up again, won't we?'

'Oh, I'm not worried about that. Come on, there's no time to lose. I'm going to the library. Perhaps there's some manuscript of Saknussemm's there, and I'd like to consult it.'

'Well, while you're there, I'll go into town. Won't you come too?'

'Oh, that doesn't interest me at all. It's not what's on this island, but what's beneath it, that interests me.'

I went out, and wandered wherever chance took me.

It would be hard to get lost in Reykjavik's two streets. I therefore had no need to ask the way, something that can easily lead to confusion when your only means of asking is by gesture.

The town stretches out along low, marshy ground between two hills. On one side there is an immense bed of lava sloping gently towards the sea. On the other side there is the vast spread of Faxa Bay, bordered to the north by the huge Snæfell glacier. The *Valkyrie* was at the time the only occupant of the bay. Usually English and French fisheries protection vessels moor there, but just then they were patrolling the eastern coasts of the island.

The longer of the only two streets in Reykjavik runs parallel to the beach. Here the merchants and traders live, in wooden cabins made of red planks set horizontally. The other street, running west, leads to a little lake and passes between the house of the bishop and other people who are not involved in trade.

I had soon explored these depressing streets. Here and there I got a glimpse of faded grass, looking like a worn-out bit of carpet, or of a kitchen garden of sorts, the sparse vegetables of which (potatoes, cabbages and lettuces) would have been suitable for a table in Lilliput[13]. A few sickly wallflowers were trying to enjoy the air and sunshine.

About halfway along the non-commercial street I found the public cemetery, enclosed by a mud wall, and where there seemed to be plenty of room.

Then a few steps brought me to the Governor's house, nothing much to look at compared with the town hall in Hamburg but a palace in comparison with the huts of the people of Iceland.

Situated between the little lake and the town, the church is built in the Protestant style, of calcined stones which the volcanoes themselves supply. It was obvious that in strong westerly winds the red tiles of the roof would be scattered in the air, to the great danger of the faithful worshippers.

On a neighbouring hill I spotted the national school, where, as I was later informed by our host, were taught Hebrew, English, French and Danish, four languages of which, I confess with shame, I knew not one word. In an exam I would have come last among the forty scholars being educated at this little college, and I would have been held unworthy to sleep with them in one of those little double closets where more delicate youths would have died of suffocation the very first night.

In three hours I had seen not only the town but its surroundings. The general appearance of the place was really dismal. No trees, and scarcely any vegetation. Everywhere bare rocks, the signs of volcanic activity. The Icelandic cottages are made of earth and turf, and the walls slope inward. They rather resemble roofs placed on the ground, but these roofs are meadows of comparative fertility. Thanks to the heat from inside, grass grows on them quite well. It is carefully mown in the haymaking season; otherwise the horses, cows and sheep would come and graze on these lush, green houses.

During my walk I only met a few people. On returning to the main street I found the greater part of the population busy drying, salting and loading cod, their main export. The men were robust but heavy, like blond Germans with pensive eyes, conscious of being far removed from the rest of humanity, poor exiles relegated to this land of ice, poor creatures who should have been Eskimos since nature had condemned them to live just outside the Arctic Circle. I tried in vain to detect a smile on their faces; sometimes they seemed to laugh, by a spasmodic and involuntary contraction of the muscles, but they never smiled.

Their clothing consisted of a coarse jacket of black woollen cloth known as *'vadmel'* in Scandinavian countries, a hat with a very broad brim, trousers trimmed with narrow red ribbon, and bits of leather rolled round their feet by way of shoes.

The women looked as sad and resigned as the men; their faces were pleasant but expressionless, and they wore dresses and petticoats of dark *vadmel*. If unmarried, they wore over their braided hair a little knitted brown cap; when married, they put a coloured kerchief round their heads, crowned with a peak of white linen.

After a good walk, I returned to Mr Fridriksson's house, where I found my uncle in the company of his host.

CHAPTER 10

INTERESTING CONVERSATIONS WITH ICELANDIC SCHOLARS

Dinner was ready. Professor Lidenbrock was devouring his platefuls with relish, as his forced fast on board the ship had turned his stomach into a vast unfathomable gulf. The meal was more Danish than Icelandic, and was nothing remarkable in itself; but the hospitality of our host reminded me of the heroes of old. It seemed to me that we were more at home than he was himself.

The conversation was carried on in the local language, which for my benefit my uncle interspersed with German and Mr Fridriksson with Latin. It was mostly about matters of science, as is quite fitting for scientists; but Professor Lidenbrock was very reserved, and at every sentence his eyes indicated that I should say absolutely nothing regarding our plans.

First Mr Fridriksson wanted to know what success my uncle had had at the library.

'Your library! Why, there's nothing there but a few tattered books on almost empty shelves.'

'What?' replied Mr Fridriksson. 'Why, we have eight thousand volumes, many of them valuable and rare, works in the old Scandinavian language, and we have all the new books that Copenhagen sends us every year.'

'Where do you keep your eight thousand volumes? As far as I could see . . .'

'Oh, Mr Lidenbrock, they're all over the country. We're fond of study in this icy region. There's not a farmer or a fisherman who cannot read and does not read. Our principle is that books, instead of growing mouldy behind an iron grating, should be worn out under the eyes of many readers. So these books are passed from one person to another, read over and over again and referred to again and again; and it often happens that they only find their way back to their shelves after an absence of a year or two.'

'And in the meantime,' said my uncle, rather spitefully, 'strangers . . .'

'Well, what would you have us do? Foreigners have their libraries at home, and the essential thing for working people is that they should be educated. I say again, the love of reading runs in Icelandic blood. In 1816 we founded a prosperous literary society; learned foreigners consider themselves honoured to become members of it. It publishes books which educate our fellow-countrymen and do the country great service. It would give us immense pleasure if you would agree to be a corresponding member, Mr Lidenbrock.'

My uncle, who had already joined about a hundred learned societies, accepted with a grace which clearly touched Mr Fridriksson.

'Now,' he said, 'if you will be kind enough to tell me what books you hoped to find in our library, I may perhaps assist you to consult them.'

My uncle's eyes met mine. He hesitated. This direct question went to the very heart of the matter. But, after a moment's reflection, he decided to speak.

'Mr Fridriksson, I wanted to know if amongst your ancient books you possessed any of the works of Arne Saknussemm.'

'Arne Saknussemm! You mean that learned sixteenth-century scholar, naturalist, chemist and traveller?'

'Exactly.'

'One of the glories of Icelandic literature and science?'

'That's the man.'

'An illustrious man anywhere!'

'Quite so.'

'And whose courage was equal to his genius!'

'I see you know him well.'

My uncle was absolutely delighted to hear his hero so described. He was feasting his eyes on Mr Fridriksson.

'Well,' he cried, 'where are his works?'

'His works? We don't have any of his works.'

'What – not in Iceland?'

'Neither in Iceland nor anywhere else.'

'Why is that?'

'Because Arne Saknussemm was persecuted for heresy, and in 1573 his books were burned by the common hangman.'

'Good! Excellent!' exclaimed my uncle, quite shocking the science teacher.

'Eh? What?' he said.

'Yes, yes. It's all clear now, it's all making sense. I see why Saknussemm, put into the Index of Prohibited Books[14] and forced to conceal the discoveries made by his genius, was obliged to bury in an incomprehensible cryptogram the secret . . .'

'What secret?' asked Mr Fridriksson with great interest.

'Oh, just a secret which . . .' stammered my uncle.

'Have you some private document in your possession?' asked our host.

'No. I was just imagining a possibility.'

'Oh, I see,' answered Mr Fridriksson, who was kind enough not to pursue the subject when he had noticed his friend's embarrassment. 'I hope you won't leave our island until you have seen some of its mineralogical wealth.'

'Certainly,' replied my uncle, 'but I'm rather a latecomer. Or have others not been here before me?'

'Oh yes, Mr Lidenbrock. The work of Olafsen and Povelsen, undertaken by order of the king, the researches of Troïl, the scientific mission of Gaimard and Robert on the French corvette *La Recherche*, and lately the observations of scientists who came in the *Reine Hortense*, have added a great deal to our knowledge of Iceland. But I assure you there is still plenty to do.'

'Do you think so?' said my uncle, pretending to look very modest and trying to hide the curiosity that was glinting in his eyes.

'Oh, yes. There are many mountains, glaciers and volcanoes left to study, as yet imperfectly known! For example, without going any further, that mountain in the horizon. That's Snæfell.'

'Oh!' said my uncle, as calmly as he was able, 'Is that Snæfell?'

'Yes, one of the most unusual volcanoes, whose crater has scarcely ever been visited.'

'Is it extinct?'

'Oh, yes, for more than five hundred years.'

'Well,' replied my uncle, who was frantically locking his legs together to keep himself from leaping up in the air, 'that is where I mean to begin my geological studies, there on that Seffel – Fessel – what do you call it?'

'Snæfell,' replied the worthy Mr Fridriksson.

This part of the conversation was in Latin. I had understood every word of it, and I could hardly conceal my amusement at seeing my uncle trying to control the excitement and satisfaction that were absolutely dripping off him. He tried hard to put on an innocent little expression of simplicity, but it looked like a diabolical grin.

'Yes,' he said, 'your words have made up me mind for me. We'll try to climb that Snæfell. Perhaps we may even carry out our studies in its crater!'

'I'm very sorry,' said Mr Fridriksson, 'that my commitments will not allow me to take time off, or I would have come with you myself for both pleasure and profit.'

'Oh, no, no!' replied my uncle with great animation, 'we wouldn't for the world put anyone out, Mr Fridriksson. Still, I thank you with all my heart: the company of such a talented man would have been very useful, but the duties of your profession . . .'

I'm glad to think that our host, innocent Icelandic soul that he was, was blind to my uncle's blatant trickery.

'I very much approve of your beginning with that volcano, Mr Lidenbrock. You will gather a harvest of interesting observations. But, tell me, how do you expect to get to the Snæfell peninsula?'

'By sea, across the bay. That's the most direct way.'

'No doubt, but it's impossible.'

'Why?'

'Because we don't have a single boat at Reykjavik.'

'Drat it!'

'You'll have to go by land, along the shore. It'll be a longer journey, but more interesting.'

'Very well, then. But I'll have to see about a guide.'

'I have one to offer you.'

'A sensible, intelligent man?'

'Yes, someone who lives on that peninsula. He is a collector of eider down, and very clever. He speaks Danish perfectly.'

'When can I see him?'

'Tomorrow, if you like.'

'Why not today?'

'Because he won't be here till tomorrow.'

'Tomorrow, then,' agreed my uncle with a sigh.

This momentous conversation ended a few moments later with warm thanks from the German professor to the Icelandic teacher. My uncle had at this dinner gained important information, amongst other things the story of Saknussemm, the reason for the mysterious document, that his host would not be accompanying him on his expedition, and that the very next day a guide would be at his disposal.

CHAPTER 11

THE FINDING OF A GUIDE TO THE CENTRE OF THE EARTH

In the evening, I took a short walk along the beach and came back early to my plank-bed, where I slept soundly all night.

When I awoke, I heard my uncle talking volubly in the next room. I immediately got dressed and joined him.

He was talking in Danish to a tall man, of robust build. This fine fellow clearly possessed great strength. His eyes, set in a large and ingenuous face, seemed to me very intelligent; they were of a dreamy sea-blue. Long hair, which would have been called red even in England, fell in long strands over his broad shoulders. The movements of this native were lithe and supple, but he made little use of his arms when speaking, like a man who knew nothing or cared nothing about the language of gestures. His whole appearance bespoke perfect calmness and self-possession, not laziness but tranquillity. I felt at once that he would be beholden to nobody, that he worked for his own convenience, and that nothing in this world would astonish him or disturb his philosophic calmness.

I caught these hints of this Icelander's character by the way he listened to the Professor's impassioned flow of words. He stood with arms crossed, perfectly unmoved by my uncle's incessant gesticulations. A negative was expressed by a slow movement of the head from left to right, an affirmative by a slight bend, so slight that his long hair scarcely moved. He took economy of movement almost to the level of niggardliness.

Looking at this man, I would certainly never have dreamt that he was a hunter. While he didn't look likely to frighten the game, it didn't seem likely that he would even get near it. But the mystery was solved when Mr Fridriksson informed me that this quiet man only hunted eider duck, whose under-plumage constitutes the chief wealth of the island. This is the celebrated eider down, and it requires no great rapidity of movement to get it.

Early in summer the female eider, a very pretty bird, goes to build her nest among the rocks of the fjords with which the coast is fringed. After building the nest, she lines it with down plucked from her own breast. Immediately the hunter, or rather the trader, comes and robs the nest, and the female starts her work all over again. This goes on as long as she has any down left. When she has stripped herself bare, the male eider takes his turn to pluck himself. But since the coarse, hard plumage of the male has no commercial value, the hunter doesn't bother to rob the nest; the female therefore lays her eggs in the spoils of her mate, the young are hatched, and the next year the harvest begins again.

Now, as the eider duck does not choose steep cliffs for her nest, but rather the smooth terraced rocks which slope down to the sea, the Icelandic hunter is able to exercise his calling without any inconvenient exertion. He is a farmer who is not obliged either to sow or reap his harvest, but merely to gather it in.

This grave, phlegmatic and silent individual was called Hans Bjelke, and he came recommended by Mr Fridriksson. He was to be our guide. His manners were in singular contrast with my uncle's.

Nevertheless, they soon came to understand each other. Neither considered the size of the payment: the one was ready to accept whatever was offered, the other was ready to give whatever was asked. Never was a bargain more easily concluded.

The result of the agreement was that Hans undertook on his part to take us to the village of Stapi on the south shore of the Snæfell peninsula, at the very foot of the volcano. By land, this would be about twenty-two miles, walkable, said my uncle, in two days. But when he learned that a Danish mile is 24,000 feet, he was obliged to modify his calculations and allow seven or eight days for the journey.

Four horses were to be placed at our disposal – two to carry my uncle and myself, two for the baggage. Hans, as was his custom, would go on foot. He knew the whole of that part of the coast perfectly, and promised to take us by the shortest route.

His engagement was not to end when we arrived at Stapi. He was to continue in my uncle's service for the whole period of his scientific research, for three rix-dollars a week; but it was an express article of the contract that his wages should be paid to him every Saturday evening at six o'clock. This, according to him, was an indispensable part of the arrangement.

The start was fixed for the 16th of June. My uncle wanted to pay the hunter part of his wages in advance, but he refused with one word:

'*Efter*,' he said.

'Afterwards,' said the Professor, for my edification.

The arrangement concluded, Hans silently withdrew.

'An excellent fellow,' exclaimed my uncle, 'but little does he know the wonderful role he is to play in the future.'

'So he is to accompany us as far as . . .'

'As far as the centre of the Earth, Axel.'

There were still forty-eight hours to go before we were to set off. To my great regret I had to spend the whole time preparing for the trip, as it took all our ingenuity to pack every article in the best way: scientific instruments here, firearms there, tools in this package, provisions in that. Four sets of packages in all.

The scientific instruments were:

1. An Eigel's centigrade thermometer, graduated up to 150 degrees, which seemed to me either too much or too little – too much if the heat in the Earth was to rise as high as that, for in that case we would be baked alive, but not enough to measure the temperature of hot springs or any matter in a state of fusion.
2. A manometer, to indicate extreme pressures of the atmosphere. An ordinary barometer would not have served the purpose, as the pressure would increase during our descent to a point where a mercury barometer wouldn't register.
3. A chronometer, made by Boissonnas Junior of Geneva, accurately set to the meridian of Hamburg.
4. Two compasses, one showing inclination and the other declination.
5. A night telescope.
6. Two Ruhmkorff's apparatuses[15], which, by means of an electric current, would provide a safe and handy portable light.

The firearms consisted of two Purdley More rifles and two Colt revolvers. But what did we want guns for? We had neither savages nor wild beasts to fear as far as I could see. But my uncle seemed as attached to his arsenal as much as to his instruments, and more especially to a considerable quantity of gun cotton, which is unaffected by moisture and the explosive force of which exceeds that of gunpowder.

The tools consisted of two pickaxes, two spades, a silk ladder, three iron-tipped sticks, an axe, a hammer, a dozen iron wedges and spikes and a long knotted rope. This made for a large load, as the ladder itself was 300 feet long.

And there were provisions too. This wasn't a large bundle, but it was comforting to know that we were taking a six-months' supply of dried beef and biscuits. The only liquid was spirits; we weren't taking any water with us, but we had flasks, and my uncle was depending on springs where we would be able to fill them. Whatever objections I raised about the quality, temperature or even absence of such springs were to no avail.

To complete the inventory of what we were taking with us, I mustn't forget to mention a pocket medicine chest containing blunt scissors, splints for broken limbs, unbleached linen tape, bandages and compresses, lint and a lancet for bleeding – each thing frightening in its implications. Then there was a row of little bottles containing dextrin, medical alcohol, lead acetate solution, ether, vinegar and sal ammoniac; these too afforded me no comfort. Finally, we had everything needed to power the Ruhmkorff's apparatuses.

My uncle hadn't forgotten a supply of tobacco, coarse-grained gunpowder and tinder, nor a leather belt in which he carried an adequate quantity of gold, silver and paper money. Six pairs of boots and shoes, made waterproof with a composition of India rubber and tar, were packed among the tools.

'Clothed, shod and equipped like this,' said my uncle, 'there's no telling how far we might go.'

The whole of the 14th was spent in organizing all these different articles. In the evening we dined with Baron Trampe; the mayor of Reykjavik and Dr Hyaltalin, the chief medical officer, were also present. Mr Fridriksson wasn't there: I learned afterwards that he and the Governor disagreed over some question of administration and didn't speak to each other. I therefore understood not a single word of what was said at this semi-official dinner, but I couldn't help noticing that my uncle talked the whole time.

On the 15th, our preparations were complete. Our host delighted the Professor by presenting him with a map of Iceland far more complete than Henderson's one. It was the map drawn by Olaf Nikolas Olsen, on the scale of 1 to 480,000, and published by the Icelandic Literary Society. Based on the geodesic work of Scheel Frisac and the topographical survey carried out by Bjorn Gumlaugsonn, it was a precious document for a mineralogist.

Our final evening was spent in close conversation with Mr Fridriksson, for whom I felt the warmest regard. After our chat, I, at least, had a disturbed and restless night.

At five in the morning I was wakened by the neighing and stamping of four horses right below my window. I dressed quickly and went down into the street. Hans was finishing our packing, almost, as it were, without moving a limb; and yet he did his work skilfully. My uncle was making a lot of noise to little purpose, and the guide seemed to be paying very little attention to his energetic instructions.

At six o'clock our preparations were finished. Mr Fridriksson shook hands with us. My uncle thanked him warmly in Icelandic for his extreme kindness. I made up a few fine Latin sentences to express my cordial farewell. Then we mounted our horses and with his last good-bye Mr Fridriksson treated me to a line of Virgil eminently applicable to such uncertain wanderers as we were likely to be:

'*Et quacumque viam dederit fortuna sequamur.*'[16]

CHAPTER 12

A BARREN LAND

We started out under a sky that was overcast but calm. There was no fear of heat, nor of disastrous rain. It was just the weather for tourists.

The pleasure of riding on horseback through an unknown country made me easy to please as we started off. I devoted myself wholly to the pleasure of the traveller, and enjoyed the feelings of freedom and expectation. I was beginning to feel really involved in the enterprise.

'Besides,' I said to myself, 'where's the risk? Here we are travelling through a most interesting country. We're about to climb a very remarkable mountain. At worst we're going to scramble down an extinct crater. It is quite obvious that Saknussemm did nothing more than this. As for a passage leading to the centre of the Earth, that's sheer nonsense! Quite impossible! Very well, then, let's get all the good we can out of this expedition, and let's not argue about our chance of success.'

By the time I had come to these conclusions, we had left Reykjavik.

Hans moved steadily on, keeping ahead of us at an even, smooth and rapid pace. The baggage horses followed him without giving any trouble. Then came my uncle and myself, looking not bad horsemen on our small but hardy animals.

Iceland is one of the largest islands in Europe. It has a surface area of 1,400 square miles[17], but only 60,000 inhabitants. Geographers have divided it into four quarters, and we were to cut diagonally across the south-west quarter, called the 'Sudvestr Fjordùngr'.

On leaving Reykjavik, Hans led us along the seashore. We passed poor pastures which were trying very hard, but in vain, to look green; they were yellow at best. The rugged peaks of the trachytic mountains presented faint outlines on the eastern horizon; here and there a few patches of snow, concentrating the diffuse light, glittered on the slopes of the distant mountains; some peaks, rising boldly towards the sky, passed through the grey clouds and reappeared above the moving mists, like rocky reefs emerging in the heavens.

Often these chains of barren rocks dipped towards the sea and encroached on the scarce pastureland, but there was always enough room to get by. Besides, our horses instinctively chose the easiest places without ever slackening their pace. My uncle didn't even get the satisfaction of urging his horse on by whip or voice. He had no excuse for impatience. I couldn't help smiling to see so tall a man on so small a pony, and as his long legs nearly touched the ground, he looked like a six-legged centaur.

'Good horse! Good horse!' he kept saying. 'You'll see, Axel, that there is no more intelligent an animal than the Icelandic horse. Neither snow, nor storms, nor impassable roads, nor rocks, nor glaciers – nothing stops him. He is courageous, sober and surefooted. He never takes a false step, never shies. If there is a river or fjord to cross (and we will meet with many), you'll see him plunge in at once, just as if he were amphibious, and reach the opposite bank. But we mustn't hurry him; let him have his way and we'll cover a steady twenty-five miles a day.'

'We may, but how about our guide?'

'Oh, never mind him. People like him stride on without a thought. The man moves so little, he'll never get tired; and besides, if he wants it, he can have my horse. I'll get cramps if I don't move about a bit. My arms are all right, but my legs need exercise.'

We were progressing at a rapid pace. The country was already almost a desert. Here and there, there was a lonely farmhouse, a *'boër'*, built of wood, turf and pieces of lava, and looking like a poor beggar by the wayside. These dilapidated huts seemed to be begging for charity from passers-by, and we weren't far off offering alms for the relief of the poor inmates.

In this country there were no roads and paths, and the poor vegetation, slow-growing as it was, would soon cover all trace of the footsteps of the infrequent travellers. Yet this part of the province, only a very small distance from the capital, is reckoned among the inhabited and cultivated parts of Iceland. What, then, must the other parts be like, even more deserted than this desert? In the first half mile we hadn't seen a single farmer standing at his cottage door, nor a single wild shepherd tending a flock rather less wild than he was; nothing but a few cows and sheep left to themselves. So what would these distorted regions that we were heading for be like, regions turned upside down by eruptions, born of volcanic explosions and underground convulsions?

We were to get to know them before long, but on consulting Olsen's map, I saw that we were for the moment avoiding them by following a winding route along the seashore. In fact, the main volcanic activity is confined to the central part of the island; there, the horizontal strata of superimposed rocks, called 'trapps' in the Scandinavian languages, the trachytic layers, the eruptions of basalt and tuffs and agglomerates, the streams of lava and molten porphyry, have made this a land of supernatural horrors. I had no idea what sight was awaiting us on the Snæfell peninsula where the destruction caused by fiery Nature has created frightful chaos.

Two hours after leaving Reykjavik, we arrived at the *'aoalkirkja'* ('main church') or village of Gufunes. There was nothing to see here but a few houses, scarcely enough to make a hamlet in Germany.

Hans stopped here for half an hour. He shared a frugal breakfast with us, answering my uncle's questions about the path with nothing but 'yes' or 'no'. When asked about our stopping-place for the night, he simply replied, 'Gardär.'

I consulted the map to see where Gardär was. I saw there was a small town of that name on the banks of the Hvalfjord, four miles from Reykjavik. I showed it to my uncle.

'Only four miles!' he exclaimed. 'Four miles out of twenty-eight. What a pleasant little walk this is!'

He tried to say something to the guide, but the latter, without answering, took up his place at the head of the horses again and went on his way.

Three hours later, still walking over the colourless grass of the pastureland, we had to work our way round the Kollafjord, a longer way but an easier one than straight across the inlet. We soon entered a *'pingstaœr'* or 'commune' called Ejulberg, on whose steeple the clock would have been striking twelve if Icelandic churches had been rich enough to have clocks. But they're like their parishioners, who have no watches and manage perfectly well without.

There our horses were fed and watered. Then, taking the narrow path to the left between a range of hills and the sea, they carried us to our next stopping-point, the *aoalkirkja* of Brantär and, one mile farther on, to Saurboër *'annexia,'* a chapel of ease built on the southern shore of the Hvalfjord.

It was now four o'clock, and we had gone four Icelandic miles.

The fjord was at least half an Icelandic mile wide at that point. The waves rolled in and crashed on the sharp-pointed rocks. The inlet widened out between high walls of rock, precipices topped by sharp peaks 2,000 feet high, and remarkable for the brown strata which separated the beds of reddish tuff. However much I might respect the intelligence of our horses, I was little inclined to put it to the test by trying to cross an arm of the sea on horseback.

If they're as intelligent as they're said to be, I thought, they won't even try it. In any case, I intend to do the thinking for them.

But my uncle wouldn't wait. He spurred his horse on down to the water's edge. His mount lowered its head to look at the nearest waves and stopped. My uncle, who had an instinct of his own, applied his spurs again, and again the horse refused, shaking its head. Then came strong language and the whip, but the animal replied to these arguments by kicking and attempting to throw its rider. At last the clever little pony, by bending its knees, got out from under the Professor's legs and left him standing on two boulders on the shore like the Colossus of Rhodes[18].

'Confounded brute!' cried the unseated rider, suddenly demoted to being a pedestrian, and just as ashamed of it as a cavalry officer would be if downgraded to being a foot soldier.

'*Färja*,' said the guide, touching him on the shoulder.

'What! A ferry?'

'*Der*,' replied Hans, pointing to one.

'Yes,' I exclaimed. 'There is a ferry.'

'Why didn't you say so, then? Come on, let's go!'

'*Tidvatten*,' said the guide.

'What's he saying?'

'He's saying 'tide',' said my uncle, translating the Danish word.

'So we have to wait for the tide, then?'

'*Förbida*?' asked my uncle.

'*Ja*,' replied Hans.

My uncle stamped his foot, while the horses headed towards the ferry.

I perfectly understood the need to wait for a particular point in the tide before undertaking the crossing of the fjord, the point when, the sea having reached its highest level, there would be slack water. At that point, the ebb and flow of the water have no noticeable effect, and there is no risk of the ferry being carried either to the top of the fjord or out to sea.

That favourable moment didn't come till six o'clock, at which time my uncle, myself, the guide, two ferrymen and the four horses, entrusted ourselves to a somewhat fragile craft. Accustomed as I was to the steamboats on the Elbe, I found the oars of the rowers a rather slow means of propulsion. It took us more than an hour to cross the fjord, but the crossing was effected without mishap.

In another half hour we had reached the *aoalkirkja* of Gardär.

CHAPTER 13

HOSPITALITY UNDER THE ARCTIC CIRCLE

It should have been dark, but on the 65th parallel there was nothing surprising about the nocturnal polar light. In Iceland during the months of June and July, the sun never sets.

But the temperature had gone down. I was cold, and even more hungry than cold. Welcome indeed was the sight of the *boër* which was hospitably opened to receive us.

It was a peasant's house, but as far as hospitality was concerned it was the equal of a king's palace. On our arrival, the master came out to shake our hands and without further ado beckoned us to follow him inside.

Follow him was what we did, because it would have been impossible to walk with him down the long, narrow, dark passage. The building was constructed of roughly squared timbers, and along the passage were four rooms – the kitchen, the weaving workshop, the *'badstofa'* or family bedroom and the visitors' room, which was the best of all. My uncle, whose height had not been taken into consideration in the construction of the house, of course hit his head several times on the beams that projected from the ceiling.

We were shown into our bedroom, a large room with a floor of hard-packed earth and lit by a window, the panes of which consisted of sheep's bladders and therefore didn't let in much light. The sleeping accommodation consisted of dry straw thrown into two wooden frames which were painted red and decorated with Icelandic sayings. I was hardly expecting so much comfort; the only discomfort came from the strong smell of dried fish, hung meat and sour milk, which my nose didn't like at all.

When we had laid aside our travelling gear, the voice of our host was heard inviting us to come into the kitchen, the only room where a fire was lit even in the severest cold weather.

My uncle wasted no time in obeying this friendly invitation, nor was I slow to follow him.

The kitchen chimney was constructed in the ancient style: in the middle of the room there was a stone for a hearth, and over it a hole in the roof to let the smoke escape. The kitchen also served as the dining-room.

As we came in, the host, as if he had never seen us before, greeted us with the word *'sællvertu'*, which means 'be happy', and came and kissed us on the cheek.

His wife greeted us in the same manner, and then, placing their hands on their hearts, the two bowed deeply.

I hasten to say that this Icelandic lady was the mother of nineteen children, all of whom, big and little alike, were swarming around in the midst of the dense coils of smoke with which the fire on the hearth was filling the room. At every moment I saw some fair-haired and rather melancholy face emerge from the rolling clouds of smoke – they were a perfect band of unwashed angels.

My uncle and I welcomed this little tribe kindly, and in a very short time we each had three or four of these kids on our shoulders, as many on our laps, and the rest between our knees. Those who could speak kept repeating *'Sællvertu'*, in every conceivable tone; those that could not speak made up for that lack by shrill cries.

This concert was brought to a close by dinner being announced. At that moment our hunter returned; he had been seeing to the horses, which is to say he had let them loose in the fields, where the poor beasts had to content themselves with the scanty moss they could pull off the rocks and a few meagre clumps of seaweed. The next day they would be sure to come of their own accord and resume the labours of the previous day.

'Sællvertu,' said Hans.

Then calmly, automatically and dispassionately he kissed the host, the hostess and their nineteen children.

This ceremony over, we sat at table, all twenty-four of us, and therefore literally one on top of another. The luckiest ones among us only had two urchins on their knees.

But silence reigned in this little world when the soup was served, and the natural taciturnity of the Icelander took over again, even among the children. The host served us soup made of lichen, by no means unpleasant, then a huge piece of dried fish floating in butter that, having been kept for twenty years, had turned rancid and was therefore, according to Icelandic gastronomy, greatly preferable to fresh butter. Along with this, we had *'skyr'*, a sort of clotted milk, flavoured with the juice of juniper berries and served with biscuits; and to drink, we had whey mixed with water, known as *'blanda'* in this country. It is not for me to say whether this diet is healthy or not; all I can say is that I was desperately hungry, and that when it came to dessert, I swallowed every last mouthful of a thick broth made from buckwheat.

As soon as the meal was over, the children disappeared, and their elders gathered round the fire, in which was burning such miscellaneous fuel as peat, heather, cow-dung and fishbones. After warming ourselves a little, the different groups retired to their respective rooms. In accordance with Icelandic custom, our hostess hospitably offered us her assistance in getting undressed, but on our gracefully declining her offer, she didn't insist on it, and I was able at last to curl up in my bed of straw.

At five o'clock next morning, we said good-bye to our host, my uncle only with difficulty managing to persuade him to accept proper payment for his hospitality, and Hans gave the signal for us to start.

A hundred yards from Gardär, the landscape began to change in appearance. The ground became boggy, and our progress became more difficult. To our right, the chain of mountains stretched out like an immense system of natural fortifications, of which we were following the counterscarp; often we met with streams, which we had to ford with great care in order not to get our packs wet.

The deserted countryside was becoming more and more of a wasteland, yet from time to time we could make out a human figure who fled at our approach. Sometimes a sharp turn in the path would bring us suddenly within a short distance of one of these spectres, and I was filled with loathing at the sight of a huge deformed head with shiny, hairless skin and repulsive sores visible through the holes in the poor creature's wretched rags.

These unhappy beings would not come near us and offer us their misshapen hands. They fled away, but not before Hans had greeted them with the customary *'Sællvertu'*.

'Spetelsk,' Hans would say.

'A leper!' my uncle would repeat.

This word always had a repulsive effect. The horrible disease of leprosy is all too common in Iceland; it is not contagious, but hereditary, and lepers are therefore forbidden to marry.

These apparitions were not likely to add any charm to the increasingly unattractive landscape. The last tufts of grass had disappeared from beneath our feet. Not a tree was to be seen, unless we except a few dwarf birches as low as brushwood. Not an animal but a few wandering ponies that their owners would not feed. Sometimes we could see a hawk gliding through the grey cloud and then darting away south with rapid flight. I was affected by the melancholy of this wild land, and my thoughts drifted away to the more cheerful scenes I had left far to the south.

We had to cross a few narrow fjords, and finally quite a wide bay. It being high tide, we were able to cross without delay and reach the hamlet of Alftanes a mile further on.

That evening, after having forded two rivers full of trout and pike, the Alfa and the Heta, we were obliged to spend the night in a deserted building worthy of being haunted by all the elves of Scandinavia. The ice-king certainly held court there, and all night long showed us what he could do.

Nothing of note happened the next day. Just the same bogs, the same monotonous landscape, the same melancholy desert tracks. By nightfall we had covered half the distance we had to travel, and we stopped for the night at the *annexia* at Krösolbt.

On the 19th of June, we walked for about a mile – that is, an Icelandic mile – over hardened lava. This ground is called *'hraun'* in Iceland. The wrinkled surface has the appearance of distorted, twisted cables, sometimes stretched out lengthwise, sometimes twisted together. An immense torrent of lava, once liquid, now solid, flowed down from the nearest mountains, now extinct volcanoes, but the debris all around us indicated the violence of past eruptions. Here and there, there were still a few jets of steam from hot springs.

We had no time to study these phenomena; we had to continue on our way. Soon the boggy land reappeared under the feet of our horses, interspersed by little lakes. Our route now lay westward; we had made our way round the great bay of Faxa, and the twin peaks of Snæfell rose white into the cloudy sky less than five miles away.

The horses walked on well; no difficulties stopped them in their steady progress. I was getting tired, but my uncle held himself as stiff and erect as he did when we first started out. I couldn't help admiring his persistence, and that of the hunter, who was treating our expedition as nothing more than a little stroll.

On June the 20th, at six o'clock, we reached Büdir, a village on the seashore. The guide was asking for his wages, and my uncle settled up with him. It was Hans's own family, that is, his uncles and cousins, who gave us hospitality. We were kindly received, and without abusing too much the goodness of these people, I would willingly have stayed here for a while to recover from my tiring journey. But my uncle, who had no need of time to recover, wouldn't hear of it, and the next morning we had to mount our horses again.

The soil showed the effects of being close to the mountain, whose granite foundations rose from the earth like the knotted roots of some huge oak. We were going round the immense base of the volcano. The Professor hardly took his eyes off it. He waved his arms about and seemed to be challenging it, saying, 'There stands the giant that I shall conquer.' After about four hours' walking, the horses stopped of their own accord at the door of the priest's house at Stapi.

CHAPTER 14

BUT ARCTIC PEOPLE CAN BE INHOSPITABLE, TOO

Stapi is a village of about thirty huts, built of lava, at the south side of the base of the volcano. It extends along the inner edge of a small fjord, enclosed between basaltic walls of the strangest construction.

Basalt is a brownish rock of igneous origin. It assumes regular forms, the arrangement of which is often very surprising. Here nature had done her work geometrically, with set-square, compasses and plumb line. Everywhere else her art consists in simply throwing down huge masses together in disorder; you see imperfectly formed cones, irregular pyramids, a strange confusion of lines. But here, as if to exhibit an example of regularity in advance of the very earliest architects, she has created a severely simple order of architecture, never surpassed either by the splendours of Babylon or the wonders of Greece.

I had heard of the Giant's Causeway in Ireland, and Fingal's Cave on Staffa, one of the Hebrides, but I had never before seen a basaltic formation.

At Stapi I beheld this phenomenon in all its beauty.

The wall that held in the fjord, like the whole coast of the peninsula, was composed of a series of vertical columns thirty feet high. These straight shafts, of perfect proportions, supported an architrave of horizontal slabs, the overhanging portion of which formed a semi-arch over the sea. At intervals, under this natural shelter, vaulted entrances spread out in beautiful curves, into which the waves dashed with foam and spray. A few shafts of basalt, torn from their hold by the fury of storms, lay along the soil like remains of an ancient temple, in ruins that remained forever fresh, and over which centuries passed without leaving a trace of age upon them.

This was the last stage of our journey above ground. Hans had shown great intelligence, and it gave me some little comfort to think then that he was not going to leave us.

On arriving at the door of the rector's house, which was no different from the others, I saw a man shoeing a horse, hammer in hand, and with a leather apron on.

'*Sællvertu*,' said the hunter.

'*God dag*,' said the blacksmith in good Danish.

'*Kyrkoherde*,' said Hans, turning to my uncle.

'The rector,' repeated the Professor. 'It seems, Axel, that this good man is the rector.'

Our guide in the meanwhile was telling the *kyrkoherde* what we were doing there. Stopping his work for a moment, the latter shouted something that could no doubt be understood between horses and horse dealers, and immediately a tall, ugly hag of a woman appeared from the hut. She must have been six feet tall, or as near as doesn't matter. I was afraid she might treat me to the 'Icelandic kiss' but thankfully she didn't, nor did she show us into her house with very good grace.

The visitors' room seemed to me the worst in the whole hut. It was narrow, dirty and smelly. But we had to be content with it. The rector obviously did not to go in for old-fashioned hospitality. Far from it. Before the day was over, I saw that we were dealing with a blacksmith, a fisherman, a hunter, a joiner but not at all with a minister of the Gospel. To be sure, it was a week-day; perhaps he made amends on Sundays.

I don't mean to say anything against these poor priests, who after all are absolutely destitute. They receive a ridiculously small pittance from the Danish government, and from the parish they get a quarter of the tithe, which doesn't amount to sixty marks a year. Hence the need to work for their living; but after fishing, hunting and shoeing horses for any length of time, one soon gets into the ways and manners of fishermen, hunters and farriers and other uncultivated people; and that evening I found out that temperance too was not among the virtues of our host.

My uncle soon discovered what sort of a man he was dealing with. Instead of a good and learned man, he found a rude and coarse peasant. He therefore decided to start out at once on the great expedition and to leave this inhospitable rectory. He cared nothing about fatigue, and resolved to spend a few days in the mountains.

The preparations for our departure were therefore made the very day after our arrival at Stapi. Hans hired the services of three Icelanders to carry our packs instead of the horses, but as soon as we had arrived at the crater, these men were to turn back and leave us on our own. This was made absolutely clear.

My uncle now took the opportunity of explaining to Hans that it was his intention to explore the interior of the volcano to its farthest limits.

Hans merely nodded. Heading there or elsewhere, down into the bowels of the Earth or anywhere on the surface of the globe, was all the same to him. For my own part, the events of the journey had kept me amused up to this point and made me forget the evils to come, but now my fears were again beginning to get the better of me. But what could I do? The place to stand up to the Professor would have been Hamburg, not at the foot of Snæfell.

One thought, above all others, particularly alarmed me, one that would have rattled firmer nerves than mine.

Now, I thought, here we are about to climb Snæfell. Fine. We'll explore the crater. That's fine, too; others have done as much without dying for it. But that's not all. If there is a way to penetrate into the very bowels of the island, if what that foolish Saknussemm said is true, we will lose our way among the deep subterranean passages of this volcano. Now, there's no proof that Snæfell is extinct. Who can reassure us that an eruption is not brewing at this very moment? Does it follow that just because the monster has slept since 1229, it will therefore never wake again? And if it does awaken in the near future, where shall we be?

It was worthwhile considering this question, and I did consider it. I couldn't sleep for dreaming about eruptions. I had no desire to play the role of ejected scoriae and ashes.

So, at last, when I couldn't stand it any longer, I made up my mind to put the question to my uncle, as prudently and as cautiously as possible, in the form of an almost impossible hypothesis.

I approached him. I communicated my fears to him, and stepped back to give him room for the explosion which I knew would follow. But I was wrong.

All he said was, 'I was thinking of that.'

What could those words mean? Was he actually going to listen to reason? Was he contemplating abandoning his plans? This was too good to be true.

After a few moments' silence, during which I dared not question him, he went on:

'I was thinking of that. Ever since we arrived at Stapi, my mind has been occupied with the important question you have just raised, because we mustn't be guilty of imprudence.'

'No, indeed!' I replied emphatically.

'For six hundred years Snæfell has been silent, but it might speak again. Now, eruptions are always preceded by certain well-known phenomena. I have therefore questioned the locals, I have studied the land, and I can assure you, Axel, that there will be no eruption.'

At this positive assertion, I just stood there, amazed and speechless.

'You doubt my word?' said my uncle. 'Well, then, follow me.'

I obeyed like an automaton. Leaving the priest's house, the Professor took a straight path, which led away from the sea through an opening in the basaltic wall. We were soon in the open countryside, if one may give that name to a vast expanse of mounds of volcanic material. This part of the country seemed to have been crushed by a rain of enormous rocks – trap, basalt, granite and all kinds of igneous rock – thrown out by the volcano.

Here and there I could see curling up into the air puffs and jets of steam, called in Icelandic 'reykir', issuing from thermal springs and indicating by their movement the volcanic energy below. This seemed to justify my fears, but my new-found hopes were dashed when my uncle said:

'You see all these plumes of steam, Axel? Well, they show that we have nothing to fear from the fury of a volcanic eruption.'

'Why should I believe that?' I exclaimed.

'Listen,' said the Professor. 'If there's an eruption coming, these jets redouble their activity, but they disappear altogether during the eruption, because the gases, no longer under pressure, are released through the crater instead of escaping by their normal passage through the fissures in the soil. Therefore, if these vapours remain in their usual state and show no increase in force, and if you add to this the observation that the wind and rain are not being replaced by a still, heavy atmosphere, then you may say with certainty that no eruption is coming in the near future.'

'But . . .'

'That's enough. When science has spoken, there is nothing more to be said.'

I returned to the parsonage, completely crestfallen. My uncle had bested me with the weapons of science. Still, I had one hope left, and this was that when we reached the bottom of the crater it would be impossible, for lack of a way through, to go deeper, in spite of all the Saknussemms in Iceland.

That whole night was one long nightmare. I saw myself in the heart of a volcano and thrown up like a rock from the deepest depths of the earth into interplanetary space.

The next day, June the 23rd, Hans was waiting for us with his companions, carrying provisions, tools and scientific instruments; there were also two iron-tipped sticks, two rifles and two cartridge belts for my uncle and myself. Hans, as a cautious man, had added to our luggage a leather bottle full of water, which, with what was in our flasks, would ensure us a supply of water for eight days.

It was nine in the morning. The priest and his huge harpy of a wife were waiting for us at the door. We thought they were standing there to bid us a kind farewell, but the farewell came in the unexpected form of a large bill, in which we were charged for everything, even the very air we breathed in the pastoral house, foul as it was. This worthy couple were fleecing us just like a Swiss innkeeper might have done, and reckoned their inadequate hospitality at a very high price.

My uncle paid without demur; a man who is starting out for the centre of the Earth is hardly going to quibble over a few rix-dollars.

This matter settled, Hans gave the signal to set off and we soon left Stapi behind us.

CHAPTER 15

SNÆFELL AT LAST

Snæfell is 5,000 feet high. Its double cone forms the end of a trachytic belt which stands out distinctly in the mountain system of the island. From our starting-point we couldn't make out the two peaks against the dark grey sky; I could only see an enormous cap of snow descending low on the giant's brow.

We walked in single file, led by the hunter, climbing up along narrow tracks where two people could not have walked abreast. Conversation was therefore almost impossible.

After we had passed the basalt wall of the Stapi fjord, we walked over fibrous peaty soil, created from the ancient vegetation of this peninsula. The vast quantity of this unharvested fuel would be sufficient to warm the whole population of Iceland for a century; this huge peat-bog was as much as seventy feet deep in places, to judge from the gorges in it, and consisted of layers of the carbonized remains of vegetation interspersed with thinner layers of tufaceous pumice.

As a true nephew of Professor Lidenbrock, and in spite of my worries, I couldn't help taking an interest in the mineralogical curiosities which lay about me as if in a vast museum, and I worked out in my mind a complete geological account of Iceland.

This most curious island has evidently been forced up from the bottom of the sea at a comparatively recent date. It may possibly still be rising slowly. If this is the case, its origin may well be attributed to subterranean fires, in which case Sir Humphry Davy's theory, Saknussemm's document and my uncle's opinions would all go up in smoke. This hypothesis led me to examine even more carefully the appearance of the ground, and I soon arrived at a conclusion as to the nature of the forces operating in its formation.

Iceland, which is entirely devoid of alluvial soil, is wholly composed of volcanic tufa, that is to say, an agglomeration of porous rocks and stones. Before the volcanoes erupted, it consisted of trap rocks slowly raised to the level of the sea by the action of forces in the centre of the Earth. The internal fires had not yet forced their way through.

But at a later period a wide chasm formed diagonally from south-west to north-east, through which the trachyte that was to form a mountain chain was gradually forced out. There was no violent activity in this change; the matter was thrown out in vast quantities, and the liquid material oozing out from the abysses of the earth slowly spread in extensive plains or in hillocky masses. To this period belong the feldspars, syenites and porphyries.

But with this outflow the thickness of the island's crust increased considerably, and therefore also its powers of resistance. One can easily imagine what vast quantities of gases, what masses of molten matter, accumulated beneath its solid surface, with no possible escape after the cooling of the trachytic crust. Therefore a time came when the fluid and explosive forces of the trapped gases lifted up this heavy cover and forced openings for themselves through tall chimneys. Hence the volcano that had formed in the crust, and the crater suddenly created at its summit.

Other volcanic phenomena followed. First of all, the ejected basalt of which the plain we had just left presented such marvellous specimens escaped through the outlets that had now been made. We were walking over dense and massive grey rocks, which in cooling had formed hexagonal prisms. Everywhere around us we saw truncated cones, which had formerly been so many fiery mouths.

After that, when the basalt flow was exhausted, the volcano, whose power was increased by the extinction of the lesser craters, allowed the escape of lava, ashes and scoriae, long screes of which I could see flowing down the sides of the mountain like locks of hair.

Such was the succession of phenomena which produced Iceland, all arising from the action of internal fire, and to suppose that the material within did not still exist in a state of liquid incandescence was absurd. Nothing could surpass the absurdity of imagining that it was possible to reach the centre of the Earth.

I felt a little comforted by this thought as we advanced to the assault of Snæfell.

Walking was becoming more and more difficult, and the ascent steeper and steeper. Loose fragments of rock gave way beneath our feet, and the utmost care was needed to avoid dangerous falls.

Hans carried on as calmly as if he were on level ground. Sometimes he disappeared altogether behind the huge rocks, then a shrill whistle would direct us towards him. Sometimes he would stop, pick up a few bits of stone and build them up into a recognisable shape, so making landmarks to guide us in our way back. A very wise precaution in itself, but, as things turned out, quite pointless.

Three hours of tiring walking had only got us as far as the foot of the mountain. There Hans made us stop, and a hasty breakfast was served out. My uncle swallowed his food two mouthfuls at a time in order to get on faster; but whether he liked it or not, this was time for a rest as well as for breakfast, and he had to wait till our guide decided to move on, which he did after about an hour. The three Icelanders, just as taciturn as their friend the hunter, never spoke, and ate their breakfasts in silence.

We were now beginning to climb the steep sides of Snæfell. By an optical illusion not uncommon in mountains, its snowy summit seemed very close to us, and yet how many weary hours it took us to reach it! The stones, not held together by soil or fibrous plant roots, rolled away from under our feet, and dropped down into the precipice below with the speed of an avalanche.

At some places the sides of the mountain formed an angle with the horizon of at least 36 degrees. It was impossible to climb these stony cliffs, and we had to work our way round them, not without great difficulty. At those points we helped each other by means of our sticks.

I have to admit my uncle kept as close to me as he could. He never lost sight of me, and in many difficult places his arm gave me strong support. He himself seemed to possess an instinctive sense of balance and he never stumbled. The Icelanders, although burdened with our loads, climbed with the agility of mountaineers.

To judge by the appearance of the summit of Snæfell in the distance, it seemed too steep to climb on the side we were on. Fortunately, after an hour of exhausting exercise, a kind of staircase appeared unexpectedly in the middle of the vast plain of snow in the hollow between the two peaks, and it made our ascent much easier. It was formed by one of those torrents of stones flung up by the eruptions, called 'stinâ' by the Icelanders. If this torrent had not been arrested in its fall by the shape of the sides of the mountain, it would have carried on down to the sea and formed more islands.

Such as it was, it served us well. The steepness increased, but these stone steps allowed us to climb with ease, and even at such a speed that, having rested for a moment while my companions continued their ascent, the distance they had climbed reduced them to microscopic size.

At seven we had ascended the two thousand steps of this great staircase, and we had reached a bulge in the mountain, a kind of bed on which rested the actual cone of the crater.

Three thousand two hundred feet below us stretched the sea. We had passed the lower limit of perpetual snow, which, on account of the dampness of the climate, begins at a lower level than one might expect. It was bitingly cold. The wind was blowing violently. I was exhausted. The Professor saw that my legs were refusing to carry me any further, and in spite of his impatience he made up his mind to stop. He signalled his intention to the hunter, who shook his head, saying:

'*Ofvanför.*'

'It seems we have to go higher,' said my uncle.

He asked Hans why.

'*Mistour,*' replied the guide.

'*Ja, mistour,*' said one of the Icelanders in a tone of alarm.

'What does that word mean?' I asked uneasily.

'Look!' said my uncle.

I looked down to the plain. An immense column of pulverized pumice, sand and dust was rising with a whirling circular motion like a waterspout. The wind was lashing it on to the very side of Snæfell to which we were clinging. This dense veil hanging in front of the sun threw a deep shadow over the mountain. If that huge revolving pillar leant over, it would grasp us in its whirling eddies. This phenomenon, which is not infrequent when the wind blows from the glaciers, is called in Icelandic *'mistour'*.

'Hastigt! hastigt!' cried our guide.

Even without knowing Danish, I understood at once that we had to follow Hans as fast as we could. He began to circle round the cone of the crater, but on a slanting path so as to make our progress easier. Presently the dust storm crashed down on the mountain, which shook with the shock of it. A hail of loose stones, caught up by the irresistible blasts of wind, flew about as if in a volcanic eruption. Fortunately we were on the other side of the mountain and sheltered from harm. But for the prudence of our guide, our mangled bodies, torn and pounded into fragments, would have been carried far away like the remnants of some unknown meteor.

Nevertheless, Hans didn't think it wise to spend the night on the side of the cone. We continued on our zigzag climb. The remaining fifteen hundred feet took us five hours to cover; the diagonal path, the circuitous route, and the need to retrace our steps from time to time, must have made for a walk of at least three leagues. I could hardly keep going any longer. I was succumbing to the effects of hunger and cold. The rarefied air was scarcely enough to fill my lungs.

At last, at eleven o'clock in the sunlit night, we reached the summit of Snæfell, and before taking shelter in the crater I had time to watch the midnight sun, at its lowest point, gilding with its pale rays the island that slept at my feet.

CHAPTER 16

BOLDLY DOWN INTO THE CRATER

Supper was gobbled down, and our little company settled itself as best it could. The bed was hard, the shelter not very substantial, and our position an anxious one at five thousand feet above sea level. Yet I slept very well indeed; it was one of the best nights I had ever had, and I didn't even dream.

Next morning we awoke half frozen in the keen air, but with the light of a splendid sun. I got up from my granite bed and went out to enjoy the magnificent spectacle that lay unfolding before my eyes.

I was standing on the very summit of the southernmost of Snæfell's peaks. I could see over the whole island. By an optical effect that you get at all great heights, it seemed as if the shores had been raised up and the central part of the island had sunk down. It was as though one of Helbesmer's relief maps lay at my feet. I could see deep valleys criss-crossing each other in every direction, precipices like low walls, lakes reduced to ponds, rivers abbreviated into streams. On my right were countless glaciers and innumerable peaks, some surrounded by feathery clouds of smoke. The undulating surface of these endless mountains, crested with sheets of snow, reminded me of a stormy sea. If I looked westward, there lay the ocean spread out in all its magnificence, like a mere continuation of those fleecy summits. My eye could hardly tell where the snowy ridges ended and the foaming waves began.

I was now able to steep myself in the wonderful ecstasy which all high summits produce in the mind without any feeling of dizziness, as I was beginning to get accustomed to these sublime aspects of nature. My dazzled eyes were bathed in the bright flood of the sun's rays. I was forgetting where I was and who I was, living rather the life of elves and sylphs, those fanciful creations of Scandinavian superstition. I felt intoxicated by the sublime pleasure of lofty peaks, without thinking of the deep abysses into which I was shortly to be plunged. But I was brought back to reality by the arrival of Hans and the Professor, who joined me on the summit.

My uncle pointed out to me in the far west a light mist, a haze, a suggestion of land, on the distant horizon beyond the waves.

'That's Greenland!' he said.

'Greenland?' I exclaimed.

'Yes. We're only thirty-five leagues away; and during thaws, polar bears are carried by the ice fields from the north even as far as Iceland. But never mind that. Here we are at the top of Snæfell and here are two peaks, one to the north and one to the south. Hans will tell us the name of the one we are standing on at the moment.'

The question being asked, Hans replied:

'Scartaris.'

My uncle shot a triumphant glance at me.

'Now for the crater!' he cried.

The crater of Snæfell resembled an inverted cone, the opening of which might be half a league in diameter. It appeared to be about two thousand feet deep. Imagine what such a reservoir would look like brimful and running over with liquid fire and rumbling like rolling thunder. The bottom of the funnel was about 250 feet in circumference, so its lower edge could be reached without much difficulty down the gentle slope. I couldn't help thinking that the whole crater was like an enormous blunderbuss, and the comparison absolutely terrified me.

'What madness it is,' I thought, 'to go down into a blunderbuss, perhaps a loaded blunderbuss, to be shot up into the air without warning!'

But I didn't try to back out. Perfectly calm, Hans resumed the lead, and I followed him without a word.

To make the descent easier, Hans wound his way down the cone by a spiral path. Our route lay through rocks that were the result of past eruptions. Loosened from their beds by our feet, some of the rocks bounced down into the abyss, creating in their fall remarkable loud echoes.

In some parts of the cone there were glaciers. Here Hans moved forward with extreme caution, using his iron-tipped pole to check for crevasses. At particularly doubtful sections, we had to tie ourselves together with a long rope so that anyone who missed his footing would be held up by his companions. This was a wise move, but didn't remove all the danger.

Yet, notwithstanding the difficulties of the descent, down slopes the guide was not familiar with, it was accomplished without accident, except for the loss of a coil of rope which escaped from the hands of an Icelander and took the shortest way to the bottom of the abyss.

We arrived at midday. I looked up and saw straight above me the upper opening of the cone, framing a very small but almost perfectly round bit of sky. Just at the edge of the opening, the snowy peak of Scartaris stood out sharp and clear against the infinities of space.

At the bottom of the crater there were three chimneys through which, in its eruptions, Snæfell would have belched out fire and lava from its central furnace. Each of these chimneys was a hundred feet in diameter. They stood gaping right in front of us. I hadn't the courage to look down any of them, but Professor Lidenbrock had hastily surveyed all three. He was panting and puffing, running from one to the other, gesticulating and uttering incoherent noises. Hans and his companions were sitting on loose lava rocks, watching him; they obviously thought he was quite mad.

Suddenly my uncle gave a shout. I thought his foot must have slipped and that he'd fallen down one of the holes. But he hadn't. I could see him, arms outstretched and legs wide apart, standing in the centre of the crater in front of a granite rock that looked just like a pedestal made for a statue of Pluto. For a moment he stood like a man transfixed, but that soon gave way to delirious joy.

'Axel, Axel,' he cried. 'Come quickly, come down here!'

I ran down. Hans and the Icelanders just stayed where they were.

'Look!' cried the Professor.

And, sharing his astonishment, but not, I think, his joy, I read on the western face of the block, in Runic characters, half crumbled away with the passage of time, this thrice-accursed name:

ᚴᚿᛣ ᛋᛣᛘᚿᛋᛋᛏᛉ

'Arne Saknussemm!' replied my uncle. 'Do you still have doubts now?'

I said nothing, and returned in silence to my lava seat in a state of utter consternation. I was completely crushed by the evidence.

How long I remained deep in thought, I cannot say. All I know is that when I looked up again, I could see only my uncle and Hans at the bottom of the crater. The Icelanders had been dismissed, and they were now descending the outer slopes of Snæfell to return to Stapi.

Hans was sleeping peacefully at the foot of a rock, in a lava bed, where he had found a suitable place to lie down, but my uncle was pacing around the bottom of the crater like a wild animal in a cage. I had neither the desire nor the strength to get up, and following the guide's example, I dropped off into an unhappy slumber, imagining I could hear ominous noises or feel tremblings within the recesses of the mountain.

That is how we spent our first night in the crater.

The next morning, a grey, heavy, cloudy sky seemed to be hanging over the summit of the cone. This I discovered not from the darkness in the crater but from my uncle's uncontrollable anger.

I soon found out the cause of his anger, and for this reason hope dawned again in my heart.

Of the three paths that lay open before us, only one had been taken by Saknussemm. What that learned Icelander had hinted at in the cryptogram was that the shadow of Scartaris touched that particular opening during the final days of the month of June.

That sharp peak might therefore be considered as the gnomon of a vast sundial, the shadow projected from which on a certain day would indicate the way to the centre of the earth.

Now, no sun means no shadow, and therefore no indicator. And it was now June the 25th. If the sun stayed hidden by cloud for six days, we would have to postpone our visit till next year.

My limited powers of description would be insufficient to attempt a picture of the Professor's angry impatience. The day wore on, and no shadow came to lay itself along the bottom of the crater. Hans didn't move from the spot he had selected; yet he must have been wondering what were we waiting for, if the matter crossed his mind at all. My uncle said not a word to me. His gaze, always directed upwards, was lost in the grey and misty space beyond.

On the 26th, still nothing. A mixture of rain and snow fell all day long. Hans built a hut of pieces of lava. I felt a malicious pleasure in watching the thousand streams and cascades that came tumbling down the sides of the cone, and the continuous deafening noise made by the stones they struck in passing.

My uncle's rage knew no bounds. It was enough to infuriate a much more mild-tempered man than he was, because his plans were foundering just like a boat that hits some rocks when almost in the harbour.

But Heaven never sends unmingled grief, and for Professor Lidenbrock there was a satisfaction in store proportionate to his desperate anxieties.

The next day the sky was again overcast, but on the 29th of June, the last day of the month but one, with the change of the moon came a change of weather. The sun poured a flood of light down the crater. Every hillock, every rock and stone, every projecting surface, shared in this torrent of brightness and threw its shadow on the ground. Amongst them, Scartaris laid down his sharp-pointed angular shadow, which began to move slowly in the opposite direction to that of the shining globe.

My uncle followed the shadow as it moved.

At noon, now at its shortest, it licked gently at the edge of the middle chimney.

'There it is! There it is!' shouted the Professor.

'Now for the centre of the Earth!' he added in Danish.

I looked at Hans, to hear what he would say.

'*Forüt!*' was his calm reply.

'Forward!' replied my uncle.

It was thirteen minutes past one.

CHAPTER 17

VERTICAL DESCENT

Now our real journey began. Up to this point, our efforts had been equal to all the difficulties we had faced, but now new difficulties would spring up at every step.

I had still not taken a look down the bottomless pit into which I was about to plunge, but the moment of truth had arrived. I could now either take part in the enterprise or refuse to go on. But I was ashamed to turn back in the presence of the hunter. Hans was accepting the adventure with such calmness, such indifference, such a perfect disregard for any possible danger, that I blushed at the very thought of being less brave than him. If I'd been alone, I might have tried once again to argue my uncle out of it, but in the presence of the guide I held my peace. I thought of my sweet Virland girl, and I walked towards the central chimney.

I have already mentioned that it was a hundred feet in diameter and three hundred feet round. I leant over a projecting rock and looked down. My hair stood on end with terror. A dizzying feeling of emptiness gripped me. I felt my centre of gravity moving and a mounting giddiness was affecting my brain just as if I was like drunk. There is nothing more treacherous than this feeling of attraction down into deep abysses. I was just about to let myself fall when a hand took hold of me. It was Hans. Obviously I hadn't taken as many lessons in 'abyss exploration' as I should have done in the Frelsers Kirk in Copenhagen.

But, short as my examination of this well had been, I had formed some idea of its shape and structure. Its almost perpendicular walls were bristling with innumerable projections which would facilitate our descent. But even if there was no lack of steps, there was still no rail. A rope fastened to the edge of the aperture might have helped us down, but how would we unfasten it when we reached the other end?

My uncle used a very simple expedient to get round this difficulty. He uncoiled a rope which was about the thickness of a thumb and four hundred feet long. First he dropped half of it down, then he wound it round a lava block that was sticking out conveniently and threw the other half down the chimney. Each of us could then descend by holding both halves of the rope, which would not be able to unwind itself from where it was attached. When we got two hundred feet down, it would be easy to get the whole rope again by letting go of one end and pulling it down by the other. Then the exercise would be repeated, *ad infinitum*.

'Now,' said my uncle, after having completed these preparations, 'let's think about our packs. I'll divide what we have to carry into three bundles, and each of us will carry one on his back. I'm only talking about the fragile articles.'

We, of course, were not included under that heading.

'Hans will take charge of the tools and one part of the provisions; you, Axel, will take another third of the provisions, and the firearms; and I will carry the rest of the provisions and the delicate instruments.'

'But,' I said, 'what about the clothes and that pile of ladders and ropes? What are we going to do with them?'

'They'll go down by themselves.'

'How?' I asked.

'You'll see.'

My uncle was always willing to take drastic action unhesitatingly. As commanded by my uncle, Hans bundled up all the non-fragile articles, tied them firmly together and simply dropped them down the abyss that lay in front of us.

I listened to the dull thuds of the bundle as it fell. My uncle, leaning over the abyss, followed the descent of the luggage with a look of satisfaction, and only stood up when he could no longer see it.

'That's fine. Now it's our turn.'

Now, I would ask any sensible person, could anyone hear such words without a shudder?

The Professor fastened his pack of instruments to his back; Hans took the tools; I took the firearms; and our descent began in the following order: Hans, my uncle, myself. It was all done in a deep silence, broken only by the sound of loose stones falling down into the dark abyss.

I let myself drop, as it were, frantically clutching the double rope with one hand and using the other to keep myself off the wall by means of my stick. One thought almost overwhelmed me, a fear that the rock I was hanging from might give way. The rope seemed very flimsy to be bearing the weight of three people. I made as little use of it as possible, performing wonderful feats of balance on the lava projections which my feet tried to catch hold of like hands.

When one of these insecure footholds became dislodged under Hans's foot, he said in his calm voice:

'*Gif akt!*'

'Watch out!' repeated my uncle.

In half an hour we were standing on the surface of a rock that was jammed across the chimney.

Hans pulled on one of the ends of the rope, and the other rose in the air. After passing the rock up above, it came down again, bringing with it a rather dangerous shower of bits of stone and lava.

Leaning over the edge of our narrow perch, I could see that the bottom of the hole was still out of sight.

The same manoeuvre with the rope was repeated, and half an hour later we had descended another two hundred feet.

I don't suppose even the maddest geologist would under such circumstances have studied the nature of the rocks we were passing. I can tell you I didn't give them any thought. Pliocene, Miocene, Eocene, Cretaceous, Jurassic, Triassic, Permian, Carboniferous, Devonian, Silurian or Primitive, it was all one to me. But the Professor was certainly continuing with his observations or taking notes, as during one of our stops he said to me:

'The farther I go, the more confident I feel. The order of these volcanic formations strongly confirms Davy's theories. We are now among the earliest rocks, which have been subjected to chemical actions which are produced by the contact of elementary bases of metals with water. I reject the whole idea of central heat altogether. We'll see further proof very soon.'

Still the same conclusion. Of course, I wasn't inclined to argue. My silence was taken for consent, and our descent continued.

Another three hours, and I could still see no bottom to the chimney. When I looked up, I could see the opening, which was getting noticeably smaller. The walls, sloping gently inwards, were coming closer together. It was steadily getting darker.

Still we kept going down. It seemed to me that the dislodged stones were being swallowed up with a duller sound, and that they must be reaching the bottom of the abyss more quickly.

As I had been careful to keep an exact note of our manoeuvres with the rope, which I knew we had repeated fourteen times, and each descent had taken half an hour, it was easy to calculate that we had been working our way down for seven hours. With fourteen quarter-of-an-hour rests, that made ten and a half hours. We had started out at one o'clock, so it must now be eleven o'clock. And the depth to which we had descended must be fourteen times 200 feet, or 2,800 feet.

At that moment I heard Hans's voice.

'Halt!' he shouted.

I stopped dead just as my feet were about to land on my uncle's head.

'We're there,' he cried.

'Where?' I said, sliding down beside him.

'At the bottom of the perpendicular chimney,' he answered.

'Is there no way of going further?'

'Yes. There's a sort of passage which slopes down to the right. We'll take a look at it tomorrow. Let's have supper and go to sleep.'

We were not yet in total darkness. The food pack was opened, we had our refreshment, and then went to sleep as well as we could on a bed of stones and lava fragments.

When I was lying on my back, I opened my eyes and saw a bright shining point of light at the top of the gigantic 3,000-foot long tube, now a huge telescope.

It was a star which, seen from this depth, had lost all its twinkle, and which by my calculations would be the *beta* star of the Little Bear. Then I fell fast asleep.

CHAPTER 18

THE WONDERS OF
THE TERRESTRIAL DEPTHS

At eight o'clock in the morning, a ray of daylight came to wake us up. The thousand shining surfaces of lava on the walls picked it up on its way down, and scattered it like a shower of sparks.

There was enough light to make out the objects around us.

'Well, Axel, what do you say?' exclaimed my uncle, rubbing his hands. 'Did you ever spend a quieter night in our little house in Königsberg? No noise of cart wheels, no street-cries of women with baskets, no boatmen shouting!'

'Certainly it's very quiet at the bottom of this well, but there's something disturbing in the very quietness itself.'

'Come now!' my uncle exclaimed. 'If you're frightened already, what will you be like later on? We haven't yet gone one single inch into the bowels of the Earth.'

'What do you mean?'

'I mean we've only reached the level of the island again. This long, vertical tube which starts at the mouth of the crater has its lower end exactly at sea-level.'

'Are you sure of that?'

'Quite sure. Check the barometer.'

In fact, the mercury, which had risen in the instrument as we descended, had stopped at twenty-nine inches.

'You see,' said the Professor. 'What we have now is exactly one atmosphere of pressure, and it's about time for the manometer to replace the barometer.'

And in truth this latter instrument would become useless as soon as the weight of the atmosphere exceeded the pressure at sea-level.

'But,' I said, 'is there no reason to fear that this ever-increasing pressure will eventually become very painful?'

'No. We'll be descending slowly, and our lungs will become used to a denser atmosphere. Aeronauts experience a lack of air as they climb to the higher levels, but we may perhaps have too much: of the two, that's what I would prefer. Let's not waste a moment. Where's the bundle we threw down ahead of us?'

I remembered then that we had searched in vain for it the evening before. My uncle questioned Hans, who, after having looked around carefully with the eye of a huntsman, replied:

'*Der huppe!*'

'Up there.'

And so it was. The bundle had been caught by a projection a hundred feet above us. Immediately the Icelander climbed up like a cat, and in a few minutes the package was in our possession.

'Now,' said my uncle, 'let's have breakfast. And let's breakfast like people who may have a long journey ahead of them.'

The biscuit and meat extract were washed down with several mouthfuls of water mixed with a little gin.

Breakfast over, my uncle pulled out of his pocket a small notebook that he kept for scientific observations. He consulted his instruments, and recorded:

Monday, July 1.

'*Chronometer, 8.17 a.m.; barometer, $29^{7/12}$ in.; thermometer, 6°. Direction, E.S.E.*

This last observation applied to the dark gallery, and was as indicated by the compass.

'Now then, Axel,' exclaimed the Professor with enthusiasm, 'now we're really going into the interior of the Earth. This is the moment when our journey really begins.'

So saying, my uncle with one hand took hold of the Ruhmkorff's apparatus which was hanging round his neck and with the other hand made an electrical connection to the coil in the lamp, and there was a bright enough light to disperse the darkness in the passage.

Hans carried the other apparatus, which was also switched on. This ingenious application of electricity would enable us to continue for a long while by creating an artificial light even in the midst of the most highly inflammable gases.

'Now, let's go!' shouted my uncle.

Each of us shouldered his pack. With Hans pushing the bundle of ropes and clothes along in front of him and myself at the rear, we entered the gallery.

At the moment of becoming engulfed in this dark gallery, I looked up, and for the last time saw through the length of that vast tube the Iceland sky that I thought never to see again.

In the last eruption of the volcano, in 1229, the lava had forced a passage through this tunnel. It still lined the walls with a thick, glistening coat. Here the electric light was intensified a hundredfold by reflected light.

The only difficulty in making progress lay in not sliding too fast down an incline of about forty-five degrees. Fortunately, there were worn-away and blistered patches in the lava that formed steps, and all we had to do was continue downwards, letting our baggage slide before us at the end of a long rope.

But the material which formed steps under our feet had formed stalactites above our heads. The lava, which was porous in many places, had formed a surface covered with small rounded blisters. Crystals of opaque quartz, set with limpid tears of glass and hanging like chandeliers from the vaulted roof, seemed as it were to catch fire and form sudden illuminations as we passed on our way. It was as if the genii of the depths were lighting up their palace to receive their terrestrial guests.

'This is magnificent!' I exclaimed in spite of myself. 'Uncle, what a sight! Aren't the colours of the lava wonderful, blending together and changing by imperceptible shades from reddish brown to bright yellow? And aren't these crystals just like globes of light?'

'Ah, you think so, do you, Axel, my boy? Well, you'll see greater splendours than these, I hope. Now, let's move on. Let's go!'

He would have been better to have said 'Let's slide', because we did nothing but drop down the steep inclines. It was Virgil's *facilis descensus Averni*[19]. The compass, which I consulted frequently, gave our direction as southeast with inflexible consistency. This lava stream deviated neither to the right nor to the left.

Yet there was no noticeable increase in temperature. This justified Davy's theory, and more than once I looked at the thermometer with surprise. Two hours after we had set off, it only showed 10°, an increase of only 4°. This suggested to me that our descent was more horizontal than vertical. As for the exact depth we had reached, that was very easy to ascertain: the Professor accurately measured the angles of deviation and inclination on the road – but he kept the results to himself.

About eight o'clock in the evening, he indicated that we should stop. Hans sat down at once. The lamps were hung on a projection in the lava; we were in some sort of cavern where there was plenty of air. Currents of air were getting to us. What atmospheric disturbance was causing them? I couldn't answer that question at that moment. I was so hungry and tired that I was incapable of thinking. A descent of seven hours at one go is not made without a considerable expenditure of effort, and I was exhausted. So I was very glad to hear the order to stop. Hans spread out our provisions on a block of lava, and we ate hungrily. But one thing troubled me: our supply of water was already half used up. My uncle was counting on a fresh supply from subterranean sources, but up to that point we hadn't come across any. I couldn't help drawing his attention to this fact.

'Are you surprised at this lack of springs?' he said.

'More than that, I'm anxious about it. We've only got enough water for five days.'

'Don't worry, Axel, we'll find more than we want.'

'When?'

'When we've left this bed of lava behind us. How could springs break through walls like these?'

'But perhaps this passage runs to a very great depth. It seems to me that we've made no great progress vertically.'

'Why do you suppose that?'

'Because if we had gone deep into the crust of Earth, we would have encountered greater heat.'

'According to your way of thinking,' said my uncle. 'But what does the thermometer say?'

'Hardly fifteen degrees, an increase of only nine degrees since we set out.'

'Well, and what is your conclusion?'

'This is my conclusion. According to exact observations, the increase of temperature in the interior of the globe increases at the rate of one degree for every hundred feet. But certain local conditions may modify this rate. So, at Yakutsk in Siberia there is an increase of one degree every 36 feet. This difference is a result of the heat-conducting capacity of the rocks. Moreover, near an extinct volcano, through gneiss, it has been observed that there is only an increase of one degree every 125 feet. Let's assume this last case as the most comparable to our situation, and calculate on the basis of that.'

'Well, calculate away, my boy.'

'Nothing easier,' I said, jotting down figures in my notebook. 'Nine times a hundred and twenty-five feet gives a depth of eleven hundred and twenty-five feet.'

'That's right.'

'Well?'

'According to my observations, we're 10,000 feet below sea-level.'

'Is that possible?'

'Yes, or figures no longer tell the truth.'

The Professor's calculations were quite correct. We had already reached a point six thousand feet deeper than anywhere that the foot of man had trod, such as the mines of Kitz-Bahl in the Tyrol and Wuttemberg in Bohemia.

The temperature, which ought to have been 81°, was scarcely 15°. That was something to think about.

CHAPTER 19

GEOLOGICAL STUDIES IN SITU

Next day, Tuesday, the 30th of June, at 6 a.m., our descent began again.

We were still following the gallery of lava, a natural staircase and as gently sloping as those sloping floors which in some old houses are still found instead of flights of steps. And so we went on until 12.17, the precise moment when we caught up with Hans, who had stopped.

'Ah, here we are,' exclaimed my uncle, 'at the very end of the chimney.'

I looked around me. We were standing at the intersection of two paths, both dark and narrow. Which one should we take? We had a problem.

My uncle was unwilling to show any sign of hesitation in front of either me or the guide. He pointed to the eastern tunnel, and soon all three of us were in it. In any case, if we had hesitated over which path to take, there would have been no end to it: since there was nothing whatsoever to guide our choice, we were forced to trust to chance.

The slope of this gallery was scarcely perceptible, but it varied greatly in height and width. Sometimes we passed through a series of arches, one after the other, like the majestic arcades of a Gothic cathedral. Here the architects of the Middle Ages might have found specimens for every form of the sacred art which grew from the development of the pointed arch. A mile farther on, we had to bow our heads under corniced elliptical arches in the Romanesque style, with massive pillars standing out from the wall and bending under the vault that rested heavily on them. In other places, this magnificence gave way to narrow channels between low structures which looked like beavers' lodges, and we had to crawl along very narrow passages indeed.

The level of heat was perfectly bearable. In spite of myself, I began to think how hot it would be when the lava thrown out by Snæfell was boiling and working its way through this now silent path. I imagined the torrents of fire being forced round every bend in the gallery and the accumulation of intensely hot vapours in this confined channel.

I only hope, I thought to myself, that this so-called extinct volcano won't take a fancy in its old age to begin its activities again!

I refrained from communicating these fears to Professor Lidenbrock. He would never have understood them anyway. He had only one idea in his head – onward! He walked, he slid, he scrambled, he tumbled, with a persistence which one could not help but admire.

By six in the evening, after a not very tiring walk, we had gone two leagues southwards but scarcely a quarter of a mile downwards.

My uncle indicated it was time to sleep. We ate without talking, and went to sleep without much thought.

Our arrangements for the night were very simple: a travelling rug for each of us, that we rolled ourselves into, was our sole covering. We had neither cold nor intruders to be afraid of. Travellers who penetrate into the wilds of central Africa, and into the pathless forests of the New World, have to keep watch over one another at night. But we enjoyed absolute safety and total seclusion: no savages or wild beasts infested these silent depths.

Next morning, we awoke refreshed and in good spirits. We set off again. As on the day before, we followed the path of the lava. It was impossible to tell what sort of rocks we were passing. The tunnel, instead of heading downwards, became more and more horizontal; I even thought I perceived a slight rise. But about ten o'clock this upward tendency became so evident, and therefore so tiring, that I was obliged to slacken my pace.

'What is the matter, Axel?' demanded the Professor impatiently.

'I can't go on any longer,' I replied.

'What, after three hours walking over such easy ground?'

'It may be easy, but it's tiring all the same.'

'What, when we've nothing to do but keep going down?'

'Going up, with all due respect.'

'Going up?' said my uncle.

'Definitely. For the last half-hour the slope has gone the other way, and at this rate we shall soon be back on the level ground of Iceland.'

The Professor shook his head slowly and uneasily, like a man who is unwilling to be convinced. I tried to pursue the conversation. He made no reply, and gave the signal for us to start again. I could see that his silence was nothing but ill-humour.

Still, I courageously shouldered my pack again, and hurried after Hans, who was following my uncle. I was anxious not to be left behind. My greatest concern was not to lose sight of my companions. I shuddered at the thought of being lost in the depths of this vast subterranean labyrinth.

Besides, if the ascending path did become steeper, I was comforted by the thought that it was bringing us nearer the surface. I found hope in this. Every step confirmed this, and I was rejoicing at the thought of meeting my little Gräuben again.

By midday there was a change in the appearance of the walls of the gallery. I noticed it by a drop in the amount of light reflected from the sides; solid rock was appearing in place of the lava coating. The rock-mass was composed of inclined and sometimes vertical strata. We were passing through rocks of the Transition or Silurian system.

It's evident, I exclaimed to myself, that marine deposits formed these shales, limestones and sandstones in the second period of the Earth's development. We're turning away from the primary granite. It's just as if we were Hamburg people going to Lübeck by way of Hanover!

I would have been better to have kept my observations to myself. But my geological instinct was stronger than my prudence, and Uncle Lidenbrock heard my exclamation.

'What's that you're saying?' he asked.

'Look,' I said, pointing to the varied series of sandstones and limestones and the first indication of slate.

'Well?'

'We're at the period when the first plants and animals appeared.'

'Do you think so?'

'Take a closer look.'

I made the Professor shine his light over the walls of the gallery. I expected some signs of astonishment, but he said not a word and just carried on.

Had he understood me or not? Was he refusing to admit, out of self-pride as an uncle and a scholar, that he had made the wrong choice when he chose the eastern tunnel? Or was he determined to examine this passage to its very end? It was evident that we had left the lava path, and that this path could not possibly lead to the extinct furnace of Snæfell.

Yet I wondered if I was not depending too much on this change in the rock. Might I myself not be mistaken? Were we really crossing the layers of rock which overlie the granite foundation?

If I'm right, I thought, I must soon find some fossil remains of primitive life, and then he'll have to yield to the evidence. Let's look for some.

I hadn't gone a hundred yards before incontestable proofs presented themselves to me. It was bound to happen, as in the Silurian age the seas contained at least fifteen hundred vegetable and animal species. My feet, which had become accustomed to the hard lava floor, suddenly found themselves on dust composed of the debris of plants and shells. In the walls were distinct impressions of seaweeds and club-mosses. Professor Lidenbrock must realize what that meant, I thought, and yet he still pushed on with, it seemed to me, his eyes resolutely shut.

This was simply obstinacy taken to a ridiculous stage. I couldn't bear it any longer. I picked up a perfectly formed shell, which had belonged to an animal not unlike the modern woodlouse. Then, joining my uncle, I said:

'Look at this!'

'Fine,' said he quietly, 'it's the shell of a crustacean, of an extinct species called a trilobite. Nothing more.'

'But don't you conclude . . .?'

'Just what you conclude yourself. Yes, I do, perfectly. We've left the granite and the lava. It's possible that I may be mistaken. But I can't be sure of that until I have reached the very end of this gallery.'

'You're right in that, uncle, and I would quite approve of your determination if there were not a danger threatening us more and more.'

'What danger?'

'The lack of water.'

'That's all right, Axel, we'll ration ourselves.'

CHAPTER 20

THE FIRST SIGNS OF DISTRESS

In fact, we had no option but to ration ourselves. Our water supply couldn't last more than three more days. I found that out for certain when we took our evening meal. And, to our sorrow, we had little reason to expect to find a source in these Transition Period beds.

The whole of the next day the gallery opened before us in endless arcades. We carried on almost without a word. Hans's silence seemed to be infecting us too.

The path was no longer climbing, at least not perceptibly. Sometimes, even, it seemed to have a slight downward slope. But this tendency, which was very slight, could do nothing to reassure the Professor, because there was no change in the beds, and the Transitional characteristics became more and more obvious.

The electric light was reflected in sparkling splendour from the schist, limestone and old red sandstone of the walls. You might have thought we were passing along a trench section in Devon, which gave its name to this system. Specimens of magnificent marbles clothed the walls, some of a greyish agate fantastically veined with white, others of a rich crimson or yellow dashed with splotches of red; then came dark cherry-coloured marbles relieved by the lighter tints of limestone.

The greater part of these rocks bore impressions of primitive organisms. Creation had evidently advanced since the day before: instead of rudimentary trilobites, I noticed remains of a more developed order of beings, amongst which were ganoid fishes and some of those sauroids in which palaeontologists have discovered the earliest reptile forms. The Devonian seas were populated by animals of these species, and deposited them by thousands in the rocks of the newer formation.

It was evident that we were ascending that scale of animal life in which man fills the highest place. But Professor Lidenbrock seemed not to notice.

He was waiting for one of two things to happen – either the appearance of a vertical shaft opening before his feet, down which our descent might be resumed, or some obstacle which would force us to turn back and retrace our footsteps. But evening came and neither wish was gratified.

On Friday, after a night during which I felt pangs of thirst, our little band again plunged into the winding passages of the gallery.

After ten hours' walking, I observed a strange deadening of the reflection of our lamps from the side walls. The marble, the schist, the limestone and the sandstone were giving way to a dark and lustreless lining. At one point, the tunnel becoming very narrow, I leant against the wall.

When I took my hand off the wall, it was black. I looked closer, and found we were in a coal formation.

'A coal mine!' I exclaimed.

'A mine without miners,' my uncle replied.

'Who knows?' I asked.

'I know,' the Professor stated firmly. 'I'm certain that this gallery driven through beds of coal was never cut by human hand. But whether or not it's the work of nature doesn't matter. It's dinner-time. Let's eat.'

Hans prepared some food. I scarcely ate, and I swallowed down the few drops of water rationed out to me. One flask half full was all we had left to slake the thirst of three men.

After their meal my two companions lay down on their rugs, and found in sleep a solace from their fatigue. But I couldn't sleep, and I counted every hour until morning.

On Saturday, at six o'clock, we started off again. In twenty minutes we reached a vast open space. I knew then that human beings hadn't hollowed out this mine: the vaults would have been shored up, whereas, as it was, they seemed to be held up by some miracle of equilibrium.

The cavern was about a hundred feet wide and a hundred and fifty in height. The ground had been forced apart by some subterranean disturbance. Yielding to some great power from below, it had separated, leaving this great hollow into which human beings were now penetrating for the first time.

The whole history of the Carboniferous Period was written on these gloomy walls, and a geologist might with ease trace all its diverse phases. The beds of coal were separated by strata of sandstone or compact clays, and appeared crushed under the weight of overlying strata.

During the age of the world which preceded the Secondary Period, the Earth was covered with immense plant forms, the product of the double influence of tropical heat and constant moisture. A steamy atmosphere surrounded the Earth, still veiling the direct rays of the sun.

This gives rise to the conclusion that the high temperature then existing was due to some other source than the heat of the sun. It is even possible that the daystar might not have been ready yet to play the important role it now has. There were no 'climates' as yet, and a torrid heat, equal from pole to equator, was spread over the whole surface of the globe. Where did this heat come from? From the interior of the Earth.

Regardless of Professor Lidenbrock's theories, a violent heat *did* smoulder within the body of the sphere. Its effect was felt to the outermost layers of the terrestrial crust. The plants, deprived of the beneficial effects of the sun, produced neither flowers nor scent, but their roots drew vigorous life from the burning soil of the early days of this planet.

There were few trees. Herbaceous plants alone existed. There were tall grasses, ferns and club-mosses, besides Sigillarias and Asterophyllites, rare plants now but whose species might at that time be counted in their thousands.

The coal measures owe their origin to this period of profuse vegetation. The still elastic and yielding crust of the Earth moved with the fluid forces beneath it, whence the innumerable fissures and depressions. The plants, sinking beneath the water, gradually gathered into huge masses.

Then came the chemical action of nature. In the depths of the seas, the vegetable accumulations first became peat; then, acted on by generated gases and the heat of fermentation, they underwent a process of complete mineralization.

Thus were formed those immense layers of coal, which nevertheless are not inexhaustible and which at the present rate of over-consumption will be exhausted in three centuries unless the industrial world devises some way of avoiding this.

These thoughts came into my mind whilst I was contemplating the wealth of coal stored in this section of the globe. This, I thought, will no doubt never be discovered; the working of such deep mines would involve too large an outlay, and so what would be the point as long as coal is still spread far and wide near the surface? Just as these untouched stores are as I see them now, so will they be when this world comes to an end.

But still we marched on. I alone was forgetting the length of the path we trod by losing myself in the midst of geological contemplations. The temperature remained what it had been during our passage through the lava and schists. I was, however, strongly affected by a gassy smell. I immediately recognized the presence in the gallery of a considerable quantity of that dangerous gas that miners call firedamp, explosions of which have often caused terrible catastrophes.

Fortunately, our light came from Ruhmkorff's ingenious apparatus. If we had been unfortunate enough to have been exploring this gallery with torches, a terrible explosion would have put an end to travelling and travellers at one stroke.

This trip through the coal mine lasted until night. My uncle could scarcely control his impatience at the horizontal passage. The darkness, always deep just twenty yards in front of us, prevented us from estimating the length of the gallery, and I was beginning to think it must be endless, when suddenly at six o'clock a wall very unexpectedly rose up before us. There was no way forward, neither to the right nor to the left of it, neither at the top of it nor at its base; we were at the end of a blind alley. 'That's fine. So much the better,' exclaimed my uncle. 'Now, at any rate, we know what we are about. We're not on Saknussemm's path, and all we have to do is go back. Let's have a night's rest, and in three days we shall get to the fork in the path.'

'Yes,' I said, 'if we have any strength left.'

'Why not?'

'Because tomorrow we'll have no water.'

'Nor any courage either?' asked my uncle severely.

I didn't dare reply.

CHAPTER 21

COMPASSION MELTS
THE PROFESSOR'S HEART

Next day we started off early. We had to hurry. It was a three-day walk back to the crossroads.

I will say nothing of the sufferings we endured during our return. My uncle bore them with the angry impatience of a man obliged to admit his own weakness; Hans with the resignation of his passive nature; I, I must confess, with complaints and expressions of despair. I didn't have the mental strength to cope with this ill-fortune.

As I had warned, the water ran out by the end of the first day's march back. All we now had as liquid food was gin, but the infernal fluid burned my throat and I couldn't bear even the sight of it. I found the temperature and the air stifling. Fatigue paralysed my limbs. More than once I almost collapsed. Then there would be a stop, and my uncle and the Icelander would do their best to restore me. But I could see that the former was struggling with difficulty against extreme fatigue and the tortures of thirst.

Finally, on Tuesday, July 8, we arrived, half dead and on our hands and knees, at the junction of the two passages. I lay there like a lifeless mass, stretched out on the lava. It was ten in the morning.

Hans and my uncle, leaning on the wall, tried to nibble a few bits of biscuit. Long moans escaped from my swollen lips.

After some time my uncle came over to me and raised me in his arms.

'My poor boy!' he said, in genuine tones of compassion.

I was touched by these words, not being accustomed to see the excitable Professor in a gentler mood. I grasped his trembling hands in mine. He let me hold them and looked at me. His eyes were moist.

Then I saw him take the flask that was hanging at his side. To my amazement he placed it to my lips.

'Drink this,' he said.

Had I heard him correctly? Was my uncle mad? I stared at him in a daze, unable to grasp what he was saying.

'Drink it,' he said again.

And raising his flask he emptied it every drop between my lips.

Oh, infinite bliss! A mouthful of water came to moisten my burning mouth. It was just one sip but it was enough to bring back my ebbing life.

I thanked my uncle with clasped hands.

'Yes,' he said, 'a mouthful of water. But it's the last one – do you hear me? – the very last. I'd been keeping it as a precious treasure at the bottom of my flask. Twenty times, no, a hundred times, I fought off a terrible impulse to drink it. But no, Axel, I kept it for you.'

'My dear uncle,' I said, whilst hot tears trickled down my face.

'Yes, my poor boy, I knew that as soon as you arrived at these crossroads, you would collapse half dead, and I kept my last drop of water to refresh you.'

'Thank you, thank you,' I said. Although my thirst was only partially quenched, some strength had nevertheless returned. The muscles of my throat, tight until then, now relaxed again, my lips became a little less inflamed, and I was able to speak again.

'Well, now,' I said, 'there's only one thing we can do now. We have no water; we must go back.'

While I was saying this, my uncle was avoiding looking at me; he hung his head; his eyes avoided mine.

'We have to go back!' I exclaimed vehemently. 'We have to go back to Snæfell! May God give us the strength to climb up the crater again!'

'Go back,' said my uncle, as if he was talking to himself rather than me.

'Yes, go back, and there's not a minute to lose.'

A long silence followed.

'So, then, Axel,' replied the Professor in a strange voice, 'you've found no courage or energy in these few drops of water?'

'Courage?'

'I see you are just as weak-willed as you were before, and still expressing nothing but despair!'

What sort of a man was I dealing with here, and what schemes did he now have going round in his fearless mind?

'What? You won't go back?'

'Should I give this expedition up just when we have the best chance of success? Never!'

'Then must we resign ourselves to perishing?'

'No, Axel, no. You go back. Hans will go with you. Leave me here myself!'

'Leave you here?'

'Leave me, I tell you. I have undertaken this expedition. I'll carry it out to the end, and I will not go back. Go on, Axel, just go!'

My uncle was in a state of feverish excitement. His voice, which had for a moment been tender and gentle, had now become harsh and threatening. He was struggling with gloomy determination to do the impossible. I didn't want to leave him in this bottomless abyss, but on the other hand the instinct for self-preservation was prompting me to flee.

The guide watched this scene with his usual phlegmatic unconcern. Nevertheless, he understood perfectly well what was going on between his two companions. Our gestures themselves were sufficient to show that we were each bent on taking a different path. But Hans seemed to have no interest in a matter on which his life depended. He was ready either to start out at a given signal or to stay, if his master so willed it.

How I wished at this moment I could have made him understand me. My words, my complaints, my tone would have had some influence over his impassive nature. Those dangers which our guide could not understand I could have demonstrated and proved to him. Together we might have overruled the obstinate Professor. If necessary, we might perhaps have been able to force him back up the heights of Snæfell.

I approached Hans. I put my hand on his. He didn't move. My parted lips sufficiently revealed my sufferings. The Icelander slowly shook his head and, pointing calmly at my uncle, said:

'Master.'

'Master?' I shouted. 'Are you crazy? No, he isn't master over your life. We must get out of here, we must drag him with us. Do you hear me? Do you understand?'

I had seized Hans by the arm. I wanted to get him to stand up. I struggled with him. My uncle intervened.

'Be calm, Axel! You'll get nothing from that stoical servant. So listen to what I have to suggest.'

I folded my arms and faced my uncle boldly.

'The lack of water,' he said, 'is the only obstacle in our way. In this eastern gallery made up of lavas, schists and coal, we haven't come across a single drop of moisture. Perhaps we'll have better luck if we follow the western tunnel.'

I shook my head incredulously.

'Hear me out,' the Professor went on with a firm voice. 'While you were lying there motionless, I went to examine the conformation of that gallery. It goes straight down, and in a few hours it'll bring us to granite rocks. There we are bound to meet with plentiful springs of water. The nature of the rock assures me of this, and instinct agrees with logic to support my conviction. Now, this is what I suggest. When Columbus asked his ships' crews to allow him three more days to discover a new world, those crews, disheartened and sick as they were, recognized the rightness of the request, and he discovered America. I am the Columbus of this nether world, and I ask only for *one* more day. If in a single day I have not found the water we need, I swear to you we will return to the surface of the Earth.'

In spite of my irritation I was moved by these words, as well as by the violence my uncle was doing to his own desires in making so dangerous a proposal.

'Well,' I said, 'do as you will, and may God reward your superhuman energy. You have now but a few hours to tempt fate. Let's make a start!'

CHAPTER 22

A TOTAL LACK OF WATER

This time we started our descent in the new gallery. Hans led the way, as was his custom.

We hadn't gone a hundred yards when the Professor, moving his lantern along the walls, exclaimed:

'Here are some primitive rocks. Now we're on the right path. Forward!'

When in its early stages the Earth was slowly cooling, its contraction gave rise to disruptions, distortions, fissures and chasms in its crust. The passage through which we were walking was one such fissure, through which at one time granite had poured out in a molten state. Its thousand meanders formed an intricate labyrinth through the primeval mass.

As fast as we descended, the succession of strata forming the primitive foundation appeared with increasing distinctness. Geologists consider this primitive matter to be the base of the mineral crust of the Earth, and have ascertained it to be composed of three different formations, schist, gneiss and mica schist, resting on that unchangeable foundation, granite.

Never had mineralogists found themselves in such wonderful circumstances to study nature *in situ*. What the drilling machine, an ignorant and brutal contraption, was unable to bring up from the inner structures to the surface of the globe, we were able to see with our own eyes and handle with our own hands.

Through the beds of schist, coloured with delicate shades of green, ran winding threads of copper and manganese, with traces of platinum and gold. I thought to myself, what riches are buried here at an inaccessible depth, hidden for ever from the covetous eyes of the human race! These treasures have been buried at such an extreme depth by the convulsions of primeval times that they run no risk of ever being harmed by pickaxe or spade.

After the schists came gneiss, partially stratified, remarkable for the parallelism and regularity of its lamina, then mica schists, lying in large plates or flakes, revealing their structure by the sparkle of the white shining mica.

The light from our Ruhmkorff lamps, reflected from the small facets of quartz, flashed sparkling rays in every direction, and I felt as if I was moving through a diamond, within which the darting rays criss-crossed in a thousand flashing coruscations.

About six o'clock this brilliant feast of light underwent a noticeable reduction in its splendour, then almost ceased entirely. The walls took on a crystalline but sombre appearance. The mica was more intimately mixed with the feldspar and quartz to form the rock of all rocks, the hard stone that forms the foundations of the Earth and which without being crushed bears the weight of the four terrestrial rock-systems. We were walled up within prison walls of granite.

It was eight in the evening. There had been no sign yet of water. I was suffering terribly. My uncle marched on. He refused to stop. He was listening anxiously for the murmur of distant springs. But, no, there was absolute silence.

And now my legs were refusing to carry me any further. I fought the pain and torment in order not to stop my uncle, which would have driven him to despair, because the day was drawing to its close, and it would be his last.

Finally my strength gave out. I gave a cry and fell to the ground.

'Help, I'm dying.'

My uncle retraced his steps. He looked at me with his arms folded, then these muttered words passed his lips:

'It's all over!'

The last thing I saw was a terrifying gesture of rage, and my eyes closed.

When I reopened them, I saw my two companions motionless and rolled up in their coverings. Were they asleep? For my part, I couldn't get a wink of sleep. I was suffering too much, and what made my thoughts especially bitter was that there was no remedy for my condition. My uncle's last words echoed painfully in my ears: 'It's all over!' For in such a terrible state of weakness, it was madness to even think of ever reaching the upper world again.

Above us there was a league and a half of terrestrial crust. The weight of it seemed to be pressing down on my shoulders. I felt weighed down, and I exhausted myself with violent struggles to turn over on my granite bed.

A few hours passed. A deep silence reigned around us, the silence of the grave. No sound could reach us through walls, the thinnest of which were five miles thick.

But even in my stupor, I thought I could hear a noise. It was dark down the tunnel, but I thought I could see the Icelander vanishing from sight with the lamp in his hand.

Why was he leaving us? Was Hans going to abandon us? My uncle was fast asleep. I wanted to shout, but my voice died on my parched and swollen lips. The darkness became deeper, and the last sound died away in the far distance.

'Hans has abandoned us,' I shouted. 'Hans! Hans!'

But these words were only spoken within me. They went no further. Yet after the first moment of terror, I felt ashamed of suspecting a man of such extraordinary faithfulness. Instead of going up, he was going down the gallery. Any evil intention would have taken him up, not down. This thought made me calm again, and I turned to other thoughts. Only some important purpose could have induced this quiet man to give up his sleep. Was he off on a search? Had he in the silence of the night detected a sound, a murmur of something in the distance, which I had failed to register?

CHAPTER 23

WATER DISCOVERED

For a whole hour, I was trying to work out in my delirious brain the reasons which might have made this calm huntsman behave like this. The most absurd notions ran in utter confusion through my mind. I thought I was going mad!

But at last the noise of footsteps could be heard in the dark abyss. Hans was coming back. A flickering light was beginning to glimmer on the wall of our dark prison. Then it appeared at the mouth of the gallery. And then Hans appeared.

He went over to my uncle, put his hand on his shoulder, and gently woke him. My uncle got up.

'What's the matter?' he asked.

'*Vatten*,' replied the huntsman.

Under the inspiration of intense pain, no doubt everybody becomes endowed with the gift of tongues. I didn't know a word of Danish, yet instinctively I understood the word he had uttered.

'Water! Water!' I shouted, clapping my hands and waving my arms like a madman.

'Water!' repeated my uncle. '*Hvar*?' he asked, in Icelandic.

'*Nedat,*' replied Hans.

Where? Down below! I understood everything that was being said. I grasped the hunter's hands, and held them tightly while he looked at me calmly.

The preparations for our departure were not long in making, and we were soon on our way down a passage that inclined two feet in seven. In an hour we had gone a mile and a quarter, and descended two thousand feet.

Then I began to hear distinctly a new sound of something running within the thickness of the granite wall, a kind of dull, dead rumbling like distant thunder. During the first part of our march, not coming on the promised spring, I could feel my distress returning, but then my uncle acquainted me with the cause of the strange noise.

'Hans wasn't mistaken,' he said. 'What you hear is the rushing of a torrent.'

'A torrent?' I exclaimed.

'No doubt about it. There's a subterranean river flowing around us.'

We hurried on in the greatest excitement. I was no longer aware of my fatigue. This murmuring of waters close at hand was already refreshing me. It was getting increasingly loud. The torrent, after having flowed for some time above our heads, was now flowing, roaring and rushing, within the left wall.

Frequently I touched the wall, hoping to feel some indication of moisture, but I couldn't feel anything.

Another half hour passed and we'd covered another half league.

Then it became clear that the hunter hadn't managed to go any further than this point. Guided by an instinct peculiar to mountaineers and water-diviners, he had, as it were, felt this torrent through the rock, but he had certainly seen none of the precious liquid, nor had he slaked his thirst.

Soon it became clear that if we continued walking, we would increase the distance between ourselves and the stream, the noise of which was becoming fainter.

We went back. Hans stopped where the torrent seemed closest. I sat near the wall, while the waters were flowing past me violently only two feet away. But there was a thick granite wall between us and the object of our desires.

Without thinking, without wondering if there were any means of getting the water, I gave way to a feeling of despair.

Hans glanced at me with, I thought, a smile of pity.

He stood up and picked up the lamp. I followed him. He moved towards the wall, while I looked on. He put his ear against the dry stone and moved it slowly backwards and forwards, up and down, listening intently. I realized at once that he was searching to find the exact spot where the torrent could be heard the loudest. He found that spot on the left-hand side of the tunnel, three feet from the ground.

I was almost overcome with excitement. I hardly dared guess what the hunter was about to do. But I couldn't help but understand, and applaud and cheer him on, when I saw him take hold of the pickaxe to attack the rock.

'We're saved!' I cried.

'Yes,' cried my uncle, almost frantic with excitement. 'Hans is right. What an excellent fellow! Who but he would have thought of it?'

Yes, who but he? Such an expedient, simple as it was, would never have crossed our minds. True, it seemed extremely hazardous to strike this part of the Earth's structure with a hammer. What if some rocks moved and crushed us all? What if the torrent, bursting through, drowned us in a sudden flood? There was nothing foolish in these fancies. But nonetheless, no fear of falling rocks or rushing floods could stop us now, and our thirst was so intense that, to satisfy it, we would have dug down into the ocean bed itself.

Hans set about the task which my uncle and I together could not have accomplished. If impatience had given our hands the power, we would have shattered the rock into a thousand fragments. Not so Hans. Completely under control, he calmly cut his way through the rock with a steady succession of light, skilful strokes, creating an opening six inches wide. I could hear noise of flowing waters getting louder, and I fancied I could feel the delicious fluid refreshing my parched lips.

The pickaxe had soon penetrated two feet into the granite partition, and our man had been working for over an hour. I was in an agony of impatience. My uncle wanted to take stronger measures, and I had some difficulty in dissuading him. However, he had just picked up a pickaxe when a sudden hissing was heard and a strong jet of water spurted out, hitting the opposite wall.

Hans, almost thrown off his feet by the force of the shock, uttered a cry of pain, and I soon understood why, when, plunging my hands into the gushing torrent, I hastily pulled them out again: the water was scalding hot.

'The water's boiling,' I cried.

'Well, never mind, let it cool,' my uncle replied.

The tunnel was filling with steam, whilst a stream was forming, which slowly trickled away into the winding subterranean passages. Soon we had the satisfaction of swallowing our first mouthfuls.

Could anything be more delicious than the feeling that our intolerable burning thirst was easing, leaving us to enjoy comfort and pleasure? But where was this water from? It didn't matter. It was water, and though still hot, it brought back life to the dying. I drank without stopping, almost without even tasting it.

It was only after a moment of savouring the water that I exclaimed, 'Why, this spring has iron salts in it!'

'Nothing could be better for the digestion,' said my uncle. 'It's full of iron. It'll be as good for us as going to Spa or Töplitz[20].'

'Well, it's delicious!'

'Of course it is. Water should be when it's found six miles underground. It has an inky flavour, which is not at all unpleasant. What an excellent source of strength Hans has found for us here. We'll name it after him.'

'That's a good idea,' I said.

And Hans's Brook it was from that moment on.

Hans was none the prouder for this honour. After drinking moderately, he quietly went over to a corner to rest.

'Now,' I said, 'we mustn't lose this water.'

'Why trouble ourselves about that?' replied my uncle. 'I don't imagine it will ever run out.'

'Yes, but we can't be sure it won't. Let's fill the water bottle and our flasks, and then block up the opening.'

My advice was followed as far as getting in a supply of water was concerned. But blocking the hole was not so easy to accomplish. In vain we picked up pieces of granite and stuffed them in with tow; we only scalded our hands without succeeding in blocking the flow. The pressure was too great, and our efforts were fruitless.

'It's obvious,' I said, 'that the main body of this water is at a considerable height above us. The force of the jet shows that.'

'No doubt,' answered my uncle. 'If this column of water is 32,000 feet high, that is, coming from the surface of the Earth, it is equal to the weight of a thousand atmospheres. But I've got an idea.'

'Well?'

'Why bother to stop the stream coming out at all?'

'Because . . .' Well, I couldn't actually think of any reason.

'When our flasks are empty, where will we be able to fill them again? Can we know that for sure?'

No, we couldn't be sure about that.

'Well, let's let the water keep on running. It'll flow downwards, and will both guide us and refresh us.'

'That's a good plan,' I said. 'With this stream for our guide, there is no reason why we shouldn't succeed in our undertaking.'

'Ah, my boy! So you agree with me now?' exclaimed the Professor, laughing.

'I heartily agree with you.'

'Well, let's rest a while, and then we'll start off again.'

I was forgetting that it was night-time. The chronometer soon informed me of that fact. And in a very short time, refreshed and thankful, we all three fell into a sound sleep.

CHAPTER 24

WELL SAID, OLD MOLE! CANST THOU WORK I' THE GROUND SO FAST?[21]

By the next day we had forgotten all our sufferings. At first, I was surprised to find I was no longer thirsty, and I was wondering why. The answer came in the murmuring of the stream at my feet.

We had breakfast, and drank some of the excellent iron-laden water. I felt totally bucked up and quite determined to push on. Why should such a firmly convinced man as my uncle, assisted by such a hard-working guide as Hans and accompanied by such a determined nephew as myself, not succeed in his aim? This was the sort of excellent thought that was going round in my head. If anyone had suggested to me that I should return to the summit of Snæfell, I would have declined with indignation.

Fortunately, all we had to do was to go down.

'Let's make a start!' I cried, awakening by my shouts the echoes of the vaulted hollows of the Earth.

On Thursday, at 8 a.m., we started off again. The winding granite tunnel led us round unexpected bends and turns, and seemed almost to form a labyrinth, but, on the whole, its direction seemed to be south-easterly. My uncle constantly consulted his compass to keep a check on the ground we were covering.

The gallery sloped down very slightly from the horizontal, scarcely more than two inches in every six feet, and the stream ran gently burbling at our feet. I thought of it as a friendly spirit guiding us underground, and with my hand I caressed the soft water-nymph whose comforting voice accompanied our steps. With my reviving spirits, these mythological notions just seemed to spring into my mind.

As for my uncle, he was beginning to rage against our horizontal passage. He was a man for vertical paths. This route seemed to be extending indefinitely, and instead of sliding along a chord of the circle as we were now doing, he would have much preferred to drop down the Earth's radius. But there was nothing we could do about it, and so long as we were approaching the centre to some extent, we felt we mustn't complain.

From time to time, a steeper path appeared. Our naiad then began to tumble before us with a hoarser murmur, and we descended with her to a greater depth.

On the whole, that day and the next we made considerable progress horizontally, but very little vertically.

On Friday evening, the 10th of July, we were according to our calculations thirty leagues south-east of Reykjavik, and at a depth of two and a half leagues.

At our feet there now opened a terrifying abyss. My uncle, however, was not to be put off, and he clapped his hands with pleasure at the steepness of the descent.

'This will take us a long way,' he exclaimed, 'and without much difficulty, because the projections in the rock make for a good staircase.'

The ropes were fastened by Hans in such a way as to prevent any accidents, and the descent began. I can hardly call it perilous, because I was beginning to be familiar with this kind of exercise.

This well, or abyss, was a narrow cleft in the granite mass, called by geologists a 'fault' and caused by the unequal cooling of the globe of the Earth. If it had at one time been a passage for eruptive matter thrown out by Snæfell, I couldn't understand why no trace remained of it passing through. We kept going down a kind of winding staircase, which seemed almost to have been made by human hands.

Every quarter of an hour we were forced to stop for a short rest to allow our knees to recover. We would then sit down on a fragment of rock and talk as we ate and drank from the stream.

Of course, Hans's Brook was falling in a cascade down this fault, and had lost some of its volume, but there was enough and to spare to slake our thirst. Besides, when the incline became more gentle, it would naturally resume its peaceful course. At this point it reminded me of my worthy uncle, with his frequent fits of impatience and anger, while below it ran with the calmness of the Icelandic hunter.

On the 11th and 12th of July, we kept following the spiral curves of this fault, penetrating in actual distance no more than two leagues, but being carried to a depth of five leagues below sea level. But on the 13th, about noon, the fault turned towards the south-east, with a much gentler slope, one of about forty-five degrees.

Then the road became monotonously easy. It couldn't be otherwise, as there was no landscape to vary the stages of our journey.

On Wednesday, the 15th, we were seven leagues underground, and had travelled fifty leagues from Snæfell. Although we were tired, we were in perfect health, and had not yet had any reason to open the medicine chest.

Every hour, my uncle noted the readings on the compass, the chronometer, the manometer and the thermometer, exactly as he has published in his scientific report of our journey. It was therefore not difficult to know exactly where we were. When he told me that we had travelled fifty leagues horizontally, I couldn't hold back an exclamation of astonishment at the thought that we had now long since left Iceland behind us.

'What's the matter?' he exclaimed.

'I was just thinking that if your calculations are correct we are no longer under Iceland.'

'Do you think so?'

'It's easy to check,' I said, and examining the map and using a pair of compasses, I added, 'I wasn't wrong. We've passed Cape Portland, and those fifty leagues bring us out into the middle of the ocean.'

'*Under* the ocean,' my uncle said, rubbing his hands with delight.

'Can we really be?' I said. 'Is the ocean spread out above our heads?'

'Of course, Axel. What could be more natural? Aren't there coal mines at Newcastle that extend far out under the sea?'

It was all very well for the Professor to call this 'natural', but I couldn't feel entirely relaxed at the thought that the boundless ocean was rolling above my head. And yet it really mattered very little whether it was plains and mountains that covered our heads, or the Atlantic waves, so long as we were protected by an arch of solid granite. Anyway, I quickly got used to the idea, as the tunnel, at times running straight, at other times winding as capriciously in its inclines as in its turnings but constantly keeping its south-easterly direction and always going deeper, was gradually taking us to very great depths indeed.

Four days later, on Saturday the 18th of July, in the evening, we arrived at a kind of vast grotto, and here my uncle paid Hans his weekly wages, and it was agreed that the next day, Sunday, should be a day of rest.

CHAPTER 25

DE PROFUNDIS[22]

I therefore awoke next day relieved from concerns about an immediate start. And although we were in the deepest of chasms, there was something quite pleasant about it. Besides, we were beginning to get accustomed to this troglodyte life. I no longer thought about the sun, the moon and the stars, nor about trees, houses and towns, nor about any other of those superfluous things that those who live on the earth's surface consider necessities. Being fossils, we considered all those things as mere nothings.

The grotto formed an immense hall. Along its granite floor ran our faithful stream. At this distance from its spring, the water was scarcely warm, and we drank it with pleasure.

After breakfast, the Professor spent a few hours sorting his daily notes.

'First,' said he, 'I'll make a calculation to ascertain our exact position. I hope, after our return, to draw a map of our journey, which will be in reality a vertical section of the globe, containing the path of our expedition.'

'That will be very interesting, Uncle, but are your observations sufficiently accurate to enable you to do that correctly?'

'Yes. I have everywhere observed the angles and inclines. I'm sure there are no errors. Let's see where we are now. Look at the compass and tell me what direction it indicates.'

I looked, and replied carefully:

'South-east by east.'

'Well,' answered the Professor, after a rapid calculation, 'I reckon we've gone eighty-five leagues since we started.'

'And so we're under the mid-Atlantic?'

'We certainly are.'

'And perhaps at this very moment there is a storm above us, and ships above our heads are being roughly tossed about by the tempest.'

'Quite probably.'

'And there are whales lashing the roof of our prison with their tails?'

'It may be, Axel, but don't worry, they won't do us any harm here. But let's go back to our calculations. Here we are eighty-five leagues south-east of Snæfell, and I reckon that we're at a depth of sixteen leagues.'

'Sixteen leagues?' I cried.

'No doubt.'

'Why, this is the very limit assigned by science to the thickness of the crust of the Earth.'

'I don't deny it.'

'And here, according to the law of increasing temperature, there ought to be a heat of 1,502 degrees Celsius!'

'So there should, my boy.'

'And all this solid granite ought to be in a liquid state.'

'You see that it is not so, and that, as so often happens, facts arise to overthrow theories.'

'I'm forced to agree with you, but, nevertheless, it is surprising.'

'What does the thermometer say?'

'27.6 degrees.'

'Therefore the scientists are out by 1,474.4 degrees, and the theory of proportional increase in temperature is a mistake. Therefore Humphry Davy was right, and I am not wrong in agreeing with him. What do you say now?'

'Nothing.'

In truth, I had a good deal to say. In no way did I accept Davy's theory. I still held to the notion of central heat, although I couldn't feel its effects. To tell the truth, I preferred to think that this chimney of an extinct volcano, lined with lavas, which are non-conductors of heat, simply didn't allow the heat to pass through its walls.

But without stopping to think up new arguments, I simply accepted our situation as it was.

'Well, admitting all your calculations to be quite correct, you must allow me to draw one definite conclusion from them.'

'Go ahead, my boy. Feel free to speak.'

'At the latitude of Iceland, where we now are, the radius of the Earth, the distance from the centre to the surface, is about 1,583 leagues. Let's say 1,600 leagues in round figures. So, out of 1,600 leagues, we've done twelve?'

'As you say.'

'And we have gone down these twelve leagues at a cost of 85 leagues diagonally?'

'Exactly so.'

'In about twenty days?'

'Yes.'

'Now, sixteen leagues are a hundredth part of the Earth's radius. At this rate it'll take us two thousand days, or nearly five and a half years, to get to the centre.'

The Professor didn't reply.

'And what's more, if a vertical depth of sixteen leagues can be achieved only by a diagonal descent of eighty-four, it follows that we must go eight thousand miles in a south-easterly direction. So we'll emerge at some point on the Earth's circumference instead of getting to the centre!'

'Confound your figures, and your theories,' shouted my uncle in a sudden rage. 'What are they based on? How do you know that this passage doesn't run straight to our destination? And besides, there's a precedent. What one man has done, another may do.'

'I hope so, but I still have the right to . . .'

'You have the right to hold your tongue, Axel, but not to talk in that stupid way.'

I could see the terrible Professor threatening to burst out of the skin of my uncle, and I took timely warning.

'Now look at the manometer. What does it say?'

'It says we are under considerable pressure.'

'Very good. So you see that by going down gradually and getting accustomed to the density of the atmosphere, we don't suffer at all.'

'Nothing except a little pain in the ears.'

'That's nothing, and you may get rid of even that by rapid breathing whenever you feel the pain.'

'Quite so,' I said, determined not to say anything that might run counter to my uncle's prejudices. 'There's even a positive pleasure in living in this dense atmosphere. Have you observed how intense sound is down here?'

'No doubt it is. A deaf person would eventually hear perfectly.'

'But won't this density increase?'

'Yes, according to a not quite understood law. It's well known that gravity lessens as one goes lower. You know that it's at the surface of the globe that its effect is felt most, and that at the centre of the globe objects have no weight at all.'

'I'm aware of that, but tell me, won't air end up with the density of water?'

'Of course, under a pressure of seven hundred and ten atmospheres.'

'And how about even deeper still?'

'Deeper, the density will increase even more.'

'Then how will we go down?'

'Well, we must fill our pockets with stones.'

'You've got an answer for everything, haven't you, Uncle.'

I didn't dare venture any further into the realms of hypothesis, for I might eventually have stumbled on an impossibility that would have enraged the Professor.

Still, it was clear that the air, under a pressure which might reach thousands of atmospheres, would sooner or later reach the solid state, and then, even if our bodies could bear the strain, we would be brought to a halt and no amount of reasoning would be able to take us any further.

But I didn't put forward this argument. My uncle would have countered it with his inevitable Saknussemm, a precedent which counted for nothing with me, for even if the journey of the learned Icelander really was attested, there was one very simple answer: that in the sixteenth century, there were neither barometers nor manometers, and therefore Saknussemm couldn't have known how far he had gone.

But I kept this objection to myself and waited to see how things would turn out.

The rest of the day was passed in calculations and in conversations. I remained a steadfast supporter of the opinions of Professor Lidenbrock, and I envied the stolid indifference of Hans, who, without going into causes and effects, went blindly on to wherever his destiny led him.

CHAPTER 26

THE WORST PERIL OF ALL

I must confess that up to this point things had not gone badly and I had had little reason to complain. If our difficulties got no worse, we might hope to reach our goal. And to what a height of scientific glory would we then attain! I had become quite a Lidenbrock in my thinking. Seriously, I had. But was this state of affairs due to the strange place I was now living in? Perhaps.

For several days steeper inclines, some terrifyingly close to perpendicular, took us deeper and deeper into the interior of the Earth. Some days we advanced nearer to the centre by a league and a half, or nearly two leagues. These were perilous descents, in which Hans' skill and incredible coolness were invaluable. The calm Icelander gave of himself with an incomprehensible lack of concern, and thanks to him we crossed many a dangerous spot which we would never have cleared alone.

But his habit of silence was increasing day by day, and was infecting us too. External objects produce definite effects on the brain. A man shut up between four walls soon loses the power to associate words and ideas together. How many prisoners in solitary confinement become idiots, if not mad, for lack of exercise for the faculty of thought?

During the fortnight following our last conversation, nothing happened that's worth recording. But I have good reason to remember one very serious incident which took place about this time, and of which I could scarcely even now forget the smallest details.

By the 7th of August our successive descents had brought us to a depth of thirty leagues; that is, for thirty leagues above our heads there were solid beds of rock, ocean, continents and towns. We must have been two hundred leagues from Iceland.

On that day the tunnel led down a gentle slope. I was ahead of the others. My uncle was carrying one of the Ruhmkorff lamps and I the other. I was examining the beds of granite.

Suddenly turning round, I realized I was alone.

Oh well, I thought, I've been going too fast, or Hans and my uncle have stopped along the way. Well, that won't do. I must rejoin them. Fortunately there's not much of an ascent.

I retraced my steps. I walked for a quarter of an hour. I gazed into the darkness. I shouted. No reply: my voice was lost in the midst of the cavernous echoes which alone replied to my call.

I began to feel uneasy. A shudder ran through me.

'Just keep calm!' I said aloud to myself, 'I'm sure to find my companions again. There aren't two paths. I've just got too far ahead. All I have to do is retrace my steps!'

For half an hour I climbed up. I listened for someone calling, and in that dense atmosphere a voice could carry a long way. But there was a dreary silence in the whole of that long gallery. I stopped. I wanted to believe that I was just disorientated, not lost. I was sure I would find my way again.

'Come on, now,' I repeated, 'since there's only one passage, and they're in it, I'm bound to find them again. All I have to do is keep going up. Unless, indeed, missing me, and supposing me to be behind them, they too have retraced their steps. But even in that case, all I have to do is walk faster than them. I'll find them, I'm sure I will.'

I repeated these words in the fainter tones of a man only half-convinced. Besides, to form even such simple ideas into words, and think them through, took time.

A doubt then gripped me. Was I really ahead when we became separated? Yes, I definitely was. Hans was behind me, and in front of my uncle. He had even stopped for a moment to adjust the pack on his shoulders. I could remember that little incident. It was at that very moment that I must have gone on.

Besides, I thought, have I not got a guarantee that I won't lose my way, a thread in the labyrinth[23] that cannot be broken – my faithful stream? I only have to follow it back and I'm bound to meet up with them.

This conclusion revived my spirits, and I resolved to resume my march without wasting any more time.

How I then blessed my uncle's foresight in preventing the hunter from blocking up the hole in the granite. This kindly spring, after having satisfied our thirst along the way, would now be my guide through this labyrinth in the terrestrial crust.

Before starting off again, I thought a wash would do me good. I stooped to bathe my face in Hans's Brook.

To my stupefaction and utter dismay, all I could feel was rough dry granite! The stream was no longer flowing at my feet.

CHAPTER 27

LOST IN THE BOWELS OF THE EARTH

To express my despair would be impossible. No words could describe it. I was buried alive, with the prospect before me of dying of hunger and thirst.

Automatically, I swept the ground with my hands. How dry and hard the rock seemed!

But how could I have left the course of the stream? For the terrible fact was that it was no longer running beside me. Then I understood the reason for the terrible silence when I had last listened for any sound from my companions. At the moment when I left the correct path I hadn't noticed the absence of the stream. It was clear that when I had reached a fork in the path, Hans's Brook, following the whims of another incline, had gone off with my companions into unknown depths.

How was I to get back? There was no trace of their footsteps nor of my own, for feet left no marks on the granite floor. I racked my brain for a solution to this problem. One word described my position. Lost!

Lost at an immeasurable depth! Thirty leagues of rock seemed to be weighing down on my shoulders with a dreadful pressure. I felt crushed beneath it.

I tried to make myself think about things on the surface of the Earth. I could hardly manage to. Hamburg, the house in the Königstrasse, my poor Gräuben, all that busy world underneath which I was wandering about, was passing in rapid confusion through my terrified memory. I could see again with vivid reality all the incidents of our journey, Iceland, Mr Fridriksson, Snæfell. I told myself that, in such a position as I was now in, to cling to even a single glimmer of hope would be madness, and that the best thing I could do was give myself up to despair.

What human power could restore me to the light of the sun by tearing apart the huge arches of rock which joined together over my head, buttressing each other with impregnable strength? Who could place my feet on the right path, and bring me back to my company?

'Oh, Uncle!' burst from my lips in the tone of despair.

It was the only word of reproach I uttered, for I knew how much he would be suffering looking for me, wherever he might be.

When I saw myself in this way far removed from all human help, and unable to do anything to save myself, I turned to heaven for aid. Memories of my childhood, and of my mother, whom I had only known in my tender early years, came back to me, and I knelt in prayer imploring the Divine assistance I was so little worthy of.

This return to trust in God's providence made me calmer, and I was able to concentrate the full force of my intelligence on my situation.

I had three days' provisions with me and my flask was full. But I couldn't remain alone for long. Should I go up or down?

Up, of course. Always up.

That way I would be bound to arrive at the point where I had left the stream, that fatal turning in the path. With the stream at my feet, I might hope to regain the summit of Snæfell.

Why hadn't I thought of that sooner? Here clearly was a chance of reaching safety. The most pressing need was to find the course of Hans's Brook again. I got up and, leaning on my iron-pointed stick, I ascended the gallery. The slope was rather steep. I walked on with hope and without hesitation, like a man who has only one path to follow.

For half an hour I met with no obstacle. I tried to recognize my way by the form of the tunnel, by the way certain rocks projected, by the layout of the fractures. But no particular sign struck me, and I soon found that this gallery could not take me back to the turning point. It came to an abrupt end. I met an impenetrable wall, and collapsed on the rock.

Unspeakable despair then gripped me. I lay there, overwhelmed, aghast! My last hope had been shattered against this granite wall.

Lost in this labyrinth, whose winding paths criss-crossed each other in all directions, there was no longer any point in thinking of escape. Here I must die the most dreadful of deaths. And, strange to say, the thought crossed my mind that when some day my petrified remains were found thirty leagues below the surface in the bowels of the Earth, the discovery might lead to some serious scientific discussions.

I tried to speak out loud, but only hoarse sounds passed my dry lips. I was panting for breath.

In the midst of my agony, a new terror laid hold of me. When I had fallen, my lamp had been damaged. I couldn't fix it, and its light was getting dimmer and would soon disappear altogether.

I watched the luminous current growing weaker and weaker in the wire coil. A dim procession of moving shadows seemed to be slowly unfolding down the darkening walls. I hardly dared shut my eyes for one moment, for fear of losing the slightest glimmer of this precious light. At each moment it seemed about to vanish and I could feel the dense blackness come rolling in upon me.

One last trembling glimmer shot feebly up. I watched it in trembling anxiety; I drank it in as if I could preserve it, concentrating the full power of my eyes on it, as if on the very last sensation of light they were ever to experience, and the next moment I lay in the heavy gloom of deep, thick, unfathomable darkness.

A terrible cry of anguish burst from me. On Earth, even in the middle of the darkest night, light never altogether fails in its duties. It's still there, subtle and diffuse, but no matter how little there may be, the eye still catches that little. Here there was not a glimmer; the total darkness made me totally blind.

Then I lost my head. I got up with my arms stretched out in front of me, attempting painfully to feel my way. I began to run wildly, hurrying through the inextricable maze, still going down, still running through the substance of the Earth's thick crust, a struggling denizen of geological 'faults', crying, shouting, yelling, soon bruised by banging against the jagged rock, falling and getting up again bleeding, trying to drink the blood which covered my face, and expecting at any moment to shatter my skull against some wall of rock.

I will never know where my mad dash took me. After some hours had passed, no doubt exhausted, I collapsed like a lifeless lump along the wall and lost consciousness.

CHAPTER 28

THE RESCUE IN
THE WHISPERING GALLERY

When I came to again, my face was wet with tears. How long that state of insensibility had lasted I cannot say. I had no means now of keeping track of time. Never was there solitude the like of this, never had any living being felt so utterly abandoned.

After my fall I had lost a good deal of blood. I felt covered in it. Ah! how happy I would have been to have died already, for death not still to be gone through. I no longer wanted to think. I chased away every idea, and, overcome by my grief, I rolled to the foot of the opposite wall.

I was already feeling another fainting fit coming on, and was hoping for complete annihilation, when a loud noise reached me. It was like the distant rumble of continuous thunder, and I could hear its deep sound rolling far away into the remote recesses of the abyss.

Where could this noise be coming from? It must be from some phenomenon happening in the great depths in the midst of which I lay helpless. Was it an explosion of gas? Was it the fall of some mighty pillar of the globe?

I continued to listen. I wanted to know if the noise would be repeated. A quarter of an hour passed. Silence reigned in this gallery. I couldn't even hear the beating of my heart.

Suddenly my ear, resting by chance against the wall, caught, or seemed to catch, certain vague, indescribable, distant, articulate sounds, like words. I shuddered.

'My mind is playing tricks on me,' I thought.

But it wasn't. Listening more carefully, I really did hear a murmuring of voices. My weakness prevented me from understanding what the voices were saying. But it was language, I was sure of it.

For a moment I was afraid the words might be my own, carried back to me by an echo. Perhaps I had been crying out without being aware of it. I closed my lips firmly, and laid my ear against the wall again.

'Yes, really, someone *is* speaking. Those *are* words!'

Even a few feet from the wall, I could hear it distinctly. I managed to catch uncertain, strange, undistinguishable words. They came as if pronounced in low, murmured whispers. The word '*forloräd*' was repeated several times in a sympathetic and sorrowful tone.

'Help!' I cried with all my might. 'Help!'

I listened, I waited in the darkness for an answer, a cry, a mere breath of sound, but nothing came. Some minutes passed. A flood of ideas exploded into my mind. I feared my weakened voice would never reach my companions.

'It's them,' I repeated. 'What other men could be thirty leagues underground?'

I began to listen again. Passing my ear over the wall from one place to another, I found the point where the voices seemed to be heard best. The word *'forloräd'* again came to me; then the rolling of thunder which had roused me from my lethargy.

'No,' I said, 'no, it's not through such a solid mass that a voice can be heard. I'm surrounded by granite walls, and the loudest explosion could never be heard here! This noise is coming along the gallery. It must be due to some remarkable action of acoustic laws!'

I listened again, and this time, yes, this time I did distinctly hear my name pronounced across the wide interval.

It was my uncle's own voice! He was talking to the guide. And *'forloräd'* is a Danish word.

Then it all became clear. To make myself heard, I had to speak along this wall, which would conduct the sound of my voice just as wire conducts electricity.

But there was no time to lose. If my companions moved but a few steps away, the acoustic phenomenon would cease. I therefore went close to the wall, and pronounced these words as clearly as possible:

'Uncle Lidenbrock!'

I waited with the greatest anxiety. Sound doesn't travel very quickly. Even increased density of air has no effect on its rate of travel; it merely increases its intensity. Seconds, which seemed ages, passed away, and at last these words reached me:

'Axel! Axel! Is that you?'

. . .

'Yes, yes,' I replied.

. . .

'My boy, where are you?'

. . .

'Lost, in the deepest darkness.'

. . .

'Where is your lamp?'

. . .

'It's gone out.'

. . .

'And the stream?'

. . .

'Disappeared.'

. . .

'Be brave, Axel, don't lose heart!'

. . .

'Wait a second! I'm exhausted! I can't answer. But keep talking to me!'

. . .

'Be brave,' said my uncle again. 'Don't talk. Listen to me. We've looked for you up and down the gallery. Couldn't find you. I wept for you, my poor boy. At last, supposing you were still on Hans's Brook, we fired our guns. Now at least we can hear each other even if our hands cannot touch. But don't despair, Axel! To be able to hear each other is something.'

. . .

During this time I had been thinking. A vague hope was returning to my heart. There was one thing I needed to know to begin with. I placed my lips close to the wall, saying:

'Uncle!'

. . .

'My boy!' came to me after a few seconds.

. . .

'We need to know how far apart we are.'

. . .

'That's easy.'

. . .

'Have you got your chronometer?'

. . .

'Yes.'

. . .

'Well, get ready to use it. Say my name, noting exactly the second when you speak. I'll repeat it as soon as it reaches me, and you will note the exact moment when you get my reply.'

'Yes. And half the time between my call and your answer will indicate exactly the time my voice will have taken to reach you.'

. . .

'Exactly, Uncle.'

. . .

'Are you ready?'

. . .

'Yes.'

. . .

'Now, pay attention. I'm going to call your name.'

. . .

I put my ear to the wall, and as soon as the name 'Axel' came, I immediately replied 'Axel,' then waited.

. . .

'Forty seconds,' said my uncle. 'Forty seconds between the two words, so the sound takes twenty seconds to travel between us. Now, at the rate of 1,020 feet per second, that's 20,400 feet, or just under four miles, more or less.'

. . .

'Four miles!' I murmured.

. . .

'It'll soon be over, Axel.'

. . .

'Do I need to go up or down?'

. . .

'Down, and I'll tell you why. We've reached a vast chamber with a large number of galleries. Yours must lead into it, because it looks like all the clefts and fractures of the globe radiate out from this huge cavern. So get up and start walking. Keep walking, drag yourself along if necessary, slide down the steep parts, and at the end gallery you'll find us waiting for you. Now, my boy, get going.'

. . .

These words cheered me up.

'Goodbye, Uncle.' I cried. 'I'm setting off now. There'll be no more voices heard once I've started. So goodbye!'

. . .

'Goodbye, Axel. See you soon!'

. . .

These were the last words I heard.

This wonderful underground conversation, carried on over the distance of four miles that separated us, ended with these words of hope. I thanked God from my heart, for it was He who had led me through those vast lonely places to the point where, perhaps there alone and nowhere else, the voices of my companions could reach me.

This acoustic effect is easily explained scientifically. It arose from the concave shape of the gallery and the conducting power of the rock. There are many examples of this transmission of sounds which remain unheard in the intervening space. I remember that a similar phenomenon has been observed in many places, amongst others on the internal surface of the 'Whispering Gallery' of the dome of St. Paul's in London and especially in the middle of the strange caverns in the quarries near Syracuse, the most wonderful of which is called Dionysius' Ear.

As I remembered these things, I could see clearly that, since my uncle's voice had reached me, there could be no barrier between us. Following the direction from which the sound came, I would without a doubt arrive where he was, if my strength didn't fail me.

So I got up. I dragged myself more than walked. The slope descended rapidly, and I slid down.

Soon the speed of the descent increased frighteningly and threatened to become a fall. I no longer had the strength to stop myself.

Suddenly there was no ground under me. I felt myself spinning in the air, striking and rebounding from the rocky projections of a vertical gallery, virtually a well. My head hit a sharp rock, and I lost consciousness.

CHAPTER 29

THE SEA! THE SEA!

When I came to, I was lying stretched out in semi-darkness, covered with thick coats and blankets. My uncle was watching over me, looking for the slightest signs of life. At my first sigh, he took hold of my hand; when I opened my eyes, he uttered a cry of joy.

'He's alive! He's alive!' he shouted.

'Yes, I'm still alive,' I answered weakly.

'My dear nephew,' said my uncle, hugging me to his breast, 'you're safe.'

I was deeply touched by the tenderness of his manner as he uttered these words, and still more with the care with which he watched over me. But it took trials such as this for the Professor to show his more tender emotions.

At that moment, Hans appeared. He saw my hand in my uncle's, and I may safely say that there was an expression of pleasure on his face.

'*God dag*,' he said.

'Good day, Hans, good day. And now, uncle, tell me where we are at this particular moment.'

'Tomorrow, Axel, tomorrow. You're too weak today. I've bandaged your head with compresses which mustn't be disturbed. Sleep now, and tomorrow I will tell you everything.'

'But do tell me what time it is, and what day.'

'It's Sunday the 9th of August, and it's ten o'clock at night. You must ask me no more questions until the 10th.'

Truth to tell, I was very weak, and my eyes closed of their own accord. I was needing a good night's rest. So off I went to sleep, with the knowledge that I had been four long days alone in the heart of the Earth.

Next morning when I awoke, I looked all around me. My bed, made up of all our travelling rugs, was in a charming grotto that was decorated with magnificent stalactites and whose floor consisted of fine sand. It was half-light. There was no torch and no lamp, but a certain mysterious light was coming from outside the grotto through a narrow opening. And I could also hear a vague, indistinct noise, something like the murmuring of waves breaking on a shingly shore, and at times I thought I could hear wind whistling.

I wondered whether I was awake or dreaming, whether perhaps my brain, deranged by my fall, was being affected by imaginary noises. Yet neither my eyes nor my ears could be deceived to that extent.

It's a ray of daylight, I thought, slipping in through this cleft in the rock! And that is indeed the murmuring of waves! That's the rustling noise of wind. Am I quite mistaken, or have we returned to the surface of the Earth? Has my uncle given up the expedition, or has it come to a successful conclusion?

I was asking myself these unanswerable questions when the Professor came in.

'Good morning, Axel,' he exclaimed cheerfully. 'I expect you're feeling better.'

'Yes, I certainly am,' said I, sitting up on my bed.

'You could hardly fail to be better, since you've had a peaceful sleep. Hans and I watched over you in turn, and we could see you were evidently recovering.'

'Yes, I do feel a great deal better, and I'll prove that to you in a moment if you'll let me have my breakfast.'

'You shall have something to eat, my boy. The fever has left you. Hans rubbed your wounds with some ointment or other that the Icelanders keep the secret of, and they've healed marvellously. He's a splendid fellow, that hunter of ours!'

Whilst he went on talking, my uncle prepared some food, which I devoured eagerly, notwithstanding his advice to the contrary. All the while I was badgering him with questions which he was more than willing to answer.

I then learnt that my providential fall had brought me right to the foot of an almost perpendicular shaft; and as I had landed in the midst of an accompanying torrent of stones, the smallest of which would have been enough to crush me, the conclusion was that part of the rock-face had come down with me. This terrifying conveyance had thus carried me into the arms of my uncle, where I fell bruised, bleeding and unconscious.

'It's quite incredible that you weren't killed a hundred times over. But, for the love of God, let's stay together from now on, or we might never see each other again.'

'Stay together? Is the journey not over then?' I opened a pair of astonished eyes, which immediately prompted the question:

'What's the matter, Axel?'

'I have a question to ask you. You say that I'm safe and sound?'

'No doubt you are.'

'And all my limbs unbroken?'

'Certainly.'

'And my head?'

'Your head, except for a few bruises, is all right, and it's on your shoulders, where it ought to be.'

'Well, I am afraid my brain is affected.'

'Your mind is affected?'

'Yes, I fear so. Are we back on the surface of the globe?'

'No, certainly not.'

'Then I must be mad, because I imagine I can see the light of day, and hear the wind blowing and the sea breaking on the shore.'

'Oh! Is that all?'

'Can you explain it to me.'

'I can't explain the inexplicable, but you will soon see and understand that geology has not yet learnt all that it has to learn.'

'Then let's go,' I answered quickly.

'No, Axel, the open air might be bad for you.'

'Open air?'

'Yes, the wind is rather strong. You mustn't expose yourself.'

'But I assure you I'm perfectly well.'

'A little patience, my boy. A relapse might get us into difficulty, and we've no time to lose, as the voyage may be a long one.'

'The voyage!'

'Yes, rest today, and tomorrow we will set sail.'

'Set sail?' The words made me jump up.

What did it all mean? Was there a river, a lake or a sea for us to cross? Did we have a ship at our disposal in some underground harbour?

My curiosity was greatly aroused, and my uncle tried in vain to restrain me. When he saw that my impatience would do me more harm than giving in to it would, he relented.

I quickly got dressed. As a precaution, I wrapped myself in a blanket and left the grotto.

CHAPTER 30

A NEW *MARE INTERNUM*[24]

At first I could hardly see anything. My eyes, unaccustomed to the light, quickly closed. When I was able to reopen them, I stood more stupefied than surprised.

'The sea!' I cried.

'Yes,' my uncle replied, 'the Lidenbrock Sea, and I don't imagine any other explorer will ever dispute my claim to name it after myself as its first discoverer.'

A vast sheet of water, the start of a lake or an ocean, spread far away beyond what the eye could see. The deeply indented shoreline was lined with a stretch of fine shining sand, softly lapped by the waves, and strewn with small shells which had been inhabited by the earliest creatures of creation. The waves broke on this shore with the hollow echoing murmur peculiar to vast enclosed spaces. A light foam blew over the waves on the breath of a moderate breeze, and some of the spray fell on my face. On the other edge of this slightly sloping shore, about a hundred fathoms from the waves, was a huge wall of vast cliffs rising majestically to a great height. Some of these, dividing the beach with their sharp spurs, formed capes and promontories, worn away by the ceaseless action of the surf. Farther on, the eye could discern their massive outline sharply defined against the distant, hazy horizon.

It was certainly a real ocean, with the irregularity of the shorelines on Earth, but deserted and horribly wild in appearance.

If my eyes were able to range far over this great sea, it was because a peculiar light made every detail of it clearly visible. It wasn't the light of the sun, with its dazzling shafts of brightness and the splendour of its rays, nor was it the pale and uncertain shimmer of moonbeams, the dim reflection of a nobler body of light. No, the illuminating power of this light, its trembling diffuseness, its bright, clear whiteness and its low temperature, showed that it must be of electrical origin. It was like an aurora borealis, a continuous cosmic phenomenon filling a cavern large enough to contain an ocean.

The vault that spanned the space above, the sky (if such it could be called), seemed to be made up of vast plains of cloud, shifting and variable vapours which at certain times condensed and fell in torrents of rain. I would have thought that under so great an atmospheric pressure there could be no evaporation, and yet, by a law of physics unknown to me, there were broad tracts of vapour suspended in the air. But then, one could say it was a 'fine day'. The play of the electric light produced peculiar effects on the upper strata of cloud. Deep shadows formed on their lower curves, and often, between two separated strata of cloud, there glided down a ray of indescribable brightness. But it wasn't solar light, and there was no heat. The general effect was sad, supremely melancholy. Instead of the shining firmament, spangled with innumerable stars shining singly or in clusters, I could feel above the clouds vast granite arches which seemed to crush me with their weight; and all this space, great as it was, would not have been enough for the orbit of the humblest of satellites.

Then I remembered the theory of an English captain, who likened the Earth to a vast hollow sphere, in the interior of which the air became luminous because of the vast pressure on it, while within it two heavenly bodies, Pluto[25] and Proserpina, followed their mysterious orbits. Had he been right?

We were in reality enclosed inside a vast cavern. Its width could not be estimated, since the shore continued to widen out as far as the eye could see, nor could its length, for the dim horizon limited one's view. As for its height, it must have been several leagues high. Where this vault rested on its granite base no eye could tell, but there was a cloud hanging far above, the height of which we estimated at 12,000 feet, a greater height than that of any terrestrial vapour, and no doubt due to the great density of the air.

The word cavern does not convey any idea of this immense space. Words of human language are inadequate to describe the discoveries of one who ventures into the deep abysses of the Earth.

I couldn't decide what geological theory would account for the existence of such a cavern. Had the cooling of the globe produced it? I knew of famous caverns from the descriptions of travellers, but had never heard of any of such dimensions as this. Even if the grotto of Guachara, in Colombia, visited by Humboldt, did not fully divulge the secret of its depth to him, he did investigate it to a depth of 2,500 feet and it probably didn't extend much farther than that. The immense Mammoth Cave in Kentucky is of gigantic proportions, since its vaulted roof rises five hundred feet above an unfathomable lake and travellers have explored its ramifications for ten leagues. But what were these holes compared to that one I was admiring, with its sky of luminous vapours, its bursts of electric light and a vast sea filling its bed? My imagination was powerless before such immensity.

I gazed at these wonders in silence. I couldn't find the words to express my feelings. I felt as if I was on some distant planet such as Uranus or Neptune, and in the presence of phenomena of which my terrestrial experience gave me no knowledge. For such novel sensations, new words were wanted, and my imagination failed to supply them. I gazed, I thought, I admired, with a stupefaction tinged with fear.

The unforeseen nature of this spectacle brought back the colour to my cheeks. I was receiving a new course of treatment with the help of astonishment, and my convalescence was promoted by this novel system of therapeutics. And besides, the dense and breezy air invigorated me, supplying more oxygen to my lungs.

It will be easily conceived that after forty-seven days' imprisonment in a narrow gallery, it was the height of physical enjoyment to breathe moist air impregnated with salty particles.

I was delighted to leave my dark grotto. My uncle, already familiar with these wonders, had ceased to feel surprise.

'Do you feel strong enough to take a little walk now?' he asked.

'Yes, certainly, and nothing could be more delightful.'

'Well, take my arm, Axel, and let's follow the windings of the shore.'

I eagerly accepted, and we began to follow the coast along this new sea. On the left huge pyramids of rock, piled one upon another, created a prodigious titanic effect. Down their sides flowed countless waterfalls which wended their way in clear, gurgling streams. A few light vapours, leaping from rock to rock, indicated where there were hot springs, and streams flowed gently down to the common basin, gliding down the gentle slopes with a softer murmur.

Amongst these streams I recognized our faithful travelling companion, Hans's Brook, coming to quietly add its little volume to the mighty sea, just as if it had done nothing else since the beginning of the world.

'We won't see it again,' I said, with a sigh.

'That one or another one,' replied the professor, 'what does it matter?'

I thought him rather ungrateful.

But at that moment my attention was drawn to an unexpected sight. Five hundred yards away, along a high promontory, appeared a tall, tufted, dense forest. It was composed of trees of moderate height, umbrella-like in form, with sharp geometrical outlines. The currents of wind seemed to have had no effect on their shape, and in the midst of the windy blasts they stood unmoved and firm, just like a clump of petrified cedars.

I hurried towards them. I couldn't give any name to these singular creations. Were they among the two hundred thousand known plant species, or did they claim a place of their own in lakeland flora? No. When we arrived under their shade, my surprise turned to wonder. There before me stood products of Earth, but of gigantic proportions. My uncle immediately said what they were.

'It's just a forest of mushrooms,' he said.

And he was right. Imagine the large development attained by these plants, which prefer a warm, moist climate. I knew that the *Lycoperdon giganteum* attains, according to Bulliard, a circumference of eight or nine feet, but here there were pale mushrooms thirty to forty feet high and crowned with a cap of equal diameter. They stood there in their thousands.

No light could penetrate between their huge cones, and complete darkness reigned beneath those giants. They formed settlements of domes in close array like the round, thatched roofs of a central African city.

I wanted to walk beneath them, though a chill fell on me as soon as I came under those cellular vaults. For half an hour we wandered from side to side in the damp shade, and it was a comfortable and pleasant change to arrive once more on the seashore.

But the subterranean vegetation was not confined to these fungi. Farther on there rose groups of tall trees of colourless foliage, easy to recognize. On Earth they were lowly shrubs, but here they attained gigantic size: Lycopodia a hundred feet high; huge Sigillaria, found in our coal mines; tree ferns as tall as our fir-trees of northern latitudes; Lepidodendrons with cylindrical forked stems ending in long leaves and bristling with rough hairs.

'Wonderful, magnificent, splendid!' cried my uncle. 'Here is the entire flora of the second period of the world – the Transition Period. These, humble garden plants as they are with us now, were tall trees in the early ages. Look, Axel, and wonder at it all. Never had a botanist such a feast as this!'

'You're right, Uncle. Providence seems to have preserved in this immense conservatory the antediluvian plants which the wisdom of scientists has so sagaciously put together again.'

'It is a conservatory, Axel, but is it not also a menagerie?'

'Surely not a menagerie!'

'Yes, there's no doubt about it. Look at that dust under your feet. See the bones scattered on the ground.'

'So there are!' I exclaimed, 'the bones of extinct animals.'

I rushed to look at these remains, formed of an indestructible mineral substance, calcium phosphate, and without hesitation I identified these monstrous bones which lay scattered about like decayed tree-trunks.

'Here's the lower jaw of a mastodon,' I said. 'These are the molar teeth of the Dinotherium. This femur must have belonged to the largest of those animals, the Megatherium. It certainly is a menagerie, because these remains were not brought here by a flood. The animals they belonged to roamed on the shores of this subterranean sea, under the shade of those arborescent plants. There are entire skeletons here. And yet I can't understand how these quadrupeds appear in a granite cavern.'

'Why?'

'Because animal life existed on Earth only in the Secondary Period, when a sediment of soil had been deposited by the rivers, and taken the place of the incandescent rocks of the Primitive Period.'

'Well, Axel, there's a very simple answer to your objection, which is that this soil is alluvial.'

'What! At such a depth below the surface of the Earth?'

'Without a doubt, and there's a geological explanation for that. At a certain period the Earth consisted only of an elastic crust or bark, alternately acted on by forces from above or below, according to the laws of attraction and gravitation. Probably there were subsidences of the outer crust, when some of the sedimentary deposit was carried down through sudden openings.'

'That may be so,' I replied, 'but if there have been creatures now extinct in these underground regions, is there any reason why some of those monsters might not still be roaming through these gloomy forests or hidden behind the steep crags?'

And as this unpleasant notion gripped me, I anxiously surveyed the open spaces before me, but no living creature appeared on the barren shore.

I felt rather tired, and went to sit down at the point of a promontory, at the foot of which the waves were beating themselves into spray. From there my eye could scan every part of this bay created by an indentation in the coastline. The end of the bay formed a little harbour between the pyramidal cliffs, where the still waters slept, sheltered from the boisterous winds. A brig and two or three schooners might safely have moored within it. I almost fancied I would presently see some ship sail out under full sail, and take to the open sea in the southern breeze.

But this illusion lasted a very short time. We were the only living creatures in this subterranean world. When the wind dropped, a deeper silence than that of the deserts fell on the arid, naked rocks and weighed heavily on the surface of the ocean. I tried to see through the distant haze, and to tear apart the mysterious curtain that hung across the horizon. Anxious questions came to my lips. Where did that sea end? Where did it lead to? Would we ever know anything about its far shores?

My uncle had absolutely no doubt about it. For my part, I both wanted and feared to know.

After spending an hour contemplating this marvellous spectacle, we returned to the shore to go back to the grotto, and I fell asleep in the midst of the strangest thoughts.

CHAPTER 31

PREPARATIONS FOR
A VOYAGE OF DISCOVERY

The next morning I awoke feeling perfectly well. I thought a bathe would do me good, and I went and plunged for a few minutes into the waters of this 'Mediterranean Sea', for assuredly it better deserved this name than any other sea[26].

I came back to breakfast with a good appetite. Hans was a good caterer for our little household; he had water and fire at his disposal, so he was able to vary our bill of fare now and then. For dessert he gave us a few cups of coffee, and never was coffee so delicious.

'Now, then,' said my uncle, 'high tide is due now and we mustn't miss the opportunity to study the phenomenon.'

'What? A tide?' I exclaimed. 'Can the influence of the sun and moon be felt down here?'

'Why not? Aren't all bodies subject throughout their mass to the power of universal attraction? This mass of water cannot escape the general law. And in spite of the heavy atmospheric pressure on the surface, you will see it rise like the Atlantic itself.'

At the same moment, we reached the sand on the shore, and the waves were gradually encroaching on the shore.

'The tide *is* rising,' I exclaimed.

'Yes, Axel. And judging by these ridges of foam, you may observe that the sea will rise about twelve feet.'

'That's amazing,' I said.

'No, it's entirely natural.'

'You may say so, Uncle, but to me it's quite extraordinary, and I can hardly believe my eyes. Who would ever have imagined, under this terrestrial crust, an ocean with ebbing and flowing tides, with winds and storms?'

'Well,' replied my uncle, 'is there any scientific reason against it?'

'No, I can't think of any, as soon as the theory of central heat is abandoned.'

'Then so far,' he answered, 'Sir Humphry Davy's theory is confirmed.'

'Clearly it is. And now there's no reason why there should not be seas and continents in the interior of the Earth.'

'No doubt,' said my uncle, 'but uninhabited ones.'

'All right,' I said, 'but why shouldn't these waters hold fish of unknown species?'

'Well,' he replied, 'we haven't seen any yet.'

'Well, let's make some fishing-lines, and see if the bait will draw them to it as it does in regions under the moon.'

'We'll certainly try, Axel, for we must investigate all the secrets of these newly discovered regions.'

'But where are we, Uncle? I haven't asked you that question yet, and your instruments must be able to provide the answer.'

'Horizontally, three hundred and fifty leagues from Iceland.'

'As much as that?'

'I'm confident of not being a mile out in my reckoning.'

'And does the compass still show south-east?'

'Yes, with a westerly deviation of nineteen degrees forty-five minutes, just as above ground. As for its dip, a curious fact is coming to light, which I have observed carefully: that the needle, instead of dipping towards the pole as in the northern hemisphere, on the contrary rises from it.'

'Would you then conclude,' I said, 'that the magnetic pole is somewhere between the surface of the globe and the point where we are?'

'Exactly, and it is likely enough that if we were to reach the spot beneath the polar regions, about that seventy-first degree where Sir James Ross has discovered the magnetic pole to be situated, we should see the needle point straight up. Therefore that mysterious centre of attraction is at no great depth.'

'It must be so, and there's a fact which science has scarcely suspected.'

'Science, my lad, has been constructed on many errors, but they are errors which it was good to fall into, because they led to the truth.'

'What depth have we reached now?'

'We are thirty-five leagues below the surface.'

'So,' I said, examining the map, 'the Highlands of Scotland are over our heads, and the Grampians are raising their rugged summits above us.'

'Yes,' answered the Professor, laughing. 'It's rather a heavy weight to bear, but a solid arch spans over our heads. The Great Architect has built it with the best materials, and never could man have made it arch so wide. What are the finest arches of bridges and the arcades of cathedrals compared with this far-reaching vault with a radius of three leagues, beneath which a wide and tempest-tossed ocean may flow at its ease?'

'Oh, I'm not afraid it'll fall on my head or anything like that. But now what are your plans? Are you not thinking of returning to the surface now?'

'Return? Certainly not! We'll continue our journey, since everything has gone well so far.'

'But how are we to get down below this liquid surface?'

'Oh, I'm not going to dive in head first. But if all oceans are properly speaking just lakes, being surrounded by land, this internal sea will of course be surrounded by a coast of granite, and on the opposite shores we shall find fresh passages opening.'

'How long do you suppose this sea to be?'

'Thirty or forty leagues. So we've no time to lose, and we'll set sail tomorrow.'

I looked about for a ship.

'Set sail, will we? I'd like to see my boat first.'

'It won't be a boat at all, but a good, well-made raft.'

'Why,' I said, 'a raft would be just as hard to make as a boat, and I don't see . . .'

'I know you don't see, but you might hear if you would listen. Don't you hear a hammer at work? Hans is already busy at it.'

'What, has he already felled the trees?'

'Oh, the trees were down already. Come with me and you'll see for yourself.'

After half an hour's walk, on the other side of the promontory which formed the little natural harbour, I saw Hans at work. With a few more steps, I was at his side. To my great surprise, a half-finished raft was already lying on the sand, made of a peculiar kind of wood, and a great number of planks, both straight and bent, and of frames, were covering the ground, enough almost for a little fleet.

'What sort of wood is this, Uncle?' I asked.

'It's fir, pine and birch, and other northern conifers, mineralized by the action of the sea. It's called *'surtarbrandur'*, a variety of brown coal or lignite, found mainly in Iceland.'

'But surely, then, like other fossil wood, it must be as hard as stone and won't float?'

'Sometimes that may happen. Some of these woods become true anthracites. But others, such as this, have only gone through the first stage of fossilization. Just watch,' added my uncle, throwing one of the precious planks into the sea.

The bit of wood, after disappearing, returned to the surface and swung to and fro with the movement of the waves.

'Are you convinced?' said my uncle.

'I'm absolutely convinced, although it's incredible!'

By the following evening, thanks to the hard work and skill of our guide, the raft was completed. It was ten feet by five. The planks of *surtarbrandur*, firmly tied together with ropes, formed a flat surface, and when launched this improvised vessel floated easily on the waves of the Lidenbrock Sea.

CHAPTER 32

WONDERS OF THE DEEP

On the 13th of August, we awoke early. We were now going to adopt this speedier and less tiring mode of travelling.

A mast was made of two poles spliced together, a cross-piece was made of a third pole, a blanket borrowed from our coverings made a tolerable sail. There was no lack of rope for the rigging, and everything was well made and firmly fixed together.

The provisions, the baggage, the instruments, the guns and a good quantity of fresh water from the rocks around us, all found their proper places on board, and at six o'clock the Professor gave the signal to embark. Hans had fixed up a rudder to steer his vessel. He took the tiller, I cast off. The sail was set, and we pushed off. At the moment of leaving the harbour, my uncle, who was obsessively fond of naming his new discoveries, wanted to give it a name, and proposed mine amongst others.

'But I have a better name to suggest,' I said. 'Gräuben. Let it be called Port Gräuben. That'll look good on the map.'

'Port Gräuben it is then.'

And so the cherished memory of my Virland girl became associated with our adventurous expedition.

The wind was blowing from the north-west. We sailed with it at top speed. The dense atmosphere acted with great force and drove us along quickly like a huge fan.

An hour later, my uncle had been able to estimate our speed fairly accurately. At this rate, he said, we'll cover thirty leagues in twenty-four hours, and we'll soon come in sight of the opposite shore.

I said nothing, but went and sat forward. The northern shore was already beginning to dip under the horizon. The eastern and western shores spread out wide as if to bid us farewell. Before our eyes lay far and wide a vast sea. Shadows of great clouds swept heavily over its silver-grey surface, the glistening bluish rays of electric light, here and there reflected by the dancing drops of spray, shot out little sheaves of light from the track we left behind us. Soon we entirely lost sight of land. There was no object left for the eye to judge by, and but for the frothy track of the raft I might have thought we were standing still.

About twelve, immense tracts of seaweed came in sight. I was aware of the great vegetative power that characterizes these plants, which grow at a depth of twelve thousand feet, reproduce under a pressure of four hundred atmospheres and sometimes form barriers strong enough to impede the course of a ship. But never, I think, were there such seaweeds as those we saw floating in immense waving lines on the Lidenbrock Sea.

Our raft skirted the whole length of these seaweeds, three or four thousand feet long, undulating like vast serpents farther than the eye could see. I amused myself tracing these endless waves, always thinking I would come to the end of them, but for hour after hour my patient expectation proved wrong and my surprise increased.

What natural force could have produced such plants, and what must have been the appearance of the Earth in the first ages of its formation, when, under the action of heat and moisture, the vegetable kingdom alone was developing on its surface?

Evening came, and, as on the previous day, I perceived no change in the luminous condition of the air. It was a constant phenomenon, the permanence of which we could rely on.

After supper I lay down at the foot of the mast and fell asleep in the midst of weird reveries.

Hans, motionless at the helm, let the raft run on, which, after all, needed no steering, the wind blowing directly from behind us.

Since our departure from Port Gräuben, Professor Lidenbrock had entrusted the log to my care. I was to record every observation, make entries of interesting phenomena, the direction of the wind, the rate of sailing, the progress we made – in short, every particular of our strange voyage.

I shall therefore reproduce here these daily notes, written, so to speak, as the course of events directed, in order to furnish an exact narrative of our passage.

Friday, August 14. – Wind steady, N.W. The raft making rapid progress in a direct line. Coast thirty leagues to leeward. Nothing in sight before us. Intensity of light the same. Weather fine; that is to say, the clouds are high, light and bathed in a white atmosphere resembling molten silver. Thermometer: 32°.

At noon Hans prepared a hook at the end of a line. He baited it with a small piece of meat and flung it into the sea. For two hours he caught nothing. Are these waters, then, empty of inhabitants? No, there's a pull at the line. Hans draws it in and brings out a struggling fish.

'A fish,' exclaims my uncle.

'A sturgeon,' I exclaim in turn, 'a small sturgeon.'

The Professor studies the creature attentively, and his opinion differs from mine.

The head of this fish is flat, but rounded in front, and the anterior part of its body is plated with bony, angular scales. It has no teeth, its pectoral fins are large, and it is tailless. The animal belongs to the same order as the sturgeon, but differs from that fish in many essential particulars. After a short examination my uncle states his opinion.

'This fish belongs to an extinct family, of which only fossil traces are found in the Devonian formations.'

'What?' I cried. 'Have we taken alive an inhabitant of the seas of primitive ages?'

'Yes,' says the professor, continuing his observations, 'and you will observe that these fossil fishes have no identity with any living species. To have in one's possession a living specimen is a happy event for a naturalist.'

'But to what family does it belong?'

'It is of the order of Ganoids, of the family of the Cephalaspidae, genus . . .'

'Well?'

'It's a species of Pterichthys, I'm sure. But this one shows a peculiarity confined to fishes that inhabit subterranean waters. It's blind.'

'Blind?

'Not only blind, but actually has no eyes at all.'

I took a look at it. Yes, my uncle was absolutely right. But thinking that it might be a solitary case, we baited our line again and tossed it out. This ocean is clearly well stocked with fish, for in another couple of hours we catch a large quantity of Pterichthydes as well as other fish belonging to the extinct family of Dipterides, but of which species my uncle could not say. None had organs of sight. This unexpected catch makes a useful addition to our stock of provisions.

It thus becomes clear that this sea contains nothing but species known to us in their fossil state. In the fossil records, fish as well as reptiles are the more perfectly formed the farther back their time of creation.

Perhaps we may yet meet with some of those saurians which science has reconstructed out of a bit of bone or cartilage. I pick up the telescope and scan the whole horizon. The sea is deserted everywhere. No doubt we are still too close to the shore.

I gaze up into the air. Why should some of the strange birds reconstructed by the immortal Cuvier[27] not flap their wings again in this dense and heavy atmosphere? There are sufficient fish to support them. I survey the whole space that stretches overhead; it is as deserted as the shore was.

Nevertheless, my imagination carries me away amongst the wonderful speculations of palaeontology. Though awake, I fall into a dream. I imagine I can see floating on the surface of the waters enormous Chelonia, antediluvian tortoises, resembling floating islands. Over the dimly lit strand there tread the huge mammals of the earliest ages of the world: the Leptotherium, found in the caverns of Brazil, and the Merycotherium, found in ice-clad Siberia. Farther on, the elephant-like Lophiodon, a gigantic tapir, hides behind the rocks to dispute its prey with an Anoplotherium, a strange creature which looked like a mixture of horse, rhinoceros, camel and hippopotamus, as if the Creator, in too much of a hurry in the earliest hours of the world, had combined several animals into one. A colossal mastodon twists and untwists his trunk, and with his huge tusks pounds and crushes the fragments of rock that cover the shore, whilst a Megatherium, buttressed on its enormous paws, grubs in the soil, awaking the sonorous echoes of the granite rocks with his tremendous roarings. Higher up, a Protopithecus – the first monkey to appear on the globe – is climbing up the steep slopes. Higher still, a pterodactyl darts to and fro in irregular zigzags in the heavy air. In the uppermost regions of the air immense birds, more powerful than the cassowary and larger than the ostrich, spread their vast wings and strike their heads against the granite vault that bounds the sky.

All this fossil world rises to life again in my vivid imagination. I return to the scriptural periods or ages of the world, conventionally called 'days', long before the appearance of man, when the unfinished world was as yet unfitted for his support. Then my dream goes back even farther into the ages before the creation of living beings. The mammals disappear, then the birds vanish, then the reptiles of the Secondary Period, and finally the fish, the crustaceans, molluscs and articulated creatures. Then the zoophytes of the Transition Period also return to nothing. I am the only living thing in the world: all life is concentrated in my beating heart alone. There are no longer any seasons nor any climates; the heat of the globe continually increases and neutralizes that of the sun. Plant growth becomes accelerated. I glide like a shade amongst arborescent ferns, treading with unsteady feet the coloured marls and the particoloured clays; I lean for support against the trunks of immense conifers; I lie in the shade of Sphenophylla, Asterophylla and Lycopods a hundred feet high.

Ages seem no more than days! I pass willy-nilly back through the long series of terrestrial changes. Plants disappear; granite rocks soften; intense heat converts solid bodies into thick fluids; the waters again cover the face of the Earth; they boil, they rise in whirling eddies of steam; mists wrap round the shifting forms of the Earth, which by imperceptible degrees dissolves into a gaseous mass, glowing fiery red and white, as large and as shining as the sun.

I myself am floating in the middle of this nebulous mass, fourteen hundred thousand times the volume of the Earth into which it will one day be condensed, and am being carried forward amongst the planetary bodies. My body has split into its constituent atoms, rarefied, volatilized. Sublimated into vapour, I mingle and am lost in the endless clouds of those vast globular volumes of vaporous mists, which roll in their flaming orbits through infinite space.

But is it not a dream? Where is it taking me? My feverish hand is vainly attempting to describe on paper its strange and wonderful details. I have forgotten everything that surrounds me. The Professor, the guide, the raft – all are gone from my mind. A hallucination has taken hold of me.

'What's the matter?' my uncle breaks in.

My staring eyes fix vacantly on him.

'Take care, Axel, or you'll fall overboard.'

At that moment I feel Hans' sinewy hand seizing me firmly. But for him, carried away by my dream, I would have thrown myself into the sea.

'Is he mad?' shouts the Professor.

'What's going on?' I say at last, coming to myself again.

'Do you feel ill?' asks my uncle.

'No, but I've had a strange hallucination. It's gone now. Is everything all right on the raft?'

'Yes, it's a fair wind and a fine sea. We're sailing along rapidly, and if I'm not out in my reckoning, we'll strike land soon.'

At these words I stood up and gazed round at the horizon, still bounded everywhere by clouds alone.

CHAPTER 33

A BATTLE OF MONSTERS

Saturday, August 15. – The sea unbroken all round. No land in sight. The horizon seems extremely distant.

My head is still stupefied by the vivid reality of my dream.

My uncle has had no dreams, but he's in a bad mood. He scans the horizon all round with his telescope, and folds his arms with a disgruntled look.

I notice that Professor Lidenbrock is tending to relapse into his impatient moods, and I make a note of it in my log. It took all the danger I was in and all my sufferings to coax a spark of human feeling out of him, but now that I am well again his basic nature has resumed its control over him. And yet, what reason is there to be angry? Is the voyage not prospering as favourably as possible under the circumstances? Is the raft not scudding along marvellously?

'You seem anxious, Uncle,' I said, seeing him continually with his telescope at his eye.

'Anxious! No, not at all.'

'Impatient, then?'

'One might well be, with less justification than now.'

'Yet we're going very fast.'

'So what? I'm not complaining that our speed is slow but that the sea is so wide.'

I then remember that the Professor, before starting out, had estimated the length of this underground sea at thirty leagues. Now we have covered three times that distance, but the southern coast is still not in sight.

'We aren't going down as we ought to be,' says the Professor. 'We're wasting time, and the fact is I haven't come all this way to take a little sail on a pond on a raft.'

He calls this sea a pond, and our long voyage taking a little sail!

'But,' I remark, 'since we've followed the path that Saknussemm has shown us . . .'

'That's the very question. *Have* we followed that path? Did Saknussemm reach this stretch of water? Did he cross it? Has the stream that we followed not completely led us astray?'

'At any rate we can't feel sorry to have come so far. This view is magnificent, and . . .'

'But I don't care for views. I came with a purpose, and I mean to achieve it. So don't talk to me about views and prospects.'

I take this as my answer, and I leave the Professor to bite his lips with impatience. At six in the evening Hans asks for his wages, and his three rix-dollars are counted out to him.

Sunday, August 16. – Nothing new. Weather unchanged. The wind is freshening. On awaking, my first thought is to observe the intensity of the light. I'm gripped by a fear that the electric light might grow dim or fail altogether. But there seems no reason to be afraid of that. The shadow of the raft is clearly outlined on the surface of the waves.

Truly this sea is of immeasurable width. It must be as wide as the Mediterranean, or even the Atlantic – and why not?

My uncle takes soundings several times. He ties the heaviest of our pickaxes to a long rope which he lets down two hundred fathoms. No bottom yet – and we have some difficulty in hauling up our sounding line.

But when the pickaxe is brought on board again, Hans points out deep prints on its surface as if it has been violently compressed between two hard bodies.

I look at the hunter.

'*Tänder*,' he says.

I don't understand, and turn to my uncle, who is entirely absorbed in his calculations. I prefer not to disturb him. I turn back to the Icelander. He conveys his idea to me by a snapping motion of his jaws.

'Teeth!' I cry, looking at the iron bar with more attention.

Yes, indeed, those are the marks of teeth imprinted on the metal! The jaws they line must be possessed of an amazing strength. Is there some monster beneath us belonging to the extinct races, more voracious than the shark, more fearful in its size than the whale? I can't take my eyes off this indented iron bar. Will the dream I had last night come true?

These thoughts bother me all day, and my imagination is scarcely calmer after several hours' sleep.

Monday, August 17. – I am trying to recall the peculiar instincts of the monsters of the pre-Adamite world, who, coming next in succession after the molluscs, the crustaceans and the fish, preceded the mammals on Earth. The world then belonged to the reptiles. Those monsters held mastery in the seas of the Secondary Period. They had a perfect structure, gigantic proportions, prodigious strength. The saurians of our day, the alligators and the crocodiles, are only feeble reproductions of their forefathers of primitive ages.

I shudder as I recall these monsters to my mind. No human eye has ever beheld them living. They burdened this Earth a thousand centuries before man appeared, but their fossil remains, found in the argillaceous limestone which the English call the Lias, have enabled their colossal structure to be perfectly reconstructed and anatomically ascertained.

I saw the skeleton of one of these creatures at the Hamburg museum, thirty feet in length. Am I then fated – I, an inhabitant of Earth – to be placed face to face with these representatives of long extinct families? No, surely it cannot be! Yet the deep marks on the iron pick have been made by conical teeth that certainly resemble those of a crocodile.

My eyes are fixed in terror on the sea. I dread to see one of these monsters darting forth from its undersea caverns. I suppose Professor Lidenbrock was of my opinion too, and even shares my fears, for after having examined the pickaxe, he too casts his eyes back and forth across the ocean. What a very bad idea that was of his, I thought to myself, to take depth soundings! He's disturbed some monstrous beast in its den, and now we could be attacked during our voyage . . .

I look at our guns and see that they are all right. My uncle notices, and nods his approval.

Already widely disturbed regions on the surface of the water indicate some commotion below. The danger is approaching. We must be on the look-out.

Tuesday, August 18. – Evening comes, or rather the time comes when sleep weighs down weary eyelids, for there is no night here, and the ceaseless light wearies the eyes with its persistence just as if we were sailing under an Arctic sun. Hans is at the helm. During his watch I sleep.

Two hours afterwards a terrible shock awakes me. The raft is heaved up on a watery mountain and pitched down again, at a distance of twenty fathoms.

'What's the matter?' shouts my uncle. 'Have we struck land?'

Hans points at a dark mass six hundred yards away, rising and falling alternately with heavy plunges. I look at it and exclaim:

'It's an enormous porpoise.'

'Yes,' replies my uncle, 'and there's an enormous sea lizard too.'

'And farther over a monstrous crocodile. Look at its huge jaws and its rows of teeth! It's diving down!'

'There's a whale, a whale!' cries the Professor. 'I can see its massive fins. See how it's throwing out air and water through his blowholes.'

And in fact two columns of liquid are rising to a considerable height above the sea. We stand amazed, thunderstruck, at the presence of such a herd of marine monsters. They are of supernatural dimensions; the smallest of them could crunch up our raft, crew and all, with one snap of its huge jaws. Hans wants to tack to get away from this dangerous area, but in the other direction he sees enemies no less terrible: a tortoise forty feet long and a thirty-foot serpent, lifting its fearsome head and gleaming eyes above the surface of the ocean.

Flight is out of the question now. The reptiles rise up; they wheel around our little raft faster than an express train. They swim around us in gradually narrowing circles. I pick up my rifle. But what could a bullet do against the scaly armour these enormous beasts are clad in?

We just stand there, struck dumb with fear. They come closer: on one side the crocodile, on the other the serpent. The other sea monsters have disappeared. I prepare to fire. Hans signals to me not to. The two monsters pass within a hundred and fifty yards of the raft, and hurl themselves one upon the other, with a fury which prevents them from noticing us.

The battle is fought three hundred yards away from us. We can clearly see the two monsters engaged in deadly conflict. But it now seems to me that the other animals are taking part in the fray – the porpoise, the whale, the lizard, the tortoise. At every moment I seem to see one or other of them. I point them out to the Icelander. He shakes his head.

'*Tva*,' he says.

'What, two? Does he mean there are only two animals?'

'He's right,' says my uncle, whose telescope has never left his eye.

'Surely you must be mistaken,' I exclaim.

'No. The first of those monsters has a porpoise's snout, a lizard's head and a crocodile's teeth; hence our mistake. It is an ichthyosaurus, the most terrible of the ancient monsters of the deep.'

'And the other?'

'The other is a plesiosaurus, a serpent protected by the shell of a turtle. It's the mortal enemy of the other.'

Hans was quite right. Only two monsters are disturbing the surface of the ocean, and in front of my eyes are two reptiles of the primitive world. I can see the eye of the ichthyosaurus, glowing like a red-hot coal and as large as a man's head. Nature has endowed it with optical apparatus of extreme power and capable of resisting the pressure of the great volume of water in the depths it inhabits. It has been appropriately called the saurian whale, for it has both the speed and the rapid movements of this monster of our own time. This one is not less than a hundred feet long, and I can judge its size when it sweeps the vertical coils of its tail over the water. Its jaws are enormous, and according to naturalists it is armed with no less than one hundred and eighty-two teeth.

The plesiosaurus, a serpent with a cylindrical body and a short tail, has four flippers or paddles that act like oars. Its body is entirely covered with a thick shell, and its neck, as flexible as a swan's, rises thirty feet above the waves.

Those huge creatures attack each other with indescribable fury. Around them they create liquid mountains, which roll as far as our raft and rock it dangerously. Twenty times we come near to capsizing. We can hear incredibly loud hissing. The two beasts are locked together; I can't distinguish the one from the other. The winner's probable rage terrifies us.

One hour, two hours, pass. The struggle continues with unabated ferocity. The combatants alternately approach our raft and swim away again. We remain motionless, ready to fire. Suddenly the ichthyosaurus and the plesiosaurus disappear below the waves, leaving a whirlpool eddying in the water. Several minutes pass while the fight continues under water.

Suddenly an enormous head rises up out of the water, the head of the plesiosaurus. The monster is mortally wounded. I can no longer see its scaly armour. Only its long neck shoots up, drops again, coils and uncoils, droops, lashes the waters like a gigantic whip and writhes like a worm when you cut it in two. The water is splashed about over a long distance and blinds us. But soon the reptile's agony draws to an end; its movements become weaker, its contortions become less violent, and the long serpentine form lies like a lifeless log on the water, now calm once more.

As for the ichthyosaurus, has it returned to its undersea cavern? Or will it reappear on the surface of the sea?

CHAPTER 34

THE GREAT GEYSER

Wednesday, August 19. – Fortunately the wind is blowing violently, and has enabled us to flee from the scene of the recent terrible struggle. Hans sticks to his post at the helm. My uncle, whom the absorbing incidents of the combat had drawn away from his contemplations, begins once more to look impatiently around him.

The voyage resumes its uniform tenor, which I don't care to see broken by a repetition of such events as yesterday's.

Thursday, August 20. – Wind N.N.E., unsteady and fitful. Temperature high. Rate: three and a half leagues an hour.

About noon, we hear a distant noise. I note the fact without being able to explain it. It's a continuous roaring sound.

'There's a rock or small island in the distance,' says the Professor, 'and the sea is breaking against it.'

Hans climbs the mast, but can't see any breakers. The ocean is smooth and unbroken to its farthest limit.

Three hours pass. The roaring seems to come from a very distant waterfall.

I mention this to my uncle, who shakes his head. However, I'm sure I'm right. Are we, then, speeding forward towards some waterfall which will toss us down into the abyss? This method of progressing may please the Professor, because it's vertical, but for my part . . .

At any rate, some leagues to windward there must be some noisy phenomenon, for now the roaring is getting very loud. Is it coming from the sky or the ocean?

I look up at the atmospheric vapours and try to fathom their depths. The sky is calm and motionless. The clouds have reached the utmost limit of the lofty vault, and there they lie still bathed in the bright glare of the electric light. It isn't there that we must look for the cause of this phenomenon. Then I study the horizon, which is unbroken and completely clear of mist. There's no change in how it looks. But if this noise is being produced by a waterfall, if all this ocean is flowing headlong into an even lower basin, if that deafening roar is produced by a mass of falling water, there must be a current, and its increasing speed will allow me to estimate the danger that threatens us. I check the current: there isn't any. I throw an empty bottle into the sea: it floats to leeward of us without moving.

About four o'clock, Hans gets up, grips the mast and climbs to the top.

From there his eye sweeps across a large expanse of sea and fixes on a point. His face shows no surprise, but his eyes remain fixed on something.

'He can see something,' says my uncle.

'I believe he can.'

Hans comes down, then stretches out his arm towards the south, saying:

'*Der nere*!'

'Over there?' replies my uncle.

Then, taking hold of his telescope, he looks attentively for a minute, which seems to me an age.

'Yes, yes!' he exclaims.

'What can you see?'

'I can see a huge plume of water rising from the surface of the ocean.'

'Is it another sea animal?'

'Perhaps.'

'Then let's steer farther to the west, because we know something of the danger of meeting with monsters of that sort.'

'Let's keep going straight on,' replies my uncle.

I appeal to Hans. He maintains our course inflexibly.

But if at our present distance from the animal, a distance of at least twelve leagues, the column of water forced through its blowholes may be seen distinctly, it must be enormous. Common sense would suggest immediate flight, but we haven't come this far to be sensible.

Imprudently, therefore, we continue on our way. The nearer we get, the higher the jet of water shoots into the air. What monster can possibly fill itself with such a quantity of water, and spurt it up so continuously?

At eight in the evening we aren't more than two leagues away from it. Its dusky, enormous, hillocky body lies spread over the sea like a small island. Is it an illusion, is it something fear is creating in our minds? It seems to me to be about a couple of thousand yards in length. What can this cetacean monster be, this creature which neither Cuvier nor Blumenbach knew anything about? It lies motionless, as if asleep; the sea seems unable to move it at all, and it is the waves that are undulating on its sides. The column of water thrown up to a height of five hundred feet falls like rain with a deafening roar. And here we are scudding like lunatics before the wind, to get near to a monster that a hundred whales a day would not satisfy!

Terror grips me. I refuse to go any further. I'll cut the halliards if necessary! I stand in open mutiny against the Professor, but he says nothing in reply.

Suddenly Hans stands up, and pointing with his finger at the menacing object, says:

'*Holme*.'

'An island!' cries my uncle.

'That's not an island!' I exclaim sceptically.

'That's exactly what it is,' shouts the Professor, with a loud laugh.

'But what about that column of water?'

'*Geyser*,' says Hans.

'No doubt it's a geyser, like those in Iceland.'

At first I can't bring myself to admit that I've been so wrong as to have mistaken an island for a sea monster. But the evidence is against me, and I have to admit my mistake: it's nothing more than a natural phenomenon.

As we get nearer, the dimensions of the plume of liquid become magnificent. The little island resembles, most deceptively, an enormous whale with a head rising above the waves to a height of twenty yards. The geyser, a word that means 'fury', rises majestically at one end. From time to time, deep, heavy explosions can be heard, and then the enormous jet, even more violent than before, shakes its plumed crest and leaps up till it reaches the lowest stratum of the clouds. It stands alone. There are no steam vents or hot springs around it, and all the volcanic power of the area is concentrated in it. Sparks of electric fire mingle with the dazzling plume of liquid, every drop sparkling with all the colours of a prism.

'Let's land,' says the Professor.

But we have to take care to avoid this waterspout, which would sink our raft in a moment. Hans, steering with his usual skill, brings us to the other end of the island.

I leap up on to the rock. My uncle follows nimbly, while our hunter remains at his post, like a man too wise to be astonished by anything.

We walk on granite mixed with siliceous tufa. The ground shivers and shakes under our feet, like the sides of an overheated boiler filled with steam that is struggling to get out. We come to a small central basin that the geyser is rising out of. I plunge an overflow thermometer into the boiling water. It registers a temperature of 163°, which is far above boiling point; this water is therefore issuing from a fiery furnace, which is not at all in harmony with Professor Lidenbrock's theories. I can't help remarking on this.

'Well,' he replies, 'how does that go against my doctrine?'

'Oh, not at all,' I say, seeing that I am up against immovable obstinacy.

Still I'm forced to say that up till now we have been extremely fortunate, and that for some reason I don't know we have accomplished our journey under singularly favourable conditions of temperature. But it seems obvious to me that some day we will come to a region where the central heat reaches its highest limits and goes beyond a point that can be registered by our thermometers.

'We'll see,' says the Professor, who, having named this volcanic island after his nephew, gives the signal to embark again.

For some minutes I am still contemplating the geyser. I notice that it throws up its column of water with variable force: sometimes sending it to a great height, then not so high; this I attribute to the variable pressure of the steam accumulated in its reservoir.

At last we leave the island, sailing past the low rocks on its southern shore. Hans has taken advantage of the brief stop to repair the raft.

But before going any farther I make a few observations, to calculate the distance we have covered, and note them in my journal. We've crossed two hundred and seventy leagues of sea since leaving Port Gräuben; and we're six hundred and twenty leagues from Iceland, under England.

CHAPTER 35

AN ELECTRIC STORM

Friday, August 21. – By the next day the magnificent geyser has disappeared. The wind has risen, and has rapidly carried us away from Axel Island. The roaring becomes lost in the distance.

The weather – if I may use that term – will soon change. The atmosphere is becoming charged with vapours which carry with them the electricity generated by the evaporation of salt water. The clouds are sinking lower, and take on an olive hue. The electric light can scarcely penetrate through the dense curtain which has dropped over the theatre on which the battle of the elements is about to be waged.

I feel an odd sensation, like many creatures on Earth do at the approach of violent atmospheric changes. The piled-up cumulus clouds lower gloomily and threateningly; they wear that implacable look which I have sometimes noticed at the outbreak of a great storm. The air is heavy; the sea is calm.

In the distance, the clouds look like great bales of cotton, piled up in picturesque disorder. They gradually swell up, and gain in size what they lose in number. Such is their ponderous weight that they cannot rise from the horizon, but, under the impulse of currents of air they merge and darken, and soon present to our view a level surface of menacing appearance. From time to time a fleecy tuft of mist, still with some gleaming light left on it, drops down on the dense floor of grey and loses itself in the opaque and impenetrable mass.

The atmosphere is evidently saturated with electrical charge. My whole body is impregnated with it; my hair is standing on end just like when you stand on an insulated stool and are affected by the action of an electrical machine. It seems to me that if my companions touched me, they would get a severe shock.

At ten in the morning, the storm symptoms get worse. You would say that the wind seems to drop only to acquire even greater strength. The huge bank of heavy clouds is a vast reservoir of fearsome windy gusts and rushing storms.

I am loath to believe these atmospheric threats, and yet I can't help muttering:

'Here comes some very bad weather.'

The Professor doesn't reply. He's in a foul mood, seeing this vast stretch of ocean stretching out interminably before him. At my words, he shrugs his shoulders.

'There's a heavy storm coming,' I shout, pointing towards the horizon. 'Those clouds look as if they're about to crush the sea.'

A deep silence falls all around us. The winds that have been roaring now drop to a dead calm; nature seems to stop breathing and to sink into the stillness of death. On the mast I can already see the light play of tongues of St Elmo's fire; the outstretched sail catches not a breath of wind and hangs like a sheet of lead. The raft is sitting motionless in a sluggish, waveless sea. But if we are now no longer moving forward, why have we still got the sail up, since it could cause us to capsize at the first shock of the storm?

'Let's reef the sail and cut the mast down!' I shout. 'That would be the safest thing to do.'

'No, no! Never!' shouts my uncle. 'Never! Let the wind catch us if it will, let the storm sweep us away! Let me have at least a glimpse of a rock or shore, even if our raft should be smashed to pieces on it!'

The words are hardly out of his mouth when a sudden change takes place in the southern sky. The accumulated vapours condense into water, and the air, forced into violent action to supply the vacuum left by the condensation of the mists, turns into a hurricane. It's blowing from the farthest recesses of the vast cavern. The darkness deepens; I scarcely manage to jot down a few hurried notes.

The raft lifts and tosses. My uncle is thrown down full length on the deck; I drag myself over beside him. He has taken a firm hold on a rope and appears to be watching this awful display of elemental strife with grim satisfaction.

Hans doesn't move. His long hair blown by the storm and laid flat across his immovable countenance makes him a strange figure, as the end of each lock of loose flowing hair is tipped with little luminous radiations. This frightening mask of electrical sparks puts me in mind of pre-Adamite man, the contemporary of the ichthyosaurus and the Megatherium.

The mast is still holding. The sail is stretched tight like a bubble ready to burst. The raft is racing along at a rate I cannot calculate, but not as fast as the drops of spray which it's throwing out on both sides in its headlong speed.

'The sail! the sail!' I cry, motioning to lower it.

'No!' replies my uncle.

'*Nej*!' repeats Hans, gently shaking his head.

But now the rain is forming a rushing waterfall in front of the horizon towards which we are racing like madmen. But before it has reached us, the rain cloud splits, the sea boils, and the electricity is brought into violent action by some strong chemical reaction operating in the upper regions. Intensely vivid flashes of lightning mingle with the violent crash of constant thunder. Fiery arrows dart continuously in and out amongst the flying thunder-clouds; the vaporous mass is soon glowing with incandescent heat; hailstones rattle down fiercely, and as they strike our iron tools they too emit gleams and flashes of lurid light. The heaving waves look like fiery volcanic hills, each belching out its own interior flames, and every crest is plumed with dancing fire.

My eyes are blinded by the dazzling light, my ears are deafened with the incessant crash of thunder. I have to cling to the mast, which bends like a reed before the mighty strength of the storm.

(Here my notes become vague and incomplete. I have only been able to find a few which I seem to have jotted down almost unconsciously. But their very brevity and their obscurity reveal the intensity of the excitement I felt, and describe the actual situation even better than my memory could do.)

Sunday, August 23. – Where are we? Being driven forward at a speed beyond measurement.

Last night has been terrible; no abatement of the storm. The din and uproar never stop; our ears are bleeding; to exchange words is impossible.

The lightning flashes with intense brilliance and seems never to stop for a moment. Zigzag streams of bluish-white fire flash down to the sea and rebound, flying upward again till they strike the granite vault that arches over our heads. What if that solid roof should collapse on our heads? Other lightning flashes become forked or form themselves into balls of fire which explode like bombshells. The general level of noise doesn't seem to be increased by this. We have already passed the limit of sound intensity within which the human ear can distinguish one sound from another. If all the powder magazines in the world were to explode at once, we would hear no more than we do now.

From the under-surface of the clouds come continual emissions of lurid light; electricity is constantly being given off by their component molecules. Apparently the gaseous elements of the air are undergoing a transformation. Innumerable columns of water spring upwards into the air and fall back again as white foam.

Where are we heading? My uncle is lying stretched out at the edge of the raft.

The heat increases. I check the thermometer; it indicates . . . (the figure is illegible).

Monday, August 24. – Will there never be an end to this? Is the atmospheric condition, having now reached this density, to going to stay like this?

We are almost prostrate with fatigue. But Hans is the same as ever. The raft is still heading south-east. We've done two hundred leagues since we left Axel Island.

At noon the violence of the storm redoubles. We're forced to fasten down every item of our cargo as securely as possible. Each of us is lashed to some part of the raft. The waves rise above our heads.

For three days now, we have not been able to make each other hear a word we say. Our mouths open, our lips move, but not a word can be heard. We can't even make ourselves heard by putting our mouth close to the other person's ear.

My uncle has crawled close to me. He has uttered a few words. He seems to be saying 'We're done for' but I'm not sure.

Finally I write down the words: 'We should lower the sail.'

He signals his agreement.

He scarcely has time to nod his head again before a disc of fire appears right beside our raft. In an instant the mast and sail together fly up into the air, and I see them carried up to a prodigious height, looking just like a pterodactyl, one of those fantastic birds of the earliest ages of the world.

We lie there, our blood running cold with unspeakable terror. The fireball, half white, half azure blue, and the size of a ten-inch shell, moves around slowly while revolving on its own axis with astonishing speed due to the force of the hurricane. Here it comes, there it glides, now it is up on the ragged stump of the mast, from there it leaps lightly on to the provisions bag, descends lightly again and just touches the powder magazine. Horror of horrors! We're going to be blown up! But no, the dazzling disc of mysterious light leaps nimbly to one side; it heads towards Hans, who steadily fixes his blue eyes on it. It threatens my uncle, who drops to his knees to avoid it. And now it's my turn, as I stand pale and trembling in the blinding splendour and the melting heat. It drops at my feet, spinning silently round on the deck. I try to move my foot away, but can't.

A stifling smell of nitrous gas fills the air. It gets into our throats and lungs. We choke on it.

Why can't I move my foot? Is it riveted to the planks? Oh, I see! This electric globe falling on to our ill-fated raft has magnetized every article of iron on board. The instruments, the tools, our guns, are clattering and clinking as they collide with each other. The nails of my boots are clinging firmly to a piece of iron embedded in the timbers, and I can't pull my foot away. At last, by a violent effort, I release myself at the very instant when the spinning ball is about to grip my foot and carry me off, if . . .

Ah! what a flood of intense and dazzling light! The globe bursts, and we are deluged with tongues of fire!

Then the light disappears. I just have time to see my uncle stretched out on the raft, and Hans still at the helm and emitting sparks of fire because of the electricity that has saturated him.

But where are we going? Where?

Tuesday, August 25. – I come out of a long faint. The storm continues to rage; the flashes of lightning flicker here and there, like broods of fiery serpents filling the air. Are we still at sea? Yes, we are being borne along at incalculable speed. We've been carried under England, under the Channel, under France, perhaps under the whole of Europe.

We can hear a new noise! Clearly the sea breaking on rocks! And then . . .

CHAPTER 36

CALM PHILOSOPHICAL DISCUSSIONS

Here ends what I may call my log, fortunately saved from the shipwreck, and I take up my narrative as before.

What happened when the raft was dashed against the rocks on the coast is more than I can tell. I felt myself thrown into the waves; and if I escaped death, and if my body was not torn on the sharp edges of the rocks, it was because Hans's powerful arm came to my rescue.

The brave Icelander carried me out of reach of the waves, on to a burning sand where I found myself by my uncle's side.

Then he returned to the rocks, against which the waves were beating furiously, to save what he could. I was unable to speak. I was shattered with fatigue and emotion. It took me a whole hour to recover.

But rain was still falling in a deluge, though with that violence which generally means that a storm is nearly over. A few overhanging rocks afforded us some shelter from the storm. Hans prepared some food, which I couldn't touch; and each of us, exhausted from three sleepless nights, fell into a disturbed and painful sleep.

The next day, the weather was splendid. The sky and the sea had suddenly become calm. Every trace of the terrible storm had disappeared. The happy voice of the Professor reached my ears as I awoke; he was ominously cheerful.

'Well, my boy,' he shouted, 'have you slept well?'

Anyone would have thought we were still in our little house in the Königstrasse and that I was just coming down to breakfast, and that I was going to be married to Gräuben that day.

Alas! If the storm had only sent the raft a little farther to the east, we would have passed under Germany, under my beloved town of Hamburg, under the very street where dwelt all that I loved most in the world. Then only forty leagues would have separated us! But they would have been forty vertical leagues of solid granite, and in reality we were a thousand leagues apart!

All these painful thoughts rapidly crossed my mind before I could answer my uncle's question.

'Well, now,' he repeated, 'won't you tell me how you've slept?'

'Oh, perfectly well,' I said. 'I'm still a bit bruised, but I'll soon be better.'

'Oh,' says my uncle, 'that's nothing. You're just a bit tired, that's all.'

'But you, Uncle, seem to be in very good spirits this morning.'

'I'm delighted, my boy, absolutely delighted. We've got there.'

'To our journey's end?'

'No. But we've reached the end of that seemingly endless sea. Now we shall go on by land, and really begin to go down, down, down!'

'But, my dear Uncle, let me ask you one question.'

'Of course, Axel.'

'How about getting back?'

'Getting back? Why, you're talking about the return journey before we even arrive there.'

'No, I only want to know how we are going to do it.'

'In the simplest way possible. When we have reached the centre of the globe, either we shall find some new way to get back, or rather boringly we'll come back the way we came. I'm pretty sure the path won't have closed up behind us.'

'But then we shall have to rebuild the raft.'

'Of course.'

'Then, what about provisions? Have we got enough to last us?'

'Yes, I'm sure we have. Hans is a clever fellow, and I am sure he must have saved a large part of our cargo. But nevertheless let's go and make certain.'

We left this grotto, which lay open to every gust of wind. I cherished a trembling hope which was at the same time a fear as well. It seemed to me impossible that the terrible wreck of the raft would not have destroyed everything on board. But I was wrong. Arriving on the shore, I found Hans surrounded by an assemblage of articles all laid out in good order. My uncle shook hands with him with warm gratitude. This man, with almost superhuman devotion, had been at work all the time that we had been asleep, and had saved the most precious articles at the risk of his life.

Not that we had suffered no serious losses. For instance, our firearms were gone, but we could do without them. Our stock of powder had remained unharmed after having nearly exploded during the storm.

'Well,' cried the Professor, 'since we have no guns, we can't hunt, that's all there is to it.'

'Yes, but how about the instruments?'

'Here's the manometer, the most useful of them all, and for which I would have happily given away all the others. With it, I can calculate our depth and know when we have reached the centre; without it, we might go too far, and come out at the Antipodes!'

He was in a ferociously good mood.

'But where's the compass?' I asked.

'Here it is, on this rock, in perfect condition, and so are the thermometers and the chronometer. Our hunter really is a splendid fellow.'

There was no denying it. We had all our instruments. As for tools and appliances, there they all lay on the ground – ladders, ropes, picks, spades, etc.

Still there was the question of provisions to be settled, and I asked, 'How are we off for provisions?'

'Let's look at the provisions, then.'

The boxes containing these were in a line on the shore, in a perfect state of preservation; for the most part, the sea had spared them, and what with biscuits, salt meat, spirits and salt fish, we had enough for about four months.

'Four months!' exclaimed the Professor. 'We've time to get there and come back again, and with what's left over I'll give a grand dinner to my colleagues at the Johannaeum.'

I ought by this time to have been quite used to my uncle's ways, but he always came up with something new to astonish me.

'Now,' he said, 'we'll replenish our supply of water with the rain which the storm has left in all these granite basins, so we'll have nothing to fear as far as thirst is concerned. As for the raft, I'm going to suggest to Hans that he do his best to repair it, although I don't expect it will be of any further use to us.'

'Why not?' I said.

'Just an idea of mine, my boy. I don't think we'll be leaving by the same way as we came in.'

I stared at the Professor with a good deal of mistrust. I wondered whether he might have gone a little bit crazy. And yet there was method in his madness.

'And now let's have breakfast,' he said.

I followed him to a headland, after he had given his instructions to the hunter. There we had an excellent meal of preserved meat, biscuits and tea, one of the best meals I ever remember. Hunger, the fresh air, the calm quiet weather after the turmoil we had gone through, all contributed to give me a good appetite.

Whilst breakfasting, I took the opportunity to ask my uncle where we were now.

'That seems to me,' I said, 'rather difficult to work out.'

'Yes, it is difficult to calculate that exactly,' he said. 'Perhaps even impossible, since during these three stormy days I've been unable to keep track of the speed or direction of the raft. But nevertheless we may get a rough idea.'

'The last observation,' I remarked, 'was made on the island where the geyser was . . .'

'You mean Axel Island. Don't decline the honour of having given your name to the first island ever discovered in the interior of the globe.'

'Fine,' I said, 'so be it. On Axel Island. By then we had covered two hundred and seventy leagues across the sea, and we were six hundred leagues from Iceland.'

'Very well,' replied my uncle. 'Let's start from that point and count four days of storm, during which our speed can't have been less than eighty leagues every twenty-four hours.'

'That's right. And that would make another three hundred leagues.'

'Yes, and the Lidenbrock Sea would therefore be six hundred leagues from shore to shore. Surely, Axel, it may be equal in size to the Mediterranean itself.'

'Especially,' I replied, 'if it happens that we have only sailed across it and not from one end to the other. And it is a curious circumstance,' I added, 'that if my calculations are right, and we are nine hundred leagues from Reykjavik, the Mediterranean is now right above our heads.'

'That's a good long journey, my boy. But whether we're under the Mediterranean, Turkey or the Atlantic depends very much on what direction we have been travelling in. Perhaps we have deviated from our intended course.'

'No, I don't think so. Our course has been the same all along, and I reckon this shore is south-east of Port Gräuben.'

'Well,' replied my uncle, 'we may easily ascertain this by checking the compass. Let's go and see what it says.'

The Professor walked towards the rock on which Hans had laid out the instruments. He was happy and full of spirits; he was rubbing his hands together and striking poses. I followed him, curious to know if I was right in my estimate. He was behaving like a much younger man! As soon as we reached the rock, my uncle picked up the compass, laid it down flat, and looked at the needle, which, after a few oscillations, eventually assumed a fixed position. My uncle looked, and looked, and looked again. He rubbed his eyes, and then turned to me, thunderstruck.

'What's the matter?' I asked.

He motioned to me to take a look. An exclamation of astonishment burst from me. The north pole of the needle was turned to what we had supposed to be the south. It pointed to the shore instead of out to the open sea! I shook the box and checked it again; it was in perfect condition. No matter what position I placed the box in, the needle returned every time to point in this unexpected direction. Therefore there seemed no reason to doubt that during the storm there had been a sudden change of wind that we hadn't noticed and which had brought our raft back to the shore we thought we had left so far behind us.

CHAPTER 37

THE LIDENBROCK MUSEUM OF GEOLOGY

It would be impossible to describe the emotions which in turn shook the breast of Professor Lidenbrock. First amazement, then incredulity, lastly an outburst of rage. Never had I seen a man so put out and then so exasperated. The fatigues of our crossing, the dangers we had faced, had all to be repeated. We had gone backwards instead of forwards!

But my uncle rapidly recovered himself.

'Well, then! Is fate playing tricks on me? Are the elements plotting against me? Will fire, air and water make a combined attack against me? Well, they shall know what a determined man can do. I will not yield. I will not take a single step backwards, and we'll see whether man or nature is to have the upper hand!'

Standing erect on the rock, angry and threatening, Otto Lidenbrock looked like a rather grotesque parody of the fierce Ajax[28] defying the gods. But I thought it my duty to step in and attempt to restrain this crazy fanaticism.

'Just listen to me,' I said firmly. 'There has to be some limit to this ambition of yours. We can't do the impossible. We're in no state to set out on another sea voyage. Who would dream of undertaking a voyage of five hundred leagues on a heap of rotten planks, with a ragged blanket for a sail, a stick for a mast and fierce winds in our teeth? We can't steer, we'll be blown about by the storms and we would be fools and madmen to attempt to cross a second time.'

I was able to develop this series of irrefutable reasons for ten whole minutes without interruption. It wasn't, however, that the Professor was paying any respectful attention to his nephew's arguments, but because he was deaf to all my eloquence.

'To the raft!' he shouted.

This was his only reply. There was no point in me entreating, pleading, getting angry or doing anything else by way of opposing him; I would only have been opposing a will harder than the granite rock.

Hans was finishing the repairs to the raft. It was as if this strange being was able to guess my uncle's plans. With a few more pieces of *surtarbrandur*, he had repaired our ship. A sail was already hanging at the new mast, and the wind was playing in its waving folds.

The Professor said a few words to the guide, and immediately he put everything on board and arranged everything necessary for our departure. The air was clear, and the north-west wind was blowing steadily.

What could I do? Could I make a stand against the two of them? Impossible. If only Hans had taken my side! But no, it was not to be. The Icelander seemed to have renounced all will of his own and made a vow to forget and deny himself. I could get nothing out of a servant so feudally subservient, as it were, to his master. My only course was to proceed.

I was therefore going to take my usual place on the raft when my uncle put his hand on my shoulder.

'We'll not sail until tomorrow,' he said.

I made a gesture of total resignation.

'I mustn't neglect anything,' he said. 'And since fate has driven me on to this part of the coast, I won't leave until I have examined it.'

To understand this comment, it must be borne in mind that, although we had returned to the northern shore of the sea, we were not at the spot we had set out from. Port Gräuben had to be to the west of us. It therefore made perfect sense to carefully investigate the area around our new landing place.

'Now, let's go and see what we can find,' I said.

And leaving Hans to his work, we set off together. There was some considerable distance between the water and the foot of the cliffs. It took us half an hour to reach the wall of rock. We trampled under our feet countless seashells of all the forms and sizes that existed in the earliest ages of the world. I also saw immense animal shells more than fifteen feet in diameter. They had been the coverings of those gigantic glyptodons or armadillos of the Pliocene Epoch, of which the modern tortoise is but a miniature representative. In addition, the soil was scattered with stony fragments, shingle rounded by the action of water, and formed in successive rows. I was therefore led to the conclusion that at one time the sea must have covered the ground on which we were treading. On the loose and scattered rocks, now beyond the reach of the highest tides, the waves had left clear traces of their passage.

This might to a certain extent explain the existence of an ocean forty leagues beneath the surface of the globe. But, by my theory, this mass of liquid must be gradually disappearing into the bowels of the Earth, and it clearly originated in the waters of the ocean above, which had made their way here through some fissure. Yet it must be assumed that that fissure was now closed, and that this whole cavern, or rather this immense reservoir, had filled in a very short time. Perhaps this water, subjected to the fierce action of subterranean heat, had been partially converted into vapour. This would explain the existence of those clouds hanging over our heads and the development of the electricity which raised such tempests within the body of the globe.

This theory regarding the phenomena we had witnessed seemed satisfactory to me, for no matter how great and stupendous are the phenomena of nature, established physical laws can always explain them.

We were therefore walking on sedimentary soil, the deposits of the waters of former ages. The Professor was carefully examining every little fissure in the rocks. Wherever he saw a hole, he always wanted to know how deep it was. To him, this was important.

We had been following the coast of the Lidenbrock Sea for a mile when we noticed a sudden change in the appearance of the soil. It seemed to have been turned upside down, contorted and convulsed by a violent upheaval of the lower strata. In many places depressions or elevations bore witness to some tremendous power causing the dislocation of strata.

We moved with difficulty across these granite fragments mingled with flint, quartz and alluvial deposits, when a field – no, more than a field, a vast plain – of bleached bones lay spread out before us. It looked like a huge cemetery, where the remains of twenty ages mingled their dust together. Immense mounds of bony fragments rose up in the distance. They stretched out in waves as far as the horizon, and then were lost in a faint haze. Within three square miles there were accumulated the materials for a complete history of the animal life through the ages, a history scarcely sketched out in the all too recent strata of the inhabited world.

But impatient curiosity carried us forward. Crackling and rattling, our feet were trampling on the remains of prehistoric animals and interesting fossils, the possession of which is a matter of rivalry and contention between the museums of great cities. A thousand Cuviers could never have reconstructed the organic remains deposited in this magnificent and unparalleled collection.

I stood there in amazement. My uncle had raised his long arms towards the vault which was our sky. His mouth gaping wide, his eyes flashing behind his shining spectacles, his head nodding and shaking, his whole stance denoted utter astonishment. Here he stood, looking at an immense collection of scattered Leptotheria, Mericotheria, Lophiodia, Anoplotheria, Megatheria, Protopithecae, pterodactyls, mastodons and all sorts of extinct monsters gathered here together for his private satisfaction. Imagine an enthusiastic bibliophile suddenly dropped into the middle of the famous Alexandrian library that was burnt by Omar[29] and by some miracle restored from its ashes! That was my uncle, Professor Lidenbrock.

But more was to come, when, rushing through clouds of bone dust, he put his hand on a bare skull, and exclaimed with a voice trembling with excitement:

'Axel! Axel! A human skull!'

'A human skull?' I cried, no less astonished.

'Yes, my boy. Oh, Milne-Edwards, oh, de Quatrefages[30], how I wish you were standing here with me, Otto Lidenbrock!'

CHAPTER 38

THE PROFESSOR IN HIS CHAIR AGAIN

To understand this last exclamation of my uncle's, addressed to two famous French scientists, you have to know about an event of great importance from a palaeontological point of view which had occurred shortly before our departure.

On the 28th of March, 1863, some excavators working under the direction of M. Boucher de Perthes, in the stone quarries of Moulin-Quignon near Abbeville, in the department of Somme, found a human jawbone fourteen feet beneath the surface of the ground. It was the first fossil of this sort that had ever been brought to light. Not far from it were found stone hatchets and flint tools stained with a uniform patina by the passage of time.

The impact of this discovery was immense, not just in France but also in England and Germany. Several scientists at the French Institute, amongst whom were Messrs Milne-Edwards and de Quatrefages, at once saw the importance of this discovery, proved the genuineness of the bone in question and became the most ardent defendants in what the English called the 'jawbone trial'.

The geologists of the United Kingdom – Messrs Falconer, Busk, Carpenter and others – who believed the fact as certain, were soon joined by German scholars, the most eminent, the most ardent and the most enthusiastic of whom was my Uncle Lidenbrock.

The genuineness of a fossil human relic of the Quaternary Period seemed therefore to be incontestably proved and accepted.

It is true that this theory met with a most obstinate opponent in M. Elie de Beaumont. This eminent authority maintained that the soil of Moulin-Quignon was not from the diluvial period at all, but was of much more recent formation; and, agreeing in that with Cuvier, he refused to admit that the human species could be contemporary with the animals of the Quaternary Period. My Uncle Lidenbrock, along with the great majority of geologists, had held his ground, had disputed and argued, until M. Elie de Beaumont stood almost alone in his opinion.

We knew all these details of the affair, but we were not aware that since our departure the matter had developed further. Other similar jawbones, although belonging to individuals of various types and different nations, were found in the loose grey soil of certain grottoes in France, Switzerland and Belgium, as well as weapons, tools, earthenware utensils, bones of children and adults. So the existence of man in the Quaternary Period seemed to become ever more certain as each day passed.

But that was not all. Fresh discoveries of remains in the Pliocene formation had emboldened other geologists to attribute the human species to an even earlier period. It is true that these remains were not human bones, but objects bearing the traces of human handiwork, such as fossil leg-bones of animals evidently sculptured and carved by the hand of man.

Thus, in one bound, man had risen several rungs further back up the ladder of time. He was a predecessor of the mastodon; he was a contemporary of the southern elephant; he lived a hundred thousand years ago, when, according to geologists, the Pliocene was being formed.

Such then was the state of palaeontological science, and what we knew of it was sufficient to explain our behaviour in the presence of this stupendous Golgotha. Anyone can now understand my uncle's frenzied excitement when, twenty yards further on, he found himself face to face with a primitive man!

It was a perfectly recognizable human body. Had some peculiarity of the soil, like that of the St-Michel cemetery at Bordeaux, preserved it in this condition for such a long time? It might be so. But this dried corpse, with its parchment-like skin drawn tightly over the bony frame, the limbs still preserving their shape, sound teeth, abundant hair, and finger and toe nails of a frightening length, this desiccated mummy startled us by appearing just as it had lived countless ages ago. I stood mute before this apparition of remote antiquity. My uncle, usually so garrulous, was likewise struck dumb. We lifted the body. We stood it up against a rock. It seemed to stare at us out of its empty socket. We sounded his hollow frame.

After some moments' silence, the uncle gave way to the professor again. Otto Lidenbrock, reverting to character, forgot all the circumstances of our eventful journey, forgot where we were standing, forgot the vaulted cavern which held us. No doubt in his mind he was back again at the Johannaeum, lecturing to his pupils, for he adopted a professorial tone and, addressing himself to an imaginary audience, spoke as follows:

'Gentlemen, I have the honour to introduce to you a man of the Quaternary system. Eminent geologists have denied his existence, others no less eminent have affirmed it. The Doubting Thomases of palaeontology, if they were here, might now touch him with their fingers, and would be obliged to acknowledge their error. I am quite aware that science has to be on its guard with discoveries of this kind. I know what capital enterprising individuals like Barnum have made out of fossil men. I have heard the tale of Ajax's kneecap, of the supposed body of Orestes claimed to have been found by the Spartans, and of the body of Asterius, ten cubits long, that Pausanias speaks of. I have read the reports of the skeleton of Trapani, found in the fourteenth century, and which was at the time identified as that of Polyphemus; and the history of the giant unearthed in the sixteenth century near Palermo. You know as well as I do, gentlemen, the analysis made at Lucerne in 1577 of those huge bones which the celebrated Dr Felix Plater affirmed to be those of a giant nineteen feet high. I have gone through the treatises of Cassanion, and all those memoirs, pamphlets, assertions and rejoinders published respecting the skeleton of Teutobochus, the invader of Gaul, dug out of a sandpit in the Dauphiné in 1613. In the eighteenth century I would have stood up for Scheuchzer's pre-Adamite man against Peter Campet. I have held in my hands the pamphlet entitled *Giga*—'

Here my uncle encountered his unfortunate affliction – that of being unable to pronounce difficult words in public.

'The pamphlet entitled *Gigan*—'

He could get no further.

'*Giganteo*—'

It was no good. The unfortunate word would not come out. At the Johannaeum, there would have been laughter.

'*Gigantosteology*,' at last the Professor burst out, between two words which I shall not record here.

Then rushing on with renewed vigour and great animation:

'Yes, gentlemen, I know all these things, and more. I know that Cuvier and Blumenbach have recognized in these bones nothing more remarkable than the bones of the mammoth and other mammals of the Quaternary Period. But in the presence of this specimen, to doubt would be to insult science. There stands the body! You may see it, touch it. It is not a mere skeleton; it is an entire body, preserved for a purely anthropological purpose.'

I was wise enough not to contradict this startling assertion.

'If I could only wash it in a solution of sulphuric acid,' my uncle continued, 'I would be able to rid it of all the particles of earth and the shells with which it is encrusted. But I do not have that valuable solvent here with me. Yet, such as it is, the body will tell us its own wonderful story.'

Here the Professor took hold of the fossil skeleton, and handled it with the skill and dexterity of a showman.

'You see,' he said, 'that it is not six feet tall, and that we are still a long way away from the supposed race of giants. As for the family to which it belongs, it is evidently Caucasian. It is of the white race, our own. The skull of this fossil is a regular oval, or rather ovoid. It exhibits no prominent cheekbones, no projecting jaws. It presents no appearance of that prognathism which reduces the facial angle[31]. Measure that angle. It is nearly ninety degrees. But I will go further in my deductions, and I will affirm that this specimen of the human family is of the Japhetic race, which has since spread from the Indies to the Atlantic. Do not smile, gentlemen.'

Nobody was smiling, but the learned Professor was frequently disturbed by the broad smiles provoked by his learned eccentricities.

'Yes,' he pursued with animation, 'this is a fossil man, the contemporary of the mastodons whose remains fill this amphitheatre. But if you ask me how he came to be here, how those strata on which he was lying slipped down into this enormous hollow in the globe, I confess I cannot answer that question. No doubt in the Quaternary Period considerable movement was still disturbing the crust of the Earth. The long-continued cooling of the globe gave rise to chasms, fissures, clefts and faults, into which, very probably, portions of the upper earth may have fallen. I make no rash assertions, but there is the man surrounded by his own works, by hatchets, by carved flints, which are the characteristics of the Stone Age. And unless he came here, like myself, as a tourist on a visit and as a pioneer of science, I can entertain no doubt of the authenticity of his remote origin.'

The Professor stopped speaking, and his audience broke out into loud and unanimous applause. For, of course, my uncle was right, and wiser men than his nephew would have found it hard to refute his statements.

Another remarkable thing. This fossil body was not the only one in this immense catacomb. We came across other bodies at every step amongst the dust, and my uncle could have selected any of the most curious of these specimens to demolish the incredulity of sceptics.

In fact, it was an amazing sight, these generations of men and animals mingling in their common cemetery. Then one very serious question came to our minds which we scarcely dared consider. Had all those creatures slid through a great fissure in the crust of the Earth, down to the shores of the Lidenbrock Sea, when they were dead and turning to dust, or had they lived and grown and died here in this subterranean world under a false sky, just like inhabitants of the upper Earth? Until the present time the only creatures we had seen alive were sea monsters and fish. Might not some living being, some native of the abyss, still be found on these desolate shores?

CHAPTER 39

FOREST SCENERY ILLUMINATED BY ELECTRICITY

For another half hour, we walked over a carpet of bones. We pushed on, driven by our burning curiosity. What other marvels did this cavern contain? What new treasures lay here for science to unfold? I was prepared for any surprise; my imagination was ready for any eventuality, no matter how astounding.

We had long since lost sight of the seashore behind the hills of bones. The foolhardy Professor, unconcerned about losing his way, dragged me on and on. We walked in silence, bathed in luminous waves of electricity. By some phenomenon which I am unable to explain, it lit up all sides of every object to an equal extent. It was so diffuse, there being no central point from which the light emanated, that shadows no longer existed. You might have thought yourself under the rays of a vertical sun in a tropical region at midday in the height of summer. No vapour was visible. The rocks, the distant mountains, a few isolated clumps of forest trees in the distance, presented a weird and wonderful aspect under these totally new conditions of universal diffusion of light. We were like Hoffmann's shadowless man[32].

A mile further on, we reached the edge of a vast forest, but not one of those forests of fungi which bordered Port Gräuben. Here the vegetation was of the Tertiary Period in the fullest extent of its magnificence. Tall palm-trees belonging to species no longer living, other splendid palm-like trees, firs, yews, cypresses, thujas, representatives of the conifers, were linked together by a tangled network of creepers. A soft carpet of mosses and liverworts clothed the soil luxuriously. A few sparkling streams ran almost in silence under what would have been the shade of the trees, except that there was no shadow. On their banks grew tree-ferns similar to those we grow in hothouses. But a remarkable feature was the total absence of colour in all those trees, shrubs and plants, growing without the life-giving heat and light of the sun. They all merged together in a uniform brownish colour like that of fading and faded leaves. Not a green leaf anywhere, and the flowers – which were abundant enough in the Tertiary period, which first gave birth to flowers – looked like brown-paper cut-outs, with neither colour nor scent.

Uncle Lidenbrock ventured into this colossal grove. I followed him, not without some apprehension. Since nature had provided plant nourishment here, why shouldn't there be fierce animals there too? In the broad clearings left by fallen trees, decayed with age, I could see leguminous plants, Acerinae, Rubiaceae and many other edible shrubs dear to ruminant animals of every period. Then I observed, mingling together in confusion, trees of countries far separated on the surface of the globe. The oak and the palm were growing side by side, the Australian eucalyptus leaned against the Norwegian pine, the birch-tree of the north mingled its foliage with New Zealand kauris. It was enough to drive the most ingenious classifier of terrestrial botany to distraction.

Suddenly I stopped. I held my uncle back.

The diffused light made it easy to make out even the smallest of objects in the dense thickets. I thought I could see – no! I *did* see, with my own eyes, enormous forms moving among the trees. They were gigantic animals, a herd of mastodons – not fossil remains but alive and resembling the ones whose bones were found in the marshes of Ohio in 1801. I could see those huge elephants under the trees with their trunks writhing like a host of serpents. I could hear the crashing noise of their long ivory tusks boring into the old decaying trunks. Branches were cracking, and the leaves that were torn away in cartloads were going down the monsters' cavernous throats.

So, then, the dream in which I had had a vision of the prehistoric world of the Tertiary and Quaternary Periods had become a reality. And there we were alone, in the bowels of the Earth, at the mercy of its wild inhabitants!

My uncle was gazing at the scene with intense and eager interest.

'Come on!' said he, seizing my arm. 'Let's take a closer look!'

'No, I won't!' I cried. 'We don't have any guns. What could we do in the middle of a herd of these four-footed giants? Come on, Uncle, let's just get away. No human being could safely risk upsetting these monstrous beasts.'

'No human creature?' replied my uncle in a lower voice. 'You're wrong, Axel. Look, look down there! I fancy I see a living creature similar to ourselves: it's a man!'

I looked, shaking my head incredulously. But though at first I couldn't believe it, I had to yield to the evidence of my senses.

In fact, about a quarter of a mile away, leaning against the trunk of a gigantic kauri, stood a human being, the Proteus[33] of those subterranean regions, a new son of Neptune, watching this countless herd of mastodons:

Immanis pecoris custos, immanior ipse.[34]

Immanior ipse? Yes, truly more gigantic. We were no longer dealing with a fossil being like the man whose dried remains we had easily lifted up in the field of bones. This fellow was a giant, well able to control those monsters. In stature he was at least twelve feet tall. His head, as big as a buffalo's, was half hidden in the thick, tangled growth of his unkempt hair. It most resembled the mane of the primitive elephant. In his hand he held an enormous branch, a crook worthy of this antediluvian shepherd.

We stood there, petrified and speechless with amazement. But what if he saw us? We had to get away!

'Come on, Uncle, run for it!' I said, dragging my uncle away. For once he allowed himself to be persuaded.

In quarter of an hour our feet had carried us beyond the reach of this terrifying monster.

And yet, now that I can consider the matter quietly, now that I am calm again, now that months have slipped by since this strange and supernatural meeting, what am I to think? What am I to believe? I have to conclude that the whole thing was impossible, that our senses were deceived, that our eyes didn't see what we thought they saw. No human beings live in this subterranean world, no human race lives in those deep caverns of the globe, unknown to and unconnected with the inhabitants of its surface. It would be crazy to think they did.

I prefer to think that it might have been some animal whose structure resembled that of humans, some ape or baboon of the early geological ages, some Protopithecus or Mesopithecus like the one discovered by Lartet in the deposit of bones at Sansan. But this creature was far larger than any known to modern palaeontology. No matter, it had to be an ape, yes, definitely an ape, improbable as that might be. That a human being, a living person, and therefore no doubt a whole race of humans besides him, should be entombed there in the bowels of the Earth, was impossible.

Meanwhile, we had left the clear, brightly lit forest, speechless with astonishment, overwhelmed with a stupefaction which reduced us almost to the level of dumb animals. We kept on running for fear that the horrible monster might be on our trail. We really were fleeing; it was just like the feeling of being driven along in spite of oneself that one often experiences in nightmares. Instinctively we made our way back to the Lidenbrock Sea, and I cannot say into what wandering thoughts my mind might have carried me but for a circumstance which brought me back to practical matters.

Although I was certain that we were now walking on ground never before trodden by our feet, I often noticed groups of rocks which reminded me of those around Port Gräuben. Besides, this seemed to confirm the indications of the compass needle, and to show that we had unintentionally returned to the north shore of the Lidenbrock Sea. Occasionally I felt quite sure about it. Brooks and waterfalls were tumbling everywhere from projections in the rocks. I thought I recognized the bed of *surtarbrandur*, our faithful Hans's Brook and the grotto in which I had regained life and consciousness. Then a few paces farther on, the arrangement of the cliffs, the appearance of an unrecognized stream or the strange outline of a rock, threw me into doubt again.

I expressed my doubts to my uncle. Like me, he wasn't sure. He didn't recognize anything in this unvarying landscape.

'It seems clear,' I said, 'that we haven't landed at our original starting-point, but the storm has carried us a little further up, and if we follow the shore we'll find Port Gräuben.'

'If that's the case, it'll be useless to continue our exploration, and we'd better return to our raft. But, Axel, could you be mistaken?'

'It's difficult to be sure, Uncle, because all these rocks are so very much alike. But I think I recognize the promontory where Hans built our boat. We must be very near the little port, if indeed this is not it,' I added, examining a creek which I thought I recognized.

'No, Axel, we would at least find our own tracks and I can't see anything . . .'

'But I can see something,' I exclaimed, darting towards an object lying on the sand.

And I showed my uncle a rusty dagger which I had just picked up.

'Come on, now,' he said. 'Were you carrying this weapon with you?'

'Me? No, certainly not! But were you perhaps . . .'

'Not as far as I know,' said the Professor. 'I'm not aware of ever having had this object in my possession.'

'Well, this is strange!'

'No, Axel, it's very simple. Icelanders often carry weapons of this sort. This must belong to Hans, and he's lost it.'

I shook my head. Hans had never had an object like this on him either.

'Might it not have belonged to some pre-Adamite warrior,' I exclaimed, 'to some living man, contemporary with the gigantic herdsman? But no, it can't be. This is not a relic of the Stone Age. It's not even from the Bronze Age. This blade is made of steel . . .'

My uncle stopped me abruptly on this path that my new train of thought was leading me down, and said in a cold voice:

'Calm down, Axel, and see sense. This dagger dates from the sixteenth century; it's a poniard, such as gentlemen carried in their belts to give the *coup de grace*. It's of Spanish origin. It was never yours, or mine, or the hunter's, nor did it belong to any of those human beings who may or may not inhabit this inner world. Look, it was never made jagged like this by cutting men's throats. Its blade is coated with rust that is neither a day, nor a year, nor even a hundred years old.'

The Professor was as usual getting excited and allowing his imagination to run away with him.

'Axel, we're on the way to a great discovery. This blade has been lying on the shore for a hundred years, two hundred years, three hundred years, and has become chipped and notched on the rocks that surround this subterranean sea!'

'But it hasn't got here on its own. And it hasn't got bent like that on its own. Someone has been here before us!

'Yes, some man has.'

'And who was that man?'

'A man who has engraved his name somewhere with that dagger. A man who wanted to mark once again the way to the centre of the Earth. Let's have a look around.'

And our interest now well aroused, we searched all along the high wall, looking into every fissure which might open out into a gallery.

And in this way we came to a place where the shore was much narrower. Here the sea lapped the foot of the steep cliff, leaving a passage no more than a couple of yards wide. Between two projecting rocks appeared the mouth of a dark tunnel.

There, on a granite slab, were two mysterious carved letters, half eaten away by time. They were the initials of the bold and daring traveller:

$$\cdot \ \text{⊣} \cdot \text{Ꮋ} \cdot$$

'A S,' shouted my uncle. 'Arne Saknussemm! Arne Saknussemm again!'

CHAPTER 40

PREPARATIONS FOR BLASTING A PASSAGE TO THE CENTRE OF THE EARTH

Since the start of our journey, I had been astonished so often that I might well be excused for thinking myself well inured to surprises. Yet at the sight of these two letters, engraved on this spot three hundred years ago, I just stood there in dumb amazement. Not only were the initials of the learned alchemist visible on the living rock, but I was actually holding the tool with which the letters had been carved. Unless I was totally dishonest with myself, I could no longer doubt the existence of that amazing traveller and the fact of his unparalleled journey.

Whilst these thoughts were spinning round in my head, Professor Lidenbrock had launched into a somewhat rhapsodical eulogy, of which Arne Saknussemm was, of course, the hero.

'You great genius!' he cried. 'You didn't forget anything that would serve to lay open to other mortals the road through the terrestrial crust, and your fellow men may even now, three centuries later, once again trace your footsteps through these dark underground passages. You intended that other eyes besides your own should look on these wonders. Your name, carved on each stage of the journey, leads the bold follower in your footsteps to the very centre of our planet's core, and there again we shall find your name written with your own hand. I too will inscribe my name on this dark granite page. But henceforth let this cape that you discovered be known by your own illustrious name – Cape Saknussemm.'

Those, or something like them, were the glowing words I heard, and I felt myself inspired by their enthusiasm. An inner fire was kindled afresh in me. I forgot everything, both the past perils of the journey and the dangers to come during our return. What another man had done, I reckoned we too might do, and no human endeavour seemed impossible to me.

'Forward! Forward!' I cried.

I was already making for the gloomy tunnel when the Professor stopped me. Usually the impulsive one, it was he who was counselling patience and calmness.

'Let's first go back to Hans,' he said, 'and bring the raft to this spot.'

I obeyed, not without displeasure, and slipped between among the rocks on the shore.

'You know, Uncle,' I said, 'it seems to me that events have been amazingly kind to us up till now.'

'Do you think so, Axel?'

'No doubt about it. Even the storm carried us in the right direction. Bless that storm! It brought us back to this coast while fine weather would have taken us far away. Just suppose our prow (is there a prow on a raft?) had touched the southern shore of the Lidenbrock Sea, what would have become of us? We would never have seen the name of Saknussemm, and we would at this moment be stranded on a rocky, impassable coast.'

'Yes, Axel, it is quite providential that, while thinking we were heading south, we should simply have come back north and arrived at Cape Saknussemm. I must say it is astonishing, and I can think of no way to explain it.'

'What does that matter, Uncle? Our business is not to explain facts, but to use them!'

'Certainly, but . . .'

'But now we're going to head north again, and to pass below the countries of northern Europe – Sweden, Russia, Siberia, who knows where? – instead of burrowing under the deserts of Africa or perhaps the waves of the Atlantic, and that's all I need to know.'

'Yes, Axel, you're right. It's all for the best, since we have left that weary, horizontal sea, which was leading us nowhere. Now we shall go down, down, and further down! Do you know, it's now only 1,500 leagues to the centre of the globe.'

'Is that all?' I cried. 'Why, that's nothing. Let's make a start, then! Let's go!'

This crazy conversation was still going on when we met the hunter. Everything was made ready for our immediate departure. All our bags and packs were put on board. We took our places, and with our sail set, Hans steered us along the coast to Cape Saknussemm.

A raft is not designed for sailing close to the wind. The wind we had was unfavourable and in many places we had to push ourselves along with our iron-pointed sticks. Often sunken rocks just beneath the surface forced us to deviate from a straight course. Finally, after sailing for three hours, about six in the evening we reached a place suitable for landing. I jumped ashore, followed by my uncle and the Icelander. This short journey had in no way dampened my enthusiasm. On the contrary, I even suggested 'burning our boats', that is to say, our raft, to prevent the possibility of turning back, but my uncle would not agree to it. I thought him remarkably lukewarm.

'At least,' I said, 'let's not waste a minute before setting off.'

'Yes, yes, my boy,' he replied, 'but first let's examine this new gallery to see if we'll need our ladders.'

My uncle switched on his Ruhmkorff's apparatus. The raft, moored to the shore, was left to itself. The mouth of the tunnel was not twenty yards from us, and our party, with myself at the head, made for it without a moment's delay.

The opening, which was almost circular, was about five feet in diameter. The dark passage had been cut through the living rock and smoothed down by the eruptive matter which had formerly issued from it. The inside was level with the ground outside, so we were able to enter the passage without difficulty. We were following an almost horizontal path when, only six yards in, our progress was blocked by an enormous rock.

'Damn this rock!' I shouted angrily, finding myself suddenly confronted by an impassable obstacle.

We searched in vain for a way past, up and down, side to side, to the right and to the left; there was no way of progressing further. I was bitterly disappointed, and could not accept the existence of such an obstacle to our plans. I looked underneath the block: no opening. Above: just more granite. In vain Hans shone his lamp over every part of the barrier. We were being forced to give up all hope of passing it.

I sat down in despair. My uncle walked up and down the narrow passage.

'But how did Saknussemm do it?' I cried.

'Exactly,' said my uncle. 'Was he stopped by this stone barrier?'

'No, no,' I replied fervently. 'This piece of rock has been shaken down by some shock or convulsion or by one of those magnetic storms which disturb these regions, and has now blocked up the passage which lay open to him. Many years elapsed between Saknussemm's return to the surface and this huge rock blocking the path. Isn't it obvious that this gallery was once open to the lava flow, and that at that time there must have been free movement along it? Look, there are recent cracks grooving the granite ceiling. This roof itself is formed of fragments of rock that were carried along; it consists of enormous stones, as if some giant's hand laboured to build it. But at some time the downward pressure was greater than usual, and this block, like the falling keystone of a ruined arch, has slipped down to the ground and blocked the way. It's only a chance obstruction, not met with by Saknussemm, and if we can't destroy it we don't deserve to reach the centre of the Earth.'

Such was my opinion! The soul of the Professor had passed into me. The spirit of discovery wholly possessed me. I forgot the past, I scorned the future. I gave not a thought to the things on the surface of this globe into which I had dived: its cities and its sunny plains, Hamburg and the Königstrasse, even poor Gräuben, who must have given us up for lost, all were for the time being dismissed from the pages of my memory.

'Right,' exclaimed my uncle, 'let's make a way through with our pickaxes.'

'It's too hard for pickaxes.'

'Well, then, with the spades.'

'That would take us too long.'

'What, then?'

'Why, gunpowder, of course! Let's mine the obstacle and blow it up.'

'Blow it up?'

'Yes, why not? It's only a bit of rock that needs blasting.'

'Hans, to work!' shouted my uncle.

The Icelander returned to the raft and soon came back with a pickaxe which he used to make a hole for the charge. This was no easy task. It required a hole large enough to hold fifty pounds of guncotton, whose explosive force is four times that of gunpowder.

I was almost beside myself with excitement. While Hans was at work, I was helping my uncle prepare a slow match of wetted powder wrapped in linen.

'This will do the trick,' I said.

'It certainly will,' replied my uncle.

By midnight our mining preparations were complete. The charge was rammed into the hole, and the slow match uncoiled along the gallery, with its end outside the opening.

A spark would now be enough to set the whole device off .

'Tomorrow,' said the Professor.

I had to resign myself to waiting six long hours.

CHAPTER 41

THE GREAT EXPLOSION AND THE RUSH DOWN BELOW

The next day, Thursday, the 27th of August, was an important date in our subterranean journey. I never think of it without a shudder of horror that makes my heart pound. From that time on, we had no further opportunity to use our reason or judgement or skill or ingenuity. Henceforth we were to be carried along, the playthings of the fierce elements of the deep.

At six o'clock, we were up and about. The moment had come for us to clear a path for ourselves by blasting through the mass of granite that was blocking our way.

I begged the honour of lighting the fuse. This done, I was to join my companions on the raft, which had not yet been unloaded. We would then push out to sea as far as we could and avoid the dangers that would arise from the explosion, the effects of which were not likely to be confined to the rock itself.

The fuse was calculated to burn for ten minutes before setting off the explosive, so I had time enough to escape to the raft.

I got ready to carry out my task, not without some anxiety.

After a hasty meal, my uncle and the hunter embarked on the raft while I remained on shore. I was equipped with a burning lantern with which to set fire to the fuse.

'Now, on you go,' said my uncle, 'and come back to us immediately.'

'Don't worry,' I replied. 'I'll not stop to play on the way.'

I went at once to the mouth of the tunnel. I opened my lantern. I took hold of the end of the match. The Professor stood, chronometer in hand.

'Ready?' he cried.

'Ready.'

'Light it!'

I immediately plunged the end of the fuse into the lantern. It spluttered and burst into flame, and I ran back to the raft at top speed.

'Get on board quickly, and let's shove off.'

Hans, with a vigorous thrust, pushed us away from the shore. The raft shot forty yards out to sea.

It was a moment of intense excitement. The Professor was watching the hand of the chronometer.

'Five minutes to go!' he said. 'Four! . . . Three! . . .'

My pulse was beating every half second.

'Two! . . . One! . . . Down you go, you mountain of granite, you!'

What happened then? I don't think I actually heard the dull roar of the explosion. But the rocks suddenly took on a new shape: they separated like curtains. I saw a bottomless pit open up on the shore. The sea, lashed into a sudden fury, rose up in an enormous billow, on the ridge of which our unfortunate raft was lifted bodily in the air with all its crew and cargo.

All three of us were thrown down flat. In less than a second we were in deep, impenetrable darkness. Then I felt as if the raft, not just me, had nothing supporting it. I thought it was sinking, but it wasn't. I tried to speak to my uncle, but the roaring of the waves prevented him from hearing even the sound of my voice.

In spite of the darkness and noise, and my astonishment and terror, I understood what had happened.

On the other side of the blown-up rock, there was an abyss. The explosion had caused a kind of earthquake in this fissure-ridden region, a great chasm had opened up, and the sea, now changed into a torrent, was rushing us along into it.

I gave myself up for lost.

An hour passed – two hours, perhaps; I can't be sure. We clung to each other to stop ourselves being thrown off the raft. We felt a violent shock whenever we were thrown against projecting rocks. However, these shocks were not very frequent, from which I concluded that the gully was widening. It was no doubt the same road that Saknussemm had taken, but instead of walking peacefully down it as he had done, we were taking a whole sea along with us.

These ideas, you understand, presented themselves to my mind in a vague and undetermined form. I had difficulty in putting any thoughts together during this headlong race, which seemed like a vertical descent. To judge by the air which was whistling past me and making a whizzing noise in my ears, we were moving faster than the fastest express train. To light a torch under these conditions would have been impossible, and our last electrical lighting-apparatus had been shattered by the force of the explosion.

I was therefore very surprised to see a clear light shining near me. It lit up Hans's calm face. The skilful huntsman had succeeded in lighting the lantern, and although it flickered so much that it nearly went out, it threw a fitful light across the awful darkness.

I was right in my supposition. It was a wide gallery. The dim light could not show us both its walls at once. The fall of the waters which were carrying us away exceeded that of the swiftest rapids in American rivers. Its surface seemed to consist of a sheaf of arrows hurled with inconceivable force; I cannot convey my impressions by a better comparison. The raft, occasionally seized by an eddy, spun round as it flew along. When it approached the walls of the gallery, I lit them up with the light of the lantern, and I could more or less judge just how fast we were moving by noticing how the jagged projections of the rocks spun into endless ribbons and bands, so that we seemed to be held within a network of shifting lines. I reckoned we must be travelling at thirty leagues per hour.

My uncle and I looked at each other with haggard eyes, clinging to the stump of the mast, which had snapped off at the first shock of our great catastrophe. We kept our backs to the wind, so as not to be suffocated by the rapidity of a movement which no human power could restrain.

Hours passed. No change in our situation. But then I discovered something that complicated matters and made them even worse than we thought.

Attempting to put our cargo into somewhat better order, I found that the greater part of the articles we had loaded on to the raft had disappeared at the moment of the explosion, when the sea broke in on us with such violence. I wanted to know exactly what we had saved, and with the lantern in my hand I began to check. Of our instruments, none were saved except the compass and the chronometer; our stock of ropes and ladders was reduced to the bit of cord rolled round the stump of the mast. Not a spade, not a pickaxe, not a hammer remained; and – a disaster we could least cope with – we had only one day's provisions left.

I searched in every crack and cranny on the raft. There was nothing else there. Our provisions were reduced to one bit of salt meat and a few biscuits.

I stared at the remains of our supplies blankly. My mind could not take in the seriousness of our loss. And yet what was the use of worrying about it? Even if we'd had provisions enough to last for months, or even years, how were we to get out of the abyss into which we were being hurled by this irresistible torrent? Why should we fear the horrors of starvation, when death was swooping down upon us in a multitude of other forms? Would we actually survive long enough to starve to death?

However, by some inexplicable trick of the mind I forgot my present dangers to contemplate the menacing horrors still to come. In any case, was there still a chance that we might escape the fury of this rushing torrent and return to the surface of the globe? How? I had no idea. Where? It wouldn't matter. But one chance in a thousand is still a chance, whilst contemplating death from starvation left us no hope at all.

I considered telling my uncle the whole truth, showing him the dreadful straits to which we were reduced, and calculating how long we might expect to live. But I had the courage to stay silent. I wanted to leave him calm and under control.

At that moment, the light from our lantern slowly dimmed and then went out. The wick had burnt itself out. Black night reigned again; and there was no hope left of our being able to dissipate a darkness we could almost feel. We still had one torch left, but we couldn't have kept it lit. Like a child, I closed my eyes firmly, so as not to see the darkness.

After quite some time, our speed increased. I could tell by the way the currents of air were blowing into my face. The descent became steeper. I thought we were no longer slipping down, but falling down. I had the impression we were dropping vertically. My uncle's hand, and the strong arm of Hans, held me tightly.

Suddenly, after a period of time I couldn't measure, I felt a shock. The raft hadn't collided with something hard but had suddenly been checked in its fall. A waterspout, an immense column of liquid, rained down on it. I was suffocating, I was drowning . . .

But this sudden flood didn't last long. In a few seconds, I found myself in air again, which I inhaled to the fullest extent of my lungs. My uncle and Hans were still holding me firmly by my arms, and the raft was still carrying us along.

CHAPTER 42

HEADLONG SPEED UPWARD THROUGH THE HORRORS OF DARKNESS

It must have been, I reckon, about ten o'clock at night. The first of my senses which came into play after this latest assault was my hearing. All at once I could hear – and it really was something to hear: I could hear the silence in the gallery after the din which for hours had stunned me. Eventually these words of my uncle's came to me as a vague murmur:

'We're ascending.'

'What do you mean?' I cried.

'We're going up, we're going up!'

I stretched out my arm. I touched the wall, and pulled back my hand. It was bleeding. We were climbing extremely quickly.

'The torch! Light the torch!' shouted the Professor.

Not without some difficulty, Hans managed to light the torch, and the flame, rising on the wick in spite of our rapid ascent, threw out enough light to show us what kind of a place we were in.

'Just as I thought,' said the Professor. 'We're in a narrow shaft not twenty-four feet wide. The water had reached the bottom of the gulf. Now it's rising to find its level, and is carrying us with it.'

'Where to?'

'I've no idea, but we must be ready for anything. We're rising at a speed which I would estimate at twelve feet per second, which makes 720 feet per minute or a little over eight miles an hour. At that speed we could go far.'

'Yes, if nothing stops us, and if this shaft has a way out. But supposing it's blocked. If the air is condensed by the pressure of this column of water, we'll be crushed.'

'Axel,' replied the Professor with perfect calmness, 'our situation is almost desperate, but there are some possibilities of deliverance, and it is these that I'm considering. If at any moment we may perish, so equally at any moment we might be saved. So let's be prepared to grasp even the slightest opportunity.'

'But what will we do now?'

'Recover our strength by eating.'

At these words I fixed a haggard eye on my uncle. The unpleasant truth I had been so unwilling to confess now at last had to be told.

'Eat, did you say?'

'Yes, at once.'

The Professor added a few words in Danish, but Hans shook his head mournfully.

'What!' cried my uncle. 'Have we lost our provisions?'

'Yes. Here is all we have left – one bit of salt meat for the three of us.'

My uncle stared at me as if he couldn't understand what I was saying.

'Well,' I said, 'do you still think we've any chance of being saved?'

My question remained unanswered.

An hour passed. I began to feel the pangs of violent hunger. My companions were suffering too, and not one of us dared touch the wretched remains of our once plentiful store.

But now we were climbing at great speed. Sometimes the air would stop us breathing, as happens to aeronauts who ascend too rapidly. But whereas they suffer from cold in proportion to their ascent, we were beginning to feel the opposite effect. The heat was increasing in a way that was causing us great anxiety; by now the temperature was certainly up around 40°.

What could such a change mean? Up to this point, the evidence had supported the theories of Davy and Lidenbrock. Until now, the particular conditions of non-conducting rocks, of electricity and of magnetism, had tempered the general laws of nature, giving us only a moderately warm climate – for the theory of a central fire remained to my mind the only one that was true and explicable. Were we then heading to where the phenomena of central heat ruled in all their rigour and would reduce the most solid of rocks to a state of molten liquid? I feared so, and said as much to the Professor:

'If we aren't drowned, or shattered to pieces, or starved to death, there's still the possibility that we'll be burned alive and reduced to ashes.'

At this, he shrugged his shoulders and returned to his own thoughts.

Another hour passed, and, except for some slight increase in the temperature, nothing new happened.

'Right,' he said, 'we have a decision to make.'

'A decision about what?' I said.

'We must keep our strength up. If we ration our food in order to try to prolong our existence by a few hours, we will simply continue to be very weak right to the end.'

'And the end is not far off.'

'So, if there is any chance of us saving ourselves, if a moment for active exertion presents itself, where will we find the strength we need if we allow ourselves to be weakened by hunger?'

'Well, uncle, when we have eaten this bit of meat, what'll we have left?'

'Nothing, Axel, nothing at all. But will it do you any more good to devour it with your eyes than with your teeth? Your thinking is that of a man with neither sense nor spirit.'

'But aren't you in despair?' I shouted irritably.

'No, certainly not,' was the Professor's firm reply.

'What? Do you think there is still some chance of being saved?'

'Yes, I do. So long as one's heart beats, so long as body and soul stay together, I cannot agree that any creature endowed with a will need despair of life.'

Resolute words, these! The man who could speak in such a way, under such circumstances, was no ordinary man.

'Well, then, what do you mean to do?' I asked.

'Eat what is left to the very last crumb, and restore our fading strength. This meal will perhaps be our last. So be it, then! But at any rate we shall once more be men, and not exhausted, empty bags.'

'Right, let's eat it then,' I exclaimed.

My uncle picked up the piece of meat and the few biscuits which had escaped the general destruction. He divided them into three equal portions and gave one to each of us. This made about a pound of food each. The Professor ate his greedily, with a sort of feverish rage; I ate without pleasure, almost with disgust; Hans quietly, moderately, chewing his small mouthfuls without any noise, and relishing them with the calmness of a man above all anxiety about the future. Searching carefully, he had found a flask of gin; this he offered to us each in turn, and this generous beverage cheered us up slightly.

'*Förtrafflig*,' said Hans, drinking in his turn.

'Excellent,' replied my uncle.

A glimpse of hope had returned, although without good reason. But our last meal was over, and it was now five in the morning.

Human beings are so constituted that health is a purely negative state. Hunger once satisfied, it is difficult for a man to imagine the horrors of starvation; they cannot be understood without being felt.

So it was that, after our long fast, these few mouthfuls of meat and biscuit triumphed over our previous troubles.

But as soon as the meal was over, we each of us fell deep in thought. What was Hans thinking of – that man of the far West who nevertheless seemed to be guided by the fatalist doctrines of the East?

As for me, my thoughts consisted of memories, and they carried me up to the surface of the globe which I ought never to have left. The house in the Königstrasse, my poor dear Gräuben, that kind soul Martha, flitted like visions before my eyes, and in the dismal rumblings that were from time to time coming through the rock, I thought I could distinguish the roar of the traffic of the great cities above me on the Earth.

My uncle was still concentrating on his work. Torch in hand, he tried to get some idea of our position by observing the strata. This calculation could, at best, be but a vague approximation, but a scientist is always a scientist if he succeeds in remaining calm, and assuredly Professor Lidenbrock possessed calmness to a surprising degree.

I could hear him muttering geological terms. I could understand them, and in spite of myself I felt interested in this final geological study.

'Eruptive granite,' he was saying. 'We're still in the Primitive Period. But we're going up, higher and higher. Who knows where?'

Yes, who knows where? With his hand he was examining the perpendicular wall, and in a few more minutes he continued:

'This is gneiss! Here is some mica schist! Ah! Soon we'll come to the Transition Period, and then . . .'

What did the Professor mean? Could he be trying to measure the thickness of the crust of the Earth that lay between us and the world above? Had he any means of making this calculation? No, he hadn't got the manometer, and no guesswork could make up for that.

The temperature kept on rising; it felt like we were in an oven. I could only compare it to the heat of a furnace at the moment when the molten metal is running into the mould. Bit by bit we had been forced to throw off our coats and waistcoats; the lightest covering became uncomfortable, even painful.

'Are we heading up into a fiery furnace?' I cried at one point when the heat was increasing rapidly.

'No,' replied my uncle, 'that's impossible, quite impossible!'

'But,' I answered, feeling the wall, 'this wall is burning hot.'

At the same moment, touching the water, I had to draw back my hand quickly.

'The water's scalding,' I cried.

This time the Professor's only answer was an angry gesture.

Then I was gripped by an overwhelming terror from which I could not free myself. I felt a catastrophe was approaching, something so awful that the boldest imagination could not conceive of it. A vague notion took hold of my mind, and was fast hardening into certainty. I tried to repel it, but it kept coming back. I didn't dare put it into words. Yet a few involuntary observations confirmed my thoughts. By the flickering light of the torch I could distinguish contortions in the granite strata. A phenomenon was unfolding in which electricity would play the principal part. And then there was this unbearable heat, this boiling water! I took a look at the compass.

It had gone crazy!

CHAPTER 43

SHOT OUT OF A VOLCANO AT LAST!

Yes, our compass was no longer a guide to our movements. The needle was jumping from pole to pole in a kind of frenzy, it was rushing round the dial, it was spinning giddily backwards and forwards.

I knew quite well that, according to the most generally accepted theories, the mineral covering of the globe is never completely at rest. The changes brought about by the chemical decomposition of its component parts, the turbulence caused by great liquid torrents, and the magnetic currents, are continually tending to disturb it, even when the beings living on its surface imagine that all is quiet below. A phenomenon of this kind would therefore not have alarmed me greatly, or at any rate would not have given rise to dreadful apprehensions.

But other peculiar circumstances gradually revealed to me the true state of affairs. There were the explosions of increasing frequency and ever greater intensity. I could only compare them to the loud clatter of dozens of carts driven at full speed over cobblestones. There was a rumbling like interminable thunder.

Then the compass, that had been thrown out of action by the electric currents, confirmed my worst thoughts. The mineral crust of the globe was threatening to break up, the granite foundations were going to come together with a crash, the fissure through which we were being driven helplessly would be filled up, the space would be full of crushed fragments of rock, and we poor wretched mortals were going to be buried and annihilated in this terrible destruction.

'Uncle, Uncle' I cried, 'we're doomed now, utterly doomed!'

'What are you frightened about now?' was the calm reply. 'What's the matter with you?'

'The matter? Look at those shaking walls! Look at those quivering rocks. Don't you feel the burning heat? Don't you see how the water is boiling and bubbling? Are you blind to the dense vapours and steam that are growing thicker and denser with every minute? Look at the compass needle spinning. There's an earthquake coming.'

My uncle shook his head calmly.

'So,' he said, 'you think there's an earthquake coming?'

'I do.'

'Well, I think you're wrong.'

'What? Don't you recognize the signs?'

'Of an earthquake? No! I think it's something better than that.'

'What do you mean?'

'It's an eruption, Axel.'

'An eruption! Do you mean to say we're being carried up the shaft of a volcano?'

'I do believe we are,' said the indomitable Professor with an air of total self-possession, 'and it's the best thing that could possibly be happening to us under the circumstances.'

The best thing! Was my uncle completely mad? What did the man mean? And what was the point in making jokes at a time like this?

'What?' I shouted. 'Are we being carried upwards in an eruption? Fate has flung us here among burning lava, molten rocks, boiling water and all kinds of volcanic matter. We're going to be pitched out, expelled, tossed up, vomited, spat out high into the air, along with fragments of rock, showers of ashes and scoria, in the midst of a towering rush of smoke and flames. And you're saying it's the best thing that could happen to us?'

'Yes,' replied the Professor, looking at me over his spectacles, 'I can't see any other way of reaching the surface of the Earth.'

I will pass rapidly over the thousand ideas which went through my mind. My uncle was right, undoubtedly right, and never had he seemed to me more daring and more certain in his ideas than at this moment when he was calmly contemplating the possibility of being shot out of a volcano!

In the meantime, up we went. The night passed in continual ascent. The din and uproar around us became more and more intensified. I was stifled and stunned; I thought my last hour was approaching. And yet imagination is such a strong thing that even in this supreme hour I was preoccupied with strange and almost childish speculations. But I was the victim, not the master, of my own thoughts.

It was quite clear we were being rushed upwards on the crest of an eruptive wave. Beneath our raft were boiling waters, and under these the more sluggish lava was working its way up in a heated mass, together with hordes of fragments of rock which, when they arrived at the crater, would be flung out in all directions high and low. We were trapped in the shaft or chimney of some volcano. There was no doubt about that now.

But this time, instead of Snæfell, an extinct volcano, we were inside one that was fully active. I wondered, therefore, where this mountain could be, and what part of the world we were to be shot out into.

I had no doubt that it would be in some northern region. Before it had gone mad, the needle had never deviated from that direction. From Cape Saknussemm we had been carried due north for hundreds of leagues. Were we under Iceland again? Were we destined to be thrown up out of Hecla, or through another of the other seven fiery craters on that island? Within a radius of five hundred leagues to the west I could only remember on this parallel of latitude the not-well-known volcanoes on the north-east coast of America.

To the east there was only one at a latitude of 80 degrees north, the Esk in Jan Mayen Island, not far from Spitzbergen. Certainly there was no lack of craters, and there were some large enough to throw out a whole army! But I wanted to know which of them was to act as our exit from the interior world.

Towards morning, our ascent grew faster. If the heat was increasing, instead of diminishing, as we approached the surface of the globe, this was due to local causes alone, volcanic ones. The way we were moving left no doubt in my mind. An immense force, a force of hundreds of atmospheres, generated by the extreme pressure of confined vapours, was driving us irresistibly on. But to what countless dangers it exposed us!

Soon wild lights began to penetrate the vertical gallery which widened as we went up. To right and left I could see deep channels, like huge tunnels, out of which escaped dense volumes of smoke. Tongues of fire lapped the walls, which crackled and sputtered under the intense heat.

'Look, Uncle, look at that!' I shouted.

'That's all right, those are only sulphurous flames and vapours, which one must expect to see in an eruption. They're quite natural.'

'But suppose they envelop us?'

'But they won't envelop us.'

'We'll be suffocated.'

'We won't be suffocated at all. The gallery is widening, and if necessary, we shall abandon the raft, and creep into a crevice.'

'But what about the water, the rising water?'

'There is no more water, Axel, only a sort of lava paste which is carrying us up on its surface to the top of the crater.'

The liquid column had indeed disappeared, replaced by dense and still boiling eruptive matter of all kinds. The temperature was becoming unbearable. A thermometer exposed to this atmosphere would have indicated 150°. Perspiration streamed from my body. But for the rapidity of our ascent we would have been suffocated.

But the Professor gave up his idea of abandoning the raft, and it was a good thing he did. However roughly joined together, those planks afforded us firmer support than we could have found anywhere else.

About eight in the morning something new happened. The upward movement ceased. The raft lay motionless.

'What's happening?' I asked, shaken by this sudden halt as if by a shock.

'It's just a pause,' replied my uncle.

'Has the eruption stopped?' I asked.

'I hope not.'

I stood up and tried to look around me. Perhaps the raft itself, stopped in its course by a projection, was holding back the volcanic torrent. If that were the case, we would have to release it as soon as possible.

But it was not so. The blast of ashes, scoria and rubbish had stopped rising.

'Would the eruption stop?' I exclaimed.

'Ah!' said my uncle between his clenched teeth. 'That's what you're afraid of. But don't be alarmed, this pause can't last long. It's lasted five minutes now, and in a short time we'll resume our journey to the mouth of the crater.'

As he spoke, the Professor continued to consult his chronometer, and once again he was right in his forecast. The raft was soon pushed and driven forward with a rapid but irregular movement, which lasted about ten minutes and then stopped again.

'That's fine,' said my uncle. 'In another ten minutes we'll be off again. We've got an intermittent volcano here. It gives us time now and then to catch our breath.'

This was perfectly true. When the ten minutes were over, we started off again with even greater speed. We had to hold on tight to the planks of the raft so as not to be thrown off. Then once again the paroxysm was over.

I have since thought about this strange phenomenon without being able to explain it. At any rate it was clear that we were not in the main shaft of the volcano, but in a lateral gallery where there was some sort of counter-reaction.

How often this operation was repeated, I cannot say. All I know is, that at each fresh impulse we were hurled forward with much greater force, and it seemed as if we were mere projectiles. During the short pauses, we were stifled by the heat; whilst we were being thrown forward, the hot air almost stopped me breathing altogether. I thought for a moment how delightful it would be to find myself carried suddenly into the Arctic regions, with a temperature 30° below freezing point. My overheated brain conjured up visions of white plains of cool snow, where I might roll around and alleviate my feverish heat. Little by little my brain, weakened by so many constantly repeated shocks, seemed to be giving way altogether. But for the strong arm of Hans, I would more than once have had my head broken against the granite roof of our burning dungeon.

I have, therefore, no exact recollection of what took place during the hours that followed. I have a confused impression of continuous explosions, loud detonations, a general shaking of the rocks all around us, and of a spinning movement with which our raft was at one point whirled helplessly round. It rocked on the lava torrent, in the middle of a dense downpour of ashes. Snorting flames darted their fiery tongues at us. There were wild, fierce puffs of stormy wind from below, like the blasts of huge iron furnaces blowing out all at the same time. I caught a glimpse of the figure of Hans lit up by the fire. All I felt was what I imagine must be the feelings of an unfortunate criminal doomed to be blown apart at the mouth of a cannon, just before the shot is fired and flying limbs and rags of flesh and skin fill the quivering air and spatter the blood-stained ground.

CHAPTER 44

SUNNY LANDS IN THE BLUE MEDITERRANEAN

When I opened my eyes again, I felt the strong hand of our guide holding me by my belt. With the other arm, he was supporting my uncle. I was not seriously hurt, but I was shaken and battered and bruised all over. I found myself lying on the sloping side of a mountain only two yards from a gaping gulf, which would have swallowed me up had I leaned at all that way. Hans had saved me from death while I lay rolling on the edge of the crater.

'Where are we?' asked my uncle irascibly, as if he felt greatly put out by having landed on the surface of the Earth again.

The hunter shook his head in token of complete ignorance.

'Is it Iceland?' I asked.

'*Nej,*' replied Hans.

'What! Not Iceland?' cried the Professor.

'Hans must be mistaken,' I said, standing up.

This was our final surprise after all the astonishing events of our wonderful journey. I expected to see a white cone covered with the eternal snow of ages rising amidst the barren deserts of the icy north, faintly lit by the pale rays of the Arctic sun, far away in the highest latitudes known, but contrary to all our expectations, my uncle, the Icelander and myself were sitting half-way down a mountain baking under the burning rays of a southern sun, which was blistering us with its heat and blinding us with the fierce light of its nearly vertical rays.

I could not believe my own eyes, but the heated air and the sensation of burning left no room for doubt. We had come out of the crater half-naked, and the radiant orb to which we had been strangers for two months was lavishing on us from its blazing splendours more of its light and heat than we were able to receive with comfort.

When my eyes had become accustomed to the bright light to which they had been strangers for so long, I began to use them to put my imagination right. In my opinion, this had to be Spitzbergen, and I was in no mood to give up this notion.

The Professor was the first to speak, and said:

'Well, this isn't much like Iceland.'

'But is it Jan Mayen Island?' I asked.

'Nor that either,' he answered. 'This is no northern mountain. There are no granite peaks capped with snow here. Look, Axel, look!'

Above our heads, at a height of five hundred feet at the most, we saw the crater of a volcano, through which, at intervals of fifteen minutes or so, there issued with loud explosions lofty columns of fire, mingled with pumice stones, ashes and flowing lava. I could feel the heaving of the mountain, which seemed to breathe like a huge whale, and puff out fire and wind from its vast blowholes. Below, down a pretty steep slope, streams of lava ran for seven or eight hundred feet, meaning that the mountain couldn't be more than about 1,800 feet high. But the base of the mountain was hidden in a perfect bower of rich greenness, amongst which I was able to distinguish olive trees, fig trees and vines covered with luscious purple bunches.

I was forced to admit there was nothing of the Arctic here.

When my eye passed beyond these green surroundings, it fixed on a wide, blue expanse of sea or lake, which appeared to surround this enchanting island which was only a few leagues wide. To the east lay a pretty little white seaport town or village, with a few houses scattered around it, and in whose harbour a few vessels of peculiar rig were gently swayed by the softly swelling waves. Beyond it, groups of small islands rose from the smooth, blue waters, but in such numbers that they resembled ants on a huge ant-hill. To the west, distant coasts lined the dim horizon, on some of which rose blue mountains of smooth, undulating forms. On a more distant coast arose a huge cone crowned on its summit with a snowy plume of white cloud. To the north lay spread out a vast sheet of water, sparkling and dancing under the hot, bright rays, its uniformity broken here and there by the topmast of a gallant ship appearing above the horizon or a swelling sail moving slowly before the wind.

This unexpected sight was extremely charming to eyes long used to underground darkness.

'Where are we? Where are we?' I asked faintly.

Hans closed his eyes with complete indifference. My uncle looked round with dumb amazement.

'Well, whatever mountain this may be,' he said at last, 'it's very hot here. The explosions are continuing, and it would be pretty stupid to have come out on an eruption and then to get our heads smashed by bits of falling rock. Let's climb down. Then we'll have a better idea what we're about. Besides, I'm starving and parched with thirst.'

The Professor was definitely not given to idle contemplation. For my part, I could happily have forgotten my hunger and fatigue for another hour or two to enjoy the lovely scene in front of me, but I had to follow my companions.

The slope of the volcano was very steep in many places. We slid down screes of ashes, carefully avoiding the lava streams which glided sluggishly past us like fiery serpents. As we made our way, I chattered and asked all sorts of questions about our whereabouts, for I was far too excited not to talk a great deal.

'We're in Asia,' I exclaimed, 'on the coast of India, in the Malayan Islands or in Oceania. We've passed through half the globe and come out near the Antipodes.'

'But what about the compass?' said my uncle.

'Ah yes, the compass!' I said, greatly puzzled. 'According to the compass, we've gone north.'

'Has it lied?'

'Surely not. Could it lie?'

'Unless, indeed, this is the North Pole!'

'Oh, no, it's not the Pole, but . . .'

Well, here was something that baffled us completely. I didn't know what to say.

By now we were coming into that delightful greenery, and I was suffering a lot from hunger and thirst. Fortunately, after two hours of walking, a charming countryside lay open before us, covered with olive trees, pomegranate trees and delicious vines, all of which seemed to belong to anybody who liked to claim them. Besides, in our state of destitution and famine we were not likely to be choosy. Oh, the inexpressible pleasure of pressing those cool, sweet fruits to our lips, and eating grapes by mouthfuls off the rich, full bunches! Not far off, in the grass, under the delightful shade of the trees, I discovered a spring of fresh, cool water, in which we bathed our faces, hands and feet voluptuously.

While we were thus enjoying our much-needed rest, a child appeared out of a grove of olive trees.

'Look!' I exclaimed. 'Here's an inhabitant of this happy land!'

It was only a poor boy, miserably ill-clad, a sufferer from poverty, and our appearance seemed to alarm him a great deal. Naturally, only half-clothed and with ragged hair and beards, we were a suspicious-looking group, and if the people of the country knew anything about thieves, we were very likely to frighten them.

Just as the poor little wretch was going to take to his heels, Hans caught hold of him, and brought him to us, kicking and struggling.

My uncle began to encourage him as well as he could, and said to him in good German:

'What is this mountain called, my little friend?'

The child made no reply.

'All right,' said my uncle. 'I infer that we're not in Germany.'

He put the same question in English.

We got no further forward. I was very puzzled.

'Is the child dumb?' exclaimed the Professor, who, proud of his knowledge of many languages, now tried French.

Still silence.

'Now let's try Italian,' said my uncle:

'*Dove noi siamo?*'

'Yes, where are we?' I repeated impatiently.

But there was still no answer.

'Will you speak when you are told!' exclaimed my uncle, shaking the urchin by the ears. '*Come si noma questa isola?*'[35]

'Stromboli,' replied the little herdboy, slipping out of Hans's hands and running through the olive trees down to the plain.

We'd hardly been thinking of that possibility. Stromboli! What an effect this unexpected name had on my mind! We were in the middle of the Mediterranean Sea, on an island of the Aeolian archipelago, on the ancient Strongyle[36] where the god Aeolus kept the winds and storms chained up, to be let loose at his will. And those distant blue mountains in the east were the mountains of Calabria. And that threatening volcano far away in the south was fierce Etna.

'Stromboli! Stromboli!' I kept repeating.

My uncle accompanied my exclamations by clapping his hands and stamping his feet, as well as echoing my words. We seemed to be chanting in chorus!

What a journey we had accomplished! How fantastic! Having entered by one volcano, we had issued from another more than two thousand miles from Snæfell and barren, faraway Iceland! The strange fortunes of our expedition had carried us into the heart of the most beautiful part of the world. We had exchanged the bleak regions of perpetual snow and impenetrable barriers of ice for those of brightness and 'the rich hues of all glorious things'[37]. Over our heads we had left the murky sky and cold fogs of the frigid zone to revel under the azure sky of Italy!

After our delicious meal of fruit and cold, clear water, we set off again to reach the port of Stromboli. It would not have been wise to explain how we had arrived there. The superstitious Italians would have put us down as fire-devils vomited out of hell. So we presented ourselves in the humble guise of shipwrecked mariners. It was not so glorious, but it was safer.

On my way I could hear my uncle murmuring: 'But the compass! That compass! It pointed due north. How are we to explain that?'

'My opinion is,' I replied disdainfully, 'that it's best not to explain it. That's the easiest way to deal with the problem.'

'Indeed, sir? The occupant of a professorial chair at the Johannaeum unable to explain the reason for some cosmic phenomenon? Why, that would be simply disgraceful!'

And as he spoke, my uncle, only half dressed, in rags, looking a perfect scarecrow, with his leather belt around him, settling his spectacles on his nose and looking learned and imposing, was himself again, the formidable German professor of mineralogy.

One hour after we had left the grove of olives, we arrived at the little port of San Vicenzo, where Hans claimed his thirteenth week's wages, which was counted out to him with cordial handshakes all round.

At that moment, if he didn't share our very natural emotions, at least his expression changed in a way very unusual with him, and while he lightly pressed our hands with his fingertips, I do believe he smiled.

CHAPTER 45

ALL'S WELL THAT ENDS WELL

Such is the conclusion of a story which I cannot expect everybody to believe, since some people will believe nothing against the testimony of their own experience. However, I'm indifferent to their incredulity, and they may believe as much or as little as they please.

The people of Stromboli received us kindly as shipwrecked mariners. They gave us food and clothing. After we had waited forty-eight hours, on the 31st of August a small craft took us to Messina, where a few days' rest completely removed the effect of our exhaustion.

On Friday the 4th of September, we embarked on the steamer *Volturno*, in the service of the French Imperial Messenger Service, and in three days we were in Marseilles, with nothing to bother us except that infernal lying compass, which we had mislaid somewhere and could not now examine. But its inexplicable behaviour occupied my mind terribly. On the evening of the 9th of September, we arrived in Hamburg.

I cannot describe to you Martha's astonishment or Gräuben's joy.

'Now you're a hero, Axel,' my blushing fiancée said to me, 'you won't leave me again!'

I looked at her tenderly, and she smiled through her tears.

How can I describe the extraordinary sensation caused by the return of Professor Lidenbrock? Thanks to Martha's gossiping, the news that the Professor had gone off to find a way to the centre of the Earth had spread over the whole civilized world. People refused to believe it, and when they saw him they would not believe him any the more. Nonetheless, the appearance of Hans and sundry pieces of intelligence gained from Iceland, tended to shake the confidence of the unbelievers.

Then my uncle became a great man, and I was now the nephew of a great man – which is a privilege not to be despised.

Hamburg gave a grand banquet in our honour. The Professor gave a public lecture at the Johannaeum, in which he described everything about our expedition, with only one omission – the unexplained and inexplicable behaviour of our compass. On the same day, he deposited in the city archives the now famous document of Saknussemm and expressed his regret that circumstances over which he had no control had prevented him from following the trail of the learned Icelander to the very centre of the Earth. He was modest notwithstanding his glory, and he was all the more famous thanks to his humility.

So much honour could not but arouse envy. There were those who envied him his fame; and as his theories, based on known facts, were in opposition to current scientific theories with regard to the question of the central fire, he maintained by pen and by speech notable discussions with scholars from every country in the world.

For my part, I cannot agree with his theory of gradual cooling. In spite of what I have seen and felt, I believe, and always shall believe, in the Earth's central heat. But I admit that certain circumstances not yet sufficiently understood may tend to modify here and there the action of natural phenomena.

While these questions were being debated with great animation, my uncle met with a real sorrow. Our faithful Hans, in spite of our entreaties, had left Hamburg. The man to whom we owed all our success, and our lives too, would not allow us to reward him as we would have wished. He was stricken with homesickness.

'*Farval*,' he said one day, and with that simple word he left us and sailed for Reykjavik, which he reached in safety.

We were very attached to our brave eider-down hunter. Though far away in the remotest north, he will never be forgotten by those whose lives he protected, and I will certainly try to see him once more before I die.

To conclude, I have to add that this 'Journey to the Centre of the Earth' caused a tremendous sensation throughout the world. It was translated into all the languages of civilization. The leading newspapers printed the most interesting passages, which were commented on, picked to pieces, discussed, attacked and defended with equal enthusiasm and determination, both by believers and sceptics. A rare privilege! My uncle enjoyed during his lifetime the glory he had deservedly won, and he may even boast the distinguished honour of an offer from Mr Barnum[38] to exhibit him on most advantageous terms in all the principal cities in the United States!

But there was one 'fly in the ointment' among all this glory and honour: one fact, one incident, of the journey remained a mystery. Now, to a man eminent for his learning, an unexplained phenomenon is an unbearable hardship. Well, my uncle was still fated to be completely happy.

One day, while arranging a collection of minerals in his cabinet, I noticed in a corner the wretched compass which we had long lost sight of. It had been in that corner for six months, little mindful of the trouble it was causing. I opened it and looked at it.

Suddenly, to my intense astonishment, I noticed something strange and uttered an exclamation of surprise.

'What's the matter?' asked my uncle.

'The compass!'

'Well?'

'Look, its poles are reversed!'

'Reversed?'

'Yes, they're pointing the wrong way.'

My uncle looked at it and checked it, and the house shook with his triumphant leap of exultation.

A light suddenly shone into his mind and mine.

'See there,' he cried, as soon as he was able to speak. 'After our arrival at Cape Saknussemm, the north pole of the needle of this blasted compass began to point south instead of north.'

'Clearly!'

'Here, then, is the explanation of our mistake. But what phenomenon could have caused this reversal of the poles?'

'The reason is obvious, Uncle.'

'Tell me, then, Axel.'

'During the electric storm on the Lidenbrock Sea, that ball of fire, which magnetized all the iron on board, reversed the poles of our magnet!'

'Aha, aha!' shouted the Professor with a loud laugh. 'So it was just a trick of electricity!'

From that day on, the Professor was the happiest of scientists – and I was the happiest of men, because my pretty Virland girl, resigning her place as his ward, took her position in the old house on the Königstrasse in the double capacity of niece and wife. What need is there to add that her uncle was the illustrious Otto Lidenbrock, corresponding member of all the scientific, geographical and mineralogical societies of the civilized world?

NOTES

1 The Tugendbund or 'League of Virtue' was a patriotic body formed in Prussia in 1808.

2 Virland is in Estonia.

3 Well-known bookbinders.

4 Verne wrongly wrote *m* in his translation of this Runic character. The rune represents a double m, not a single m, as Verne himself says further on. The translation printed here is amended to this effect.

5 In Ancient Greek mythology, Oedipus solved the difficult riddle asked by the Sphinx.

6 In the Roman calendar, the calends were the first day of the month.

7 A Leyden jar was a device for storing electricity.

8 A French league is about 4 kilometres or 2½ miles.

9 The Belts are two straits on the east coast of Denmark.

10 At this time, Iceland was not an independent country but was governed by Denmark.

11 The Sound is the stretch of sea between Zealand (Sjælland) and Sweden.

12 It is actually the south-eastern part.

13 Lilliput is a fictitious country described in the novel *Gulliver's Travels*. The people of Lilliput are tiny.

14 Formerly, a list of books banned by the Roman Catholic Church.

15 The following is Verne's note: 'A Ruhmkorff's apparatus consists of a Bunsen battery activated by potassium dichromate, which is odourless. An induction coil carries the electricity generated by the battery to a lantern of peculiar construction: in this lantern there is a spiral glass tube from which the air has been expelled, and in which remains only a residue of carbon dioxide or nitrogen. When the apparatus is operated, this gas becomes luminous, producing a steady white light. The battery and coil are placed in a leather bag which the traveller carries over his

shoulders; the lantern, outside the bag, throws out sufficient light in deep darkness; it enables one to venture without fear of explosions into the midst of highly inflammable gases, and is not extinguished even in the deepest waters. M. Ruhmkorff is a learned and most ingenious man of science; his great discovery is his induction coil, which produces a powerful stream of electricity. He obtained in 1864 the quinquennial prize of 50,000 francs reserved by the French government for the most ingenious application of electricity.'

16 'And whatever path Fortune may give us, we will follow it.'

17 These must be Icelandic 'miles'. The area of Iceland is just under 40,000 sq. miles.

18 A statue of the Greek sun-god Helios at Rhodes, according to legend built astride the entrance to the harbour.

19 'An easy path down to the Underworld.'

20 Well-known spas. (The word 'spa' comes from the town of Spa.)

21 Quotation taken by Malleson from Shakespeare's *Hamlet*.

22 'Out of the depths'; quotation taken by Malleson from the Latin version of Psalm 130.

23 In an Ancient Greek myth, Theseus used a thread to guide him out of the labyrinth where the Minotaur lived.

24 The 'Internal Sea', a Roman name for the Mediterranean Sea.

25 The planet named Pluto was not discovered until 1930. The name 'Pluto' was not attached to any body in the Solar System when Verne was writing.

26 'Mediterranean' means 'in the middle of the Earth'.

27 A famous French anatomist and palaeontologist.

28 An Ancient Greek hero who defied the Greek gods and who as punishment was shipwrecked and drowned.

29 It is said that the books in the library in Alexandria were burned on the orders of the Muslim caliph Omar in the 7th century, but the story is almost certainly not true.

30 Famous French naturalists.

31 The following is Verne's note, of interest in that it illustrates then current scientific thinking: 'The facial angle is formed by two lines,

one touching the brow and the front teeth, the other from the orifice of the ear to the lower line of the nostrils. The greater this angle, the higher intelligence denoted by the formation of the skull. Prognathism, in anthropological terminology, is that projection of the jaw-bones which sharpens or lessens this angle.'

32 The person referred to is Peter Schlemihl, the hero of Adelbert von Chamisso's tale of a man who sold his shadow to the Devil. The writer E T A Hoffmann included the character in one of his tales.

33 Proteus was the herdsman of the Greek god Poseidon (or Neptune in Roman mythology).

34 'The shepherd of gigantic herds, even more gigantic himself.'

35 'What is the name of this island?'

36 The Greek and Latin name for Stromboli.

37 Quotation taken by Malleson from Mrs Hemans' poem *The Better Land*.

38 A famous American showman and circus-owner.